I've travelled the world twice over,
Met the famous: saints and sinners,
Poets and artists, kings and queens,
Old stars and hopeful beginners,
I've been where no-one's been before,
Learned secrets from writers and cooks
All with one library ticket
To the wonderful world of books.

© JANICE JAMES.

THE WINTER SPRING

Early in 1837 Thomas Winter was invited to take his theatrical company to the Earl of Bagot's country house to entertain the Earl's guests. The evening heralded the beginning of a new life for Winter's two enchanting daughters; for Isabella a dizzy rise to a great social position that was to be shadowed by scandal and the threat of public disgrace; and for Lettice the start of a career which involved the excitement of working with the greatest actor/manager of his day, the fascinating and terrifying Henry Davenant.

Books by Suzanne Goodwin in the Ulverscroft Large Print Series:

THE WINTER SISTERS
THE WINTER SPRING

SUZANNE GOODWIN

THE WINTER SPRING

Complete and Unabridged

ULVERSCROFT
Leicester

First published 1978

First Large Print Edition
published January 1982
by arrangement with
The Bodley Head Ltd.
London

British Library CIP Data

Goodwin, Suzanne
  The winter spring.—Large print ed.
  (Ulverscroft large print series: historical
  romance)
  I. Title
  823'.914 [F]   PR6057.0585

  ISBN 0-7089-0736-9

Published by
F. A. Thorpe (Publishing) Ltd.
Anstey, Leicestershire
Printed and Bound in Great Britain by
T. J. Press (Padstow) Ltd., Padstow, Cornwall

The author is grateful to her sister
Madeleine Bingham
for the expert historical advice
she has given so generously

Part One

1

(1)

LOOKING across the room at the curtained bed where her sister's peaceful figure lay, Isabella felt a surge of impatience. How late Lettice slept. And she never budged. She always lay in the position she took as Juliet after taking the sleeping potion, arms on her breast, flat on her back, her red hair round a face of perfect stillness. She didn't seem to breathe. It was a valuable gift in an actress.

Isabella longed to creep across the room, give a loud whoop and jump on her sleeping sister. But she thought better of it.

She never felt the actor's need to rebuild her energies in long hours of sleep. Every morning when the farm carts rumbled into the town she lay listening to the wheels on the cobbles, the shouts of the carters, the crack of their whips. She knew the time to expect the sweet shrill whistle of the baker's boy going by with his tray of fresh loaves. Everybody was alive and awake. How could Lettice waste time asleep?

Unable to stay in bed a minute longer, Isabella climbed out. The room was bitterly cold and in the night a glassy layer of ice had formed on top of the jug. When she poured out the water and splashed her face, her cheeks burned. She dressed, shivering.

The sisters were startlingly different in appearance—a stranger would never know they were related. Isabella was tall and thin, leggy, with an olive skin and very dark brown eyes. There was something Celtic in her looks. But Lettice was small, with a luminous white skin, wide apart green eyes and luxuriant red hair. The only single similarity between them was the shape of their short straight noses.

At the bottom of the staircase the housemaid, Milly, a sturdy thirteen-year-old, was on her knees in a cloud of dust.

"Mornin', miss."

"Good morning, Milly," said Isabella casually.

She was not yet used to the family having a maid-servant, although it was already a year since Milly had been with them.

Her mother, Ellen Winter, was sitting sedately in the front parlour, drinking coffee.

4

The room was bare and cold, although a small fire was lit. Ellen Winter was muffled in a shabby grey shawl.

She was a small woman, with Isabella's olive skin, brown hair not yet grey, and an expression in her dark eyes which changed from energetic liveliness to prim disapproval. When she saw Isabella she frowned.

"Why have you risen so early? You know I prefer you to rest."

"*You* are up, Mama."

"I am not an actress and don't need to keep fresh for the evening performance. Lettice has more sense."

"Oh, Lettice! She's so vexing, lying there looking like Juliet. One day I know I shall jump on her."

Ellen should have frowned again, but she laughed. She liked what she called "ill-discipline", enjoyed romping bad behaviour while firmly correcting it; her dark eyes always snapped with interest when her daughters quarrelled. Once when there had been a backstage fight between two actors, Ellen had stood watching attentively and cried "Good shot!" when one actor landed a savage crack on his opponent's jaw.

She poured Isabella some coffee, and

looked her over. This year, 1837, all the girls were in striped muslin, and Isabella had been enchanted with the new dress her mother had made her, white striped with marigold-coloured flowers. But the girl would wear it all the time.

"You should keep your clothes for occasions," remarked Ellen. "Or when the time arrives there will be nothing to wear."

Isabella ignored that, and buttered some bread. Her mother continued to study her. To Ellen her children were objects of the deepest interest—she made the best audience in the world. She never showed them her love by words, and would not dream of telling them they were handsome, although she thought so.

The moment she'd finished her breakfast Isabella jumped up restlessly and went to the window. She peered out into the street, saying she was sure it would snow. Suddenly she pressed closer to the window-pane.

"Goodness! A carriage stopping here!"

"Then do not be seen looking at it."

"But, Mama—"

"Come away from the window this instant. Do you wish to be thought a servant?"

At her mother's sharp voice Isabella crossly

left the window, remarking that there was a coat of arms on the carriage door and wasn't *that* interesting, at least? Ellen did not deign to reply.

A moment later Milly, distinctly dusty, came into the room.

"Letter for the Master, ma'am."

"You may take it to him, Milly."

"Not got the stairs finished, ma'am."

"Very well, give the letter to me," said Ellen, with a look of dignified dismissal. Milly still hung about, looking on with eyes like a clever terrier's.

"Waitin' outside still. Wants an answer, 'e said."

"Tell the *footman* to wait," said Ellen, closing her eyes.

Milly left the room and Isabella rushed to her mother and waited while Ellen broke the heavy seal.

"What can it be? Mama, speak!"

Reading the letter, Ellen did not look pleased. She passed it to Isabella in silence.

The paper was so thick that when it was unfolded again it creaked. The letter, written in the third person, announced it had the honour to inform Mr. Thomas Winter that Mr. Edwin Sidaway, Steward to His Lordship the Earl of Bagot, wished to enquire if Mr. Winter and his actors would consent to pay a visit to Bagot Park. Might a private performance be arranged of "some dramatic offering of suitable interest? Mr. Sidaway would do himself the honour of waiting on Mr. Winter etc. etc."

Before Isabella could exclaim, enraptured, her mother said briefly she must go and see Thomas at once.

With Ellen out of the way, Isabella ran to the window again. Rank, possessions, the world of privilege fascinated her. The Bagot carriage was certainly worth staring at. Everything shone. The beautiful chestnut horses shifting and stamping, sending out clouds of steamy breath in the cold air; the glittering brass lamps and yellow and black coachwork of the carriage, the coachman's tall hat, the silver buttons on the footman's livery . . . half in pleasure, half in envy, Isabella sighed.

Thomas Winter was upstairs in the room he called his "sanctum", a kind of office where he kept his papers. His papers indicated Thomas's state of mind, they were in wild disarray. There were heaps of unanswered letters, scrawled notes he couldn't read, bills to pay, plays to read. Thomas never admitted to being cold and there was no fire in the grate. He had a shawl of his wife's draped around the shoulders of his rusty black coat and was writing with a scratchy quill. He glanced up as his wife came into the room.

Thomas looked what he was—an actor. His face was high-cheekboned, his manner theatrical, his curling hair cut to look at its best onstage. His voice had a richness, a declamatory note. As a young man he had been handsome, with chunky russet hair and swimming eyes, but middle age had coarsened his looks and covered his cheeks with broken veins.

"Tom, do I disturb you?"

"I cannot spare any time just now, my dear."

But she came into the room and closed the door. The air was so cold that their breath was like smoke. It's very stubborn of Tom, she thought, to keep his sanctum as cold as the street. She draped the shawl closely round his shoulders as if he were an ageing baby.

"I am afraid I have to speak to you. This letter has come from the Earl of Bagot."

Thomas was startled. But when he had read the letter he gave a gratified smile.

"His Lordship has never honoured me before with such a request."

"Indeed, no."

At Ellen's tone, the smile on Thomas's face died and he looked anxious. Everything she said and did affected his own opinions.

"It might be the beginning of great things for us," he ventured. "You will be back in the gentry where you belong, my love."

Ellen merely said, "A servant is waiting for your reply."

"I shan't write it, I had better speak to him," he said, starting up so that the shawl hung off one shoulder. She removed it.

"Yes, tell him that you will call at Bagot Park. We do not want the steward coming here."

Thomas, throwing back his head as if about to make his entrance on a stage, hurried down the stairs.

The Bagot footman, a tall young man in beautiful livery, listened politely to Thomas's message. Had Ellen been watching she would not have liked her husband's manner, it was too friendly and actorish. She would have seen the same thought in the footman's eye.

"I will inform Mr. Sidaway that you will be waiting on him," said the footman, bowing.

The carriage clattered away, leaving the street to more workaday folk, a farmer on a donkey, a man with a milk-cart and some children bowling hoops.

Isabella moved guiltily away from the window when her parents came into the room. To avoid being scolded a second time, she said vivaciously, "Is not the news exciting, Papa? Imagine, the *Earl* has sent for you! What play shall we do? Mama, you always said you wanted to see inside Bagot Park!"

Thomas had sat down heavily and Ellen draped the little shawl round him again, solicitously poured him some coffee, generally behaving as if he were recovering from shock. Then she said mildly, "I'm afraid I shall not be going to Bagot Park."

Her husband and daughter looked aghast; Ellen was the centre of the family and nothing was done without her.

"But my dear—" began Thomas. She interrupted.

"No, Tom. Nothing would induce me to go."

"Mama—nobody at Bagot Park knows who you are!" exclaimed Isabella. "Of course you must come, you *know* you wish to come—"

11

"Isabella, your father and I want to talk. Please leave us."

Longing to stay, Isabella unwillingly left the room.

She thought of listening at the door but it was oak and very solid. Then it occurred to her that here was an excellent excuse for waking Lettice.

She burst into the dark bedroom, tugged open the curtains and rushed over to shake Lettice awake.

"Go away."

"I shall not! This time you *have* to wake up! Listen to what has happened!"

Lettice, groaning, came slowly to her senses. She tried to pay attention, but Isabella's voice was loud and excited. She lay back in sleepy silence.

Different in looks, their characters were always at variance, Isabella talkative, volatile and restless, her elder sister quiet, sometimes radiant, sometimes dreamy, her thoughts reflected in large, melting green eyes.

Isabella plumped herself down on the bed. Her weight hurt Lettice's feet and Lettice moved them.

"The parents are in the parlour now. Pa has gone into a dumpish gloom. Imagine,

Letty, Mama says she positively will not go with us to the Earl's house."

"Because she is related to them."

"Only twenty times removed!"

"She still can't forget she is gentry," said Lettice, swallowing a yawn.

"She forgot when she fell in love with Pa and eloped with him in a chaise from the vicarage."

"Isabella. Do stop shifting about."

"I know how Mama feels, you know," said Isabella, not listening. "She won't go to Bagot Park as a menial—the person who *mends the costumes*."

"Being in the theatre is not menial."

"Pooh. Trundling from town to town is. Living on a gift of the gab and a few tattered cloaks and feathered hats. If Pa hadn't known half a hundred plays, Shakespeare and Sheridan and *The Smuggler's Bride* and lord-knows-what, and if *we* hadn't danced and sung and played elves since we could walk, and if poor Mama hadn't sewn everything from Hamlet's black to Lear's rags, we'd have starved."

Lettice did not bother to reply. She was accustomed to her sister's disparagement of their profession, though neither their parents

13

nor the girls themselves ever imagined they could do anything else.

Until their mother's legacy had been spent buying the North Street theatre here in Market Chester, life had been a journey up and down England. Lettice sometimes thought they must be the descendants of Shakespeare's players in *Hamlet* with their baskets of props and Greek tags. Lettice and Isabella had learnt to dance when they learnt to walk, flitted across the stage as fairies, popped out of cardboard pies as infant blackbirds. They played the Little Princes in *Richard III* when they were six and seven years old. Thomas taught them to recite the Ten Dramatic Passions, "Joy, Grief, Fear, Anger, Pity, Scorn, Hatred, Jealousy, Wonder, Love." They learnt these when other children learnt nursery rhymes.

It was a year since their father had bought the North Street theatre and they had come to live in this plain, pleasant little house opposite the theatre. Life was different now.

"I don't know why you still grumble about the circuits when it is months and months since we travelled," Lettice said. "Besides, you may look down on being an actress, but if it weren't for that you wouldn't have this *Earl's* invitation you're so excited over."

14

"Aren't you excited?"

Lettice, her teeth chattering with cold, climbed out of bed in her long cambric nightgown and began to wash.

"I might be if I knew which play Papa will choose."

"We know which one *you* want. Juliet, of course."

Lettice dried her hands, swathed herself in one of the family's supply of woollen shawls and sat down at the dressing-table to examine her freckled face.

Impatiently watching her sister's leisurely movements, Isabella cried, "Of course you want to play Juliet at Bagot Park. Why not admit it?"

"Because it is the wrong play."

"Everybody loves *Romeo and Juliet*."

"Not the gentry."

"How can you talk such nonsense, Letty! What about old Lord Craven who has his box reserved every single week when you are Juliet."

"The Bagots will have been out hunting all day."

"How can you possibly know that? What do *you* know about the gentry?"

"Only that they'd sooner laugh than cry."

Isabella couldn't help laughing. Lettice, for all her mildness, was so absolutely certain of what she thought. She always knew exactly which plays she liked, which she thought worthless. She seemed to sense uncannily when an actor had talent. Like Thomas she thought of nothing but the theatre. But while her father's mind was full of the price of taffeta for costumes or oil for lamps, of how many tickets were sold, whether the carpenters had been paid, Lettice thought of how to conquer an audience.

During the following days the family talked of the Bagot invitation until the subject was quite worn out. Thomas was flustered. What play should he choose? What fee would be paid?

"I must decide what fee to suggest, my dear."

"Gracious, Tom, Mr. Sidaway will inform you what the Earl will pay for the evening's entertainment."

"But it might not be sufficient. Not all the gentry are open-handed," said Thomas anxiously.

"It would not be becoming to mention a fee," said Ellen.

Lettice, listening, thought this very foolish but held her tongue.

It was decided that Thomas should hire a hack and ride out to Bagot Park to meet the Earl's steward, Mr. Sidaway. Ellen helped her husband to dress. She put in his best studs, tied his satin cravat and waited upon him as if he were preparing to attend a coronation. She watched while he put on his tall hat at a rakish angle.

"You look very nice, Tom."

It was high praise.

He put his arms round her and they stood close for a moment, sharing each other's thoughts.

Thomas rode out of Market Chester along a country road deeply rutted by the carts which came and went daily. In wet weather the road was a sea of mud, but now in the cold the mud was frozen into deep ridges. On either side stretched meadows and ploughed fields white with frost. Every blade of grass glittered.

He did not like the country, thought it lonely and melancholy and tried to fix his mind on practical matters: they were worrying, too. The stage carpenters were a lazy bunch. A new actor he had engaged, a comic

17

scarcely bigger than a dwarf, had been drunk the previous evening.

"Laurie Spindle nearly fell into the pit," Ellen had said, pursing her lips. She despised drunkards.

The road straightened, and in the distance Thomas saw a high brick wall and twin stone pillars topped with heraldic animals, half-stag, half-unicorn.

The lodge-keeper, always on the lookout for the visitors who continuously drove up or left the Park, came out of his cottage to open the gates. Thomas bowed his thanks, and felt sure the man knew to a farthing how much he'd paid to hire the horse.

The avenue between the leafless trees appeared to go on for miles and as Thomas rode through the frostbound landscape he felt more and more nervous.

The aristocracy were arrogant, self-confident, sometimes rude. They were beholden to nobody for their position and their wealth. Like the countryside they owned, he did not like them.

At last the drive curved, and he saw the house in the distance. Long ago, Bagot Park had been a low, rambling Tudor place but in the 1750s one of the Bagots had visited Italy and fallen in love with classicism. The house was given a pillared façade, tall symmetrical windows, tacked unselfconsciously on to the Elizabethan manor. The house stood on a rise of ground with woods and downland in the distance. The gardens, too, had been changed, the old walled orchards and herb-beds replaced by sloping lawns, "prospects", statues, vistas of meadows set about with solitary and beautiful trees, a lake, ghostly now in the winter mist.

As he neared the house, the doors under the portico opened and a group of gentlemen came out. Round the side of the house came grooms leading what seemed to Thomas dozens of horses. Through the clear air he heard laughter and talk.

Something in the manner of the gentlemen, in the way their servants waited on them, made his nerve fail. He reined in his horse and turned to the left, riding down the side of the house, and went under the archway into a back courtyard. Here some maidservants stood at an open door gossiping to a carter. Dogs were running about. The cheerful faces of the girls made him feel comfortable and he dismounted and went to the back door to enquire for Mr. Sidaway.

He was taken first to a small woman in dark

silk who introduced herself as "Mrs. Judge, the Earl's housekeeper," and then accompanied by a footman on a journey through the house. He seemed to walk miles. Servants hurried by with armfuls of linen or trays of silver. The place hummed like a hive of bees and reminded him, in its activity, of backstage. And as in the theatre he had to go through a pass door. This one, covered in green baize and studded with brass nails, divided the servants' quarters from the main house.

The footman knocked at a door and announced, "Mr. Winter, sir."

"Ah. Winter. Good of you to make the journey. How-de-do?"

Mr. Sidaway came over to greet him.

Thomas was surprised at the steward's appearance. He was not the way he imagined the gentleman would be. Mr. Sidaway wore a plain brown coat of coarse cloth and hobnail shoes; with his red face and white stock, he might have been a rich tradesman, except that his voice drawled and there was something easy yet reserved in his manner.

"Please take a chair. I trust you do not find this room overheated? Mrs. Judge has a mistaken idea that I feel the cold and this stove is devilish fierce, but I have not the heart to tell her so."

He put Thomas at his ease.

"What size of room have you in mind for your play, sir? We have every sort of size, d'you see, big as a ballroom, small as a billiard table. Depends on the size of your audience, of course. Well, some are leavin' and some arrivin'. Shall we say fifty? Come and take a look at the Music Room."

Thomas agreed respectfully. He would have agreed to acting in the larder. Mr. Sidaway took him down a huge curving staircase to a hall, marble-floored like a chessboard, with statues in niches. Thomas caught a glimpse through an open door of a group of ladies and gentlemen breakfasting. They, too, were as plainly dressed as Mr. Sidaway. He had imagined velvets.

"This is the room," said Mr. Sidaway, opening double doors. It was a great high room, the ceiling painted with goddesses, clouds, cherubs, warriors. The walls were also covered with paintings, and behind a settee stood a larger-than-lifesize marble Venus. A great fireplace at the end of the room, in which a fire was freshly lit, had a carved chimney-piece of vine leaves, grapes and birds.

"Does it suit, do you think?" enquired the steward, looking about. "Just tell us what to push out, eh?" He gestured at the chairs and tables, a spinet, an embroidered carpet and a bronze tiger eating a dead antelope.

Thomas frowningly studied the room, wearing his most officious (and harassed) expression.

"I'm lookin' forward to hearing what play we're to see," remarked Mr. Sidaway. "I am bound to warn you, Winter, that His Lordship dislikes to weep. Always easily moved when he goes to the play. Only time in his life that happens. Ha ha!"

(2)

Ellen was waiting for him when Thomas returned home. She shooed away Milly, firmly closing the door.

"Well?"

Thomas sat down with an exaggerated air of weariness.

"Mr. Sidaway was most kind."

"And?"

"A clever man, my dear, very genteel. We

22

have been given the Music Room for the performance. A comfortably large room which in summer opens on to the garden. Mr. Swayne, the butler, will arrange rows of chairs."

Ellen sat down facing her husband.

"Tell me about the house, Tom. Somebody said the drive is four miles long and there is a waterfall. Did you see the family? How many guests have they? The Bagots gave a ball last month and had three hundred. Describe everything. Do!" She gave him a sudden, very charming smile.

But though he liked to please her, he could not give her an impression of the sumptuous house he had visited. He had lived in the world of the imagination all his life—it seemed right for a cardboard circlet to become a king's crown. But he noticed nothing except the theatre. He told her instead about the standard oil lamps, the carpet which could be rolled up and the number of gilt chairs and sofas for the audience.

Recovering from the excitement of the Bagot invitation, the Winter family settled to their occupation—acting. Thomas and his daughters played every night at his North Street theatre; Thomas was owner and manager, with attendant worries. Ellen made or refurbished the costumes and worked as the prompt. The company were rehearsing a new piece, *The Welsh Girl*, which Thomas thought might be a success. Lettice played the leading role.

Laurie Spindle, the newly-arrived comic, also settled down. The actors liked him. His manner was unusually dry and satirical but he developed a doglike devotion for Lettice. The little man, with his big long-chinned face, and the slight redheaded girl were constantly together.

He found her one morning, seated on a prop basket learning her lines for *The Welsh Girl*.

"I'll hear your lines for you, Beauty."

"You are kind, Laurie."

"Your mama does not think so. She looks on me as a drunken beast."

"You do drink rather."

"So I do. I like it."

She grinned at him disapprovingly. He had a voice with a break in it which he used in a certain way, a talent for driving a joke straight at the audience so that they caught it with both hands. When sober, his gift was remarkable: it was not inconsiderable when he was drunk.

He heard her lines for a while, then said, "What has your father decided we're to play for the nobs?"

"Sheridan, he says."

"That's a mistake, Beauty."

"But why?"

"I'll tell you. Never play the gentry *to* the gentry. You'll make them laugh at you instead of with you. Shakespeare knew it. Look at the mechanicals in the *Dream*. The Duke thought them ridiculous. What the nobs would enjoy is a comic melodrama. *The Welsh Girl*, for instance."

Lettice's large eyes grew larger.

"I see you're pleased," he said.

"Laurie, I would *love* it to be that play. But my father would never consent. And I couldn't persuade him."

"Not as you've such a thumping big part in it you couldn't," he said, laughing. "Leave it to me, Beauty."

Lettice had no idea how he persuaded Thomas to change his mind—Thomas never listened to anybody but Ellen. But somehow the "comic melodrama" began to attract him. She heard him asking Ellen whether she agreed that the gentry might be entertained by the piece with its disguises and mistaken identities.

"You could talk to Mr. Sidaway, Tom."

"Now, Ellen, that *is* an excellent idea."

The Earl's steward agreed so heartily that Thomas immediately became convinced of his own acuteness. When he announced the play to the company, Laurie looked at Lettice but did not even wink.

Lettice spent a diligent week before the Bagot Park visit studying and rehearsing. She never complained at late hours, was always on call, patient, concentrated. She stood without moving when her mother pinned her into a new costume (Isabella complained and fidgeted). Lettice was in the theatre from morning till midnight. Sometimes when Isabella was fast asleep Lettice rose quietly and sat in the ice-cold bedroom, studying by candlelight.

Isabella was in a fever of excitement at the prospect of visiting a great house; she hung round her mother tiring her with questions. At what time did the gentry dine? What did the ladies wear at home? Did each lady have one maid or two? What did one call an earl?

When the evening came, Thomas Winter closed the theatre, for the performance was to be at ten o'clock after the Bagots and their guests had dined.

26

Ellen supervised the packing, bullied the theatre dressers, chose the frocks her daughters would wear for supper at the Park after the play, criticised and enjoyed being in charge. Satisfied that she would not be demeaned by visiting the Bagots, her six-times-removed relations, Ellen was keenly interested in the visit.

An hour before they were due to leave Lettice was waiting at the Stage Door for the cart which was to collect the costume baskets. The night was frosty and blazing with stars. She wrapped her cloak round her, noticing with relief that the night was dry. She'd seen costumes sodden and scenery ruined by rain many times. Now she waited alone, determined to see her own costume basket safely placed in the cart.

As she stood under the light of an oil lamp at the Stage Door, three men lurched down the alleyway from the inn at the street corner. The doors of *The Cat and Custard Pot* swung open every night and out reeled men drunken or violent or both. Lettice was indifferent to them. The only time she hated them was when they sat in the pit and shouted oaths and threw things. She knew how to dodge bottles thrown on stage, how to use her voice

27

to drown hisses from the pit or the loud voices of the gentry talking in the boxes (sometimes with their backs to the stage). The theatre had made her a hardy little creature.

When the cart arrived, Lettice called to the Stage Door-keeper and Thomas arrived to organise the scene shifting. Two carters with backs as broad as their own horses filled the cart with screens, painted flats and skips. Lettice wedged her basket safely, and made a note of exactly where it was placed so that she herself could find it.

"So there you are, Letty," cried Isabella, darting out of the theatre without a cloak. "Why are you waiting? It isn't nearly time to go yet."

"Papa says the carriage will come directly."

"But the performance is not until ten!"

"We need time," was Lettice's brief reply.

Their mother had decided that the Winter family must have a carriage to themselves. The rest of the company would have to crowd into two broughams and sit on each other's laps.

"But a carriage only for us, my dear," demurred Thomas. "It is very extravagant."

"Remember, you *are* the owner."

When the journey began, the sisters

28

huddled together for warmth. The carriage jolted on the rutted country road and Isabella's teeth knocked together. But every bump and shudder brought her nearer to the great house.

"Surely we are there now, Papa?"

"Not yet."

"Bagot Park!" sighed Isabella. "I must remember to look at *everything*. I want to see the family and the guests, and the ladies' dresses, and the servants and the house—and everything."

"Here we are," said her father, looking from the carriage window. "Why doesn't the driver get down? He really should not shout like that. I am sure the lodge-keeper will not like it."

The driver was giving undignified halloos and cracking his whip for the gates to be opened.

"What country bumpkins drive hired coaches!" exclaimed Thomas irritably.

"We are bumpkins too," murmured Lettice. Isabella said loudly, "*You* can be if you like. I'm not."

To Isabella's disappointment the carriage did not drive up to the portico of the great house, where she could see lamps burning, but down the side of the house past many different sized buildings all joined and jumbled, until they drew up in a backyard.

Before the coachman could help her, Lettice jumped down. The cart of scenery and costumes was drawn up at the open stable; she hurried over to drag out a small basket and tuck it under her arm. Then, beckoning Isabella, she walked coolly into the house.

The passage smelled of spices, there was the hot breath of cooking from two large kitchens near by; Isabella was nervously sure the servants would come out to question them. But Lettice pulled her by the hand as if she had known the house all her life. She had an instinct about finding her own way in theatres: the same instinct worked now.

Smiling at two housemaids who passed, she went down a passage, then another, skirted a flight of uncarpeted stairs and found one of the green baize doors which divided the house like a frontier between countries.

Isabella, following her sister down a richly carpeted corridor with white and gold walls hung with paintings, felt oppressed. Her excitement evaporated—she wished she had never come. But Lettice, unconscious of the splendour of her surroundings, turned into the magnificent entrance of the hall with heroic statues lining the walls, and a vast marble staircase curving upwards to a gallery.

"There," said Lettice. "That must be it!"

She walked straight to the open doors of the Music Room and only then looked around with interest.

Isabella followed, subdued, envious and sad.

A tall young man was standing indolently by the fireplace watching the busyness in the room. The butler was in command, the chairs being arranged, the place in a turmoil. Lettice walked over to the butler and immediately engaged him in talk.

Isabella remained in the doorway, adrift, taking no part in the talk and activity. She was standing beside a wall on which hung a huge painting of warriors, horses, flags; the picture emphasised her stillness.

The young man walked over to her and bowed.

"Allow me to present myself. Carteret."

"I am Isabella Winter. My father is Thomas Winter." She gave the merest curtsy.

"So you and your sister are playing for us tonight."

They both looked across the room at Lettice, still talking energetically.

"I hope you will enjoy the play," Isabella said, almost with indifference.

She intrigued him. He liked her brown eyes, the colour of her skin, the beautiful oval of her face, her long neck. She was serious. She had none of the playful manners of girls he met in society. It was amusing to be treated coolly by an actress in one's own home.

"I have to confess I have not had the honour of visiting your father's theatre and seeing you or your family act."

"You do not go to the play, Mister—"

"Carteret. The Earl is my father."

"Oh." Isabella was confused. She must be talking to a viscount. Her manner became stiffer.

"It was my notion to ask your father if he would be good enough to give us this performance," Lord Carteret was saying in his lazy way. "It gets dull, you know, in the winter. Especially for the ladies. We hunt and shoot a good deal and they drive out and go visiting, but there are only cards in the evenings. Such a lot of evenings."

He laughed pleasantly, as if she shared with

him a dismay at the interminable games of bezique and backgammon.

She thought him handsome, in a way. Not in the dramatic, deliberate way of actors who forced people to admire them. He was unselfconscious, as if unaware of how he looked. He had a round face, dark hair rather straight and not thick which fell on his forehead, a pleasure-loving mouth. His manner was extraordinarily kind and gentle.

Feeling it ungracious not to have visited the North Street theatre, Lord Carteret murmured, "My family do sometimes go to the play, you know, at the Garden."

"Covent Garden? My sister's idea of paradise!"

"Not yours, Miss Isabella?"

She smiled for the first time. She had looked distant and discontented; he could not know how rare such an expression was for her. When she smiled her whole face changed.

She gave him a mischievous, veiled look.

"I must not say so, but the theatre has never been heaven to me, my lord. Lettice would be excessively cross if she heard me confess it."

He looked at her and then, smilingly, at

33

Lettice. The young girl was surrounded by actors, carpenters and footmen. She seemed to be playing, as to the manner born, the role of duchess in a drama of high society.

2

(1)

"MR. SWAYNE, I think?" Lettice had approached the butler. He was taking no part in the scurry of preparations, a broad-shouldered elderly man with white hair tinged with yellow. Two young men stood in attendance ready to carry out his orders.

"Madam?"

He looked down at the small figure.

"The statue over there will have to be moved, I'm afraid, Mr. Swayne."

Lettice pointed at the marble Venus, nine feet high, which dominated part of the space allotted for the actors. The Venus, naked except for a piece of drapery held in one broken hand, had stood there since her arrival sixty years before, when the Earl's grandfather had brought the statue from Italy. He'd seen the goddess fished from the Tiber.

"That is out of the question, madam." Mr. Swayne, perfectly courteous, was cold as the marble. Lettice moved closer. She did something a person of rank would never do, rested her hand lightly on his arm. Her father, looking across the room, frowned. He had already asked the butler to provide extra lamps: it had been like talking to a brick wall. Did Lettice imagine she could succeed where he failed?

"You see, sir, it is not easy when one is an actress," murmured Lettice. "That beautiful statue is a little large, you know, and I am rather small. In our profession . . ."

Modest as a daughter, she confided to the impassive old man some of the mysteries of her art.

Mr. Swayne listened in silence. Orders were then given. The Venus, up-ended with one hand accusingly pointing skywards, was borne away by four footmen.

After the removal of her rival, Lettice's enslavement of the housekeeper was a minor matter. Lettice had known how to conquer her own sex since she was a baby. Men fell under Lettice's spell, women wished to look after her. "They are so understanding," was how Lettice thought of it.

She explained to the sympathetic Mrs. Judge about such things as lamps and candles, that the dressing-rooms were a trifle crowded, so perhaps . . . ? Her father did not know whether to be pleased or angry at Lettice's success.

"Letty!" sighed Isabella, when the girls had been escorted to a large bedroom which overlooked the moonlit park. "This house!"

The sisters were resting together on a four-poster bed, Lettice in the Juliet pose she unconsciously took, relaxed and still.

"It is very splendid."

"But there are so many *things*. Even in this room. Look at the gold-framed pictures and that clock with warriors sitting by it and the vases with the birds and those screens and the chest of drawers and six chairs and a chaise longue and that alabaster bust. When you think how bare our rooms are at home! And in the corridors so many paintings and all the marbles and bronzes and tapestries—and did you see a fountain trickling into a basin full of ferns? It is so stately—so beautiful. The flowers! Where do they come from?"

"Hothouses, I suppose."

"Have you ever seen such strange flowers? Great white scentless ones like plates and little yellow ones," said Isabella dreamily. "And as for servants, it is a sort of army.

37

With the butler in command. He's the Duke of Wellington."

"Mr. Swayne is a nice man. Bella, please let me rest."

"Did you know who I met? The Earl's son. The Viscount Carteret. Wait till I tell Mama!"

(2)

It was after ten o'clock when the Music Room began to fill with people. Thomas and his daughters, the actors, some servants, much to their enjoyment ordered by Mr. Swayne to help with props, were waiting in a parlour leading into the Music Room and which tonight was being used as the back-stage. Laurie Spindle opened the door a crack and hissed, "They're coming!"

There was a murmur, a rustle of dresses, the sound of voices, noises the actors knew well as an audience takes its place. But this noise was more subdued, lacking the vitality they were accustomed to. Lettice, in her Act One costume of *The Welsh Girl*, feet bare, hair pinned on top of her head, wondered if it was her fancy that she could smell a mixture of scent and flowers, cigars and brandy.

Thomas drew on his white gloves, opened

the Music Room door, strode into the centre of the space to be used as a stage and waited. He stood erect, grizzled head thrown back. When the audience was quiet, he made his opening address:

"My Lords. Ladies. Gentlemen. We have the honour tonight to present a play for your pleasure. We cannot, of course, use all our scenery or backcloths, many of the aids to our art will be lacking. We must ask you to employ your fancy. Help us poor actors to transform this room into a scene on the Welsh hills . . ." Isabella, listening to the speech which was stylishly delivered, thought its tone obsequious. Why did he behave like that to these people? *She* would not do so. She looked at Lettice, hoping to catch her sister's glance of mutual disapproval at their father, but Lettice was in a trance. She had that actressy look, intent, withdrawn . . . Thomas stopped speaking, there was polite applause. Lettice picked up a basket of rushes and made her entrance.

(3)

Lettice was always surprised when people who had never acted believed the players

39

could scarcely see the audience, either because of the glare of lights or the actor's own concentration. The reverse was true. As she moved through the play's disguises and absurdities, she saw the old Earl of Bagot, the young man who must be the Viscount, two ladies clearly Bagot daughters and many other members of the brilliant audience. Acting in a drawing-room had gains and losses. She liked an audience to be close and they were very close. She could see the old Earl slumped sideways in his chair, his face like that of a beaky grey-feathered bird. Some of the ladies quizzed her through glasses of the kind used in the Regency. The ladies, glittering with diamonds and seeming with their draperies and bouquets and fans too large for the tiny gilt chairs, watched with attention. The gentlemen were more difficult to engage. They clearly preferred horses to actors, probably looked on acting as a game they themselves sometimes indulged in for fun, forgotten the instant it was over. She had no intention of allowing them to forget her.

The actors, excited by the rich and un-familiar atmosphere, played well; Laurie Spindle made the audience laugh time and again. When the play ended the applause was surprisingly warm. One or two of the younger gentlemen actually shouted "Hurrah".

Lettice and Isabella curtsied deeply. Thomas bowed, his hand on his heart.

The actors finally left the room and the audience, in a good humour, began to rustle away.

Isabella and Lettice left the Music Room and went back upstairs to the bedroom to change. With the rest of the actors, they had been invited to supper with the guests after the performance.

The room, their room for this evening, had been rearranged the fire made up, fresh candles burning. A young maid was waiting to help them to dress.

She unlaced Isabella's costume and when Isabella sat at the dressing-table, the girl began to brush her hair. Isabella enjoyed the sensation and sat still for a while, then suddenly exclaimed, "Letty. Stop dreaming."

Lettice, still in her Welsh petticoats, was staring into the fire.

"I think I must go home."

"But Lord Bagot has invited us to supper!"

Lettice yawned. She was very white and seemed half asleep.

"I'm sorry. I couldn't possibly talk to

people. You must make my excuses. Thank the Earl and explain."

She stood indifferently as the maid began to help her take off the petticoats; every now and again she swallowed another yawn.

When Isabella was dressed she did not say good night to her sister but left the room angrily. She might have guessed this would happen! When Lettice collapsed after a performance there was nothing to be done. What was so horrid was that everybody would want to talk to Lettice, she had played the leading role, she was the interesting one. It was too vexing of her, and rude, too. Isabella felt so miserably embarrassed that she wanted to run away.

In the distance she could hear music, and as she turned a corner at the head of the staircase she came face to face with the tall figure of Viscount Carteret.

"Miss Isabella. I was in search of you and your sister."

"I am afraid my sister is tired and wishes to go home."

Shaken from her pretended poise, she was almost on the verge of tears. How could she enjoy this evening when nobody would wish to speak to her, when the one they wanted was gone?

She did not expect any help from the elegant unknown man looking at her so attentively. It was true she asked for help by her look but she was accustomed to actors, always selfish, and never thought men could be otherwise. She'd never met a man to whom good manners were as strong as religion.

"Would you prefer me to make your sister's excuses to the Earl?"

"Oh, Lord Carteret!"

"It will be an honour and a pleasure." The formal speech did not match his expression which was kind and rather teasing.

He offered her his arm and they went to the top of the staircase down which it seemed to Isabella that they floated.

"The Earl will perfectly understand," Lord Carteret said as they walked towards the music, "what an ordeal it has been for Miss Winter to play a part of such length. He will be glad she had the wisdom to return straight home."

(4)

Thomas Winter and Isabella were driven back to the town in the Bagot coach. During

43

the drive Isabella was silent. Her father did not notice, he was impatient to be home with Ellen.

He found his wife propped up in bed wearing a little lace cap, broad awake at three in the morning. They kissed tenderly.

"We must congratulate ourselves, my dear. I think I can say only jockeys or prize-fighters please the gentry the way we did tonight," he said. "Perhaps this will be the first of other visits. And in houses where the family is not connected with your own. You will, I hope, then consent to come with us."

"Oh yes," said Ellen vigorously.

"You were much missed. Nobody keeps things as well organised as you do."

Ellen agreed.

Lying side by side in the dark, they continued to talk comfortably.

"Lord Fletcher has a country seat not far from Brighton."

"And there is the Duke of Norfolk at Arundel."

Ellen was gratified by the success of the visit, not only because of the handsome fee which relieved some of Thomas's worries, but because in future he would not be so nervous if he had to deal with people of rank.

44

She looked forward to hearing a description of the glory of the Bagots, those distant relatives she'd never met: Isabella loved describing adventures. But the next day Isabella was irritable and gloomy by turns, sat about, and blushed crimson every time there was a knock at the front door. Lettice, who described the evening to her mother, tried to smooth things.

"Perhaps she is a little in love."

"With a viscount?" said Ellen, with a hard laugh.

Lettice took her mother's unresisting hand and pressed it.

"It is not impossible. Even when I was there, and you know I did not stay for the supper, he sought her out. He was very handsome."

"I am sure."

"But, Mama—"

"It is useless being sentimental with me, Lettice. If Isabella thinks a man of title would look twice at her, she's out of her wits. The only reason he would pay her attention is a dangerous one. I shall tell her so."

Poor Isabella, thought Lettice. It was the first time her sister had shown the least sign of falling in love, and during the days that followed she had every classic symptom: she ate nothing, scarcely talked, and looked as if she did not sleep much. Lettice often had mild flirtations or little love passages with actors. Her sister had teased her about them. This seemed much more serious. And yet . . . Lettice wasn't quite convinced it was love that had so unsettled her volatile sister.

Isabella knew she was behaving badly. She didn't seem able to help it. She was like a person who has stared for too long at the sky and whose eyes are dazzled, so that when she looks back at the road it seems dusty and dingy. Or a child who, spending the afternoon in a theatre, returns home to find it the dullest place on earth.

She had been disturbed, not only by Viscount Carteret's kindness but by every person, every object she had looked at in Bagot Park. The great chains of rooms, their ceilings painted with clouds and goddesses, the ladies floating by in rose colours or pearly whites, braceleted gloved hands used for nothing rougher than holding a fan, the candelabra burning with a hundred candles, the easy formality of the world of privilege, the servants waiting to carry out the guests' smallest wishes. Had Lettice asked Isabella

46

what she wanted, she would have replied "Everything." And because the desire was absurd, she sulked.

The play in rehearsal at the North Street theatre was, as Thomas printed it on the playbills, "by popular demand". It was *King Charles's Merrie Days* and audiences enjoyed any piece on the subject of Charles II and Nell Gwyn. Lettice played Nell and Isabella was Louise, the Duchess of Portsmouth, the Frenchwoman who shared the doubtful joys of the King's bed.

Lettice disliked *King Charles's Merrie Days*. She never wished to play any character who was immoral. She was reserved, undressed beneath a wrapper, would never discuss sex even with Isabella. Her sister did not share her prudery and when the actors talked of the old wicked days, Isabella listened openly. The theatres had been filled with soliciting whores. "You should have seen the fights— heard the screams!"

"Horrible," shuddered Isabella delightedly.

But today's tastes were changing; in this new version of *King Charles's Merrie Days* there was not a single scene in a bedchamber.

On the afternoon of the first night, it began to snow. Isabella, huddled in one of her mother's shawls, sat on the window-seat. The snow whirled through the air, seeming to fly up rather than down. When the carriages and carts went by their wheels spurted up slush which spattered the clothes of the passers-by.

How pinched everybody looks, she thought. It's time to go to the theatre, I suppose. How I hate it. She watched her father picking his way across the street.

She leaned her forehead against the icy window-pane. In her imagination she saw the women in Bagot Park, exquisitely dressed, waited-upon, warm. Fires burned in great fireplaces, the Viscount—they called him "Carteret", he did not seem to have a Christian name—sat by the fire with his sisters. What did the nobility talk of? Conversation in the Winter family was theatrical and usually about money. That endless talk of money and the lack of it . . .

"Isabella. We must go."

It was Ellen in the doorway, dressed in her old black cloak with the hood, her hands in her muff. Isabella left the window-seat in silence. She glanced at her mother's stony face.

"I'm sorry if I have been disagreeable."

"You certainly have."

48

"Seeing Bagot Park and everything—I suppose it upset me. I can't *help* feeling like that, Mama!"

The cold disapproval in Ellen's face vanished as if by magic.

"Of course you can't," she said. "You have Bagot blood in your veins, my child, I would have been exactly the same. Your father and sister don't understand things like that."

She fastened Isabella's cloak—Ellen's equivalent of the tenderest kiss—and they went out of the house. They lifted their skirts as high as modesty allowed and waited for a carriage to go by, mud spattering, and the deafening noise of wheels on cobblestones.

Lettice and Isabella shared the smallest dressing-room in a row of rooms situated under the stage. The call-boy was filling the oil-lamp in his usual fashion. Lettice gave out a shriek.

"Look out for my costume, Jeffrey. You are so clumsy. That's our best lace on the cuffs."

She sat down at the dressing-table, lit the candles and began to pin up her long hair, trying to make it resemble Lely's portrait of Nell Gwyn. It took her a long time.

Watching her, Isabella said, "You should wear a wig."

49

"I detest to wear a wig."

There was no arguing with Lettice when she used that voice. Isabella laced herself into the stock costume of green taffeta, much mended and darned, which was used for Court ladies in Shakespeare, Sheridan or any other piece. She had to fasten the dress carefully in case the silk should tear.

"Mama says most of the boxes are empty, it will be a dull performance tonight."

"*I* shall not walk through my part on that account," said Lettice disdainfully.

A thump on the door.

"Beginners, please! Beginners—if you perlease!"

The girls stood up, Lettice in a blouse falling from freckled shoulders, a tray of property oranges in her hands, Isabella in the mended taffeta. They went along the narrow passage between the dressing-rooms and climbed a ladder towards the stage.

They would never climb that stairway again.

The house was not full but the audience was friendly and settled down to enjoy Nell Gwyn and her antics. Half-way through the first act there was a scene between Nell and the Duchess. Lettice had a soliloquy first,

50

ending: "Ah, but I shudder, in spite of my natural courage!"

Isabella entered. Facing Lettice haughtily and using her best French accent, she began her speech. Suddenly from nowhere a gust of smoke blew across the stage. Trained to continue, as every actor must, Isabella finished her speech and Lettice replied. The smoke belched in again, thicker and yellower. Then there was a piercing shriek from the audience, the bloodcurdling cry of, "*Fire!*"

With something between a roar and a groan every man and woman in the audience sprang to their feet and began to rush towards the doors. The smoke grew thicker, there was the noise of crackling and behind Lettice a tongue of flame licked up the painted flat showing St. James's Palace.

Lettice and Isabella fled to the Prompt side, the audience stampeded, voices shouted vainly for calm. Actors rushed by, almost knocking the girls down. In the Prompt corner Ellen was dazedly watching the fiercely burning scenery.

"Mama! Come! Come!"

They dragged her, tottering, backstage but she pulled away screaming "Your father— Thomas—"

"We'll get him!" Somehow they managed to push Ellen into a passageway and out of the Stage Door. "Thomas!" shrieked Ellen again. Laurie Spindle, bundling actors and actresses out into the snow-covered street, shouted, "I'll find him. Lettice, take your mother and get out before the doorway catches!"

Sobbing and stumbling, the girls and Ellen made their way to the front of the theatre. It was chaos. Carriages and stamping horses, shouting people, no sign of the fire-engines but only the frightened crowds, tongues of fire flaming at an upper window, the whirling snow.

Suddenly Ellen cried, "Look!"

Down the passageway from the Stage Door came Laurie Spindle and beside him, half dragging, half carrying a basket of singed costumes, was Thomas.

(5)

By the time the fire-engines galloped into North Street the theatre was burning like a torch.

The fierce flames grew higher as they were fed by stores of materials which ignited at

52

once . . . rolls of painted backcloths, sized flats of bone-dry wood, baskets of painted, gilded costumes, dozens of wigs, wooden props, oil-lamps, benches, velvet curtains. The heat was so intense that the firemen could not safely get close to the theatre . . . all they did was prevent the fire spreading down the street.

The whole of Market Chester, men, women and children, came to watch the fire. It was a spectacle of high drama. The theatre drew more crowds on the night it burned down than in all the years it had been a playhouse. The street was packed with tense, silent people staring at the fire, until tiredness and freezing cold finally drove them indoors.

Thomas, his family and most of the actors stood at the windows of the house opposite, shocked, white-faced, their faces and clothes smeared and blackened with smoke. Thomas watched the fire in a dreadful silence. It was a holocaust of his life. Scenery, props, costumes, the building his wife's inheritance had bought for him, his hopes, all, all consumed in roaring flames, like hell itself. The very bricks of the building were burned—later they fell to powder. The smell, acrid and bitter, filled the town afterwards for nearly a week.

At last the actors crept away. Ellen put her arm round Thomas and took him up to bed.

Only Lettice stayed. She crouched on the window-seat, looking at the smouldering blackened building opposite. Great smuts floated in the air among the snowflakes and settled on a playbill bearing her name.

3

(1)

SPRING came late in Northumberland. The daffodils in the woods outside the town only budded at the beginning of May. The heather stayed for a long time a brown sea of dry stems. In Sussex, Lettice thought, the bluebells would have come and gone in the hazel woods and so would the primroses.

It was over a year since the fire had destroyed the family's livelihood in Market Chester, floating away Thomas's theatre in black smuts on the winter air. But Lettice still thought of life there, the pleasure and freedom of owning their own theatre. What they had done—all they could do—was to start up the old circuit life of travelling from town to town—taking any circuit in England that would have them.

Jolting in teeth-rattling coaches, the Winters returned to the travelling life. They were often cold and miserable, racked and battered by day and night. Sometimes the coaches halted interminably at toll gates, sometimes the roads were impassable in seas of mud. Sometimes Thomas scarcely had the fares for the journey. They arrived at an unfamiliar town, met unknown actors, and unpacked their own few shabby costumes, an essential part of their livelihood.

Thomas had been stunned by the disaster. Had it not been for Ellen, he might have been gravely ill. He escaped the horror of bankruptcy and arrest by a hairsbreadth, by Ellen writing to her uncle for money. The sum needed to rescue Thomas was sent, with a contemptuous "Do not make such a request again. It will not be granted."

Ellen had no time to suffer over such a humiliation, she was too relieved at saving her husband from prison. Everything had to be sold: the costumes and properties saved from the fire, a few pieces of undamaged scenery, all the furniture in the North Street house, even Ellen's diamond ring and the gold watch Thomas had inherited from his father. When actors and creditors were paid, Thomas breathed again. By the grace of God, the Winters obtained an engagement on the Manchester circuit. They left Market

Chester with luggage consisting of a single box, and a bag containing two of Ellen's bonnets.

Thomas might have had a stroke, might have died, but he could not afford it. He obeyed his wife's repeated entreaty: "Tom. Don't be ill, *please!*"

He took his family to Manchester and began to work again. He was short-tempered and looked older.

Lettice was more unhappy than she admitted to anyone but she fixed her mind on her work and tried, in small ways, to comfort her father, who scarcely noticed her. The two who came out best during the time of the disaster were Ellen and Isabella. Ellen was positively cheerful: she enjoyed drama. When their furniture was sold, she attended the auction with interest, returned to the stripped house and made a picnic on upturned boxes. When she said goodbye to the actors, she gave them words of advice. She bade Milly goodbye as if parting with a family retainer.

"We must give the servant a farewell gift. She has served us faithfully," said Ellen, tipping her. It was a maxim of Ellen's that one might be poor, but one must never look poor.

Isabella, too, behaved well during the days following the fire, helping to pack the scorched costumes, counting spoons, suggesting her trinkets should be sold.

But such heroism could not last and Isabella soon became very low-spirited. The drama was over, Market Chester left behind. The life which began again was poor and hard. Thomas called himself "Stage Manager" but he often did the work of six stage carpenters, setting the stage himself. When there was no money for coach fares, the family walked from one engagement to the next on the open road in pouring rain or icy winds. Once they acted in an old malt house to an audience of three boys and an old woman.

Thomas's face grew pinched. Sometimes he was morose, sometimes his worry took the form of harassing his daughters. He began to insist that they should say their lines aloud at breakfast-time. He would stare at them with a grey unsmiling face and say, "What comes next? And then? And then?"

Ellen supported him, she called it "bolstering him up" to herself though not to the girls. With Thomas's lost confidence and Isabella's gloom, she and Lettice had the worst of the family's trouble.

But now they were settled for a season in Newcastle and after their adventures in barns or disused stables in inn-yards (when they had no circuit engagement they became strolling players), the family were acting in a good theatre again. Things were better.

Lettice sat in a lean-to whitewashed attic at the top of the lodgings where the family were installed. The room was so small that the girls had to sleep together in the narrow bed, top to toe, and when they dressed they edged past each other to fetch a comb or a petticoat.

Uncomfortable and cramped, Lettice felt cheerful. The sun was shining as she brushed her bright hair. Something delightful had happened yesterday. She had been in her dressing-room when the door had creaked, and a voice chanted in sepulchral tones: "I ha' summat to say, summat at my tongue's end—it must come out. Do you recollect when you sent me away fra' your service? Because I wore given to drink, you turned your back on me, I ha' never been a man since that time."

"Laurie!"

A goblin face had peered round the door

and while Lettice was still laughing at the words which came from a melodrama, *Luke the Labourer*, which they had played together, they rushed into each other's arms.

Laurie had told her delightedly that he had just arrived—to join the company.

"But why did Papa not tell me you were coming?"

"Because he didn't know. I didn't know either. I was just passing through and called to see him," said Laurie, with all the player's optimism, indifferent to the risk of no work, certain his gift would not fail him.

What a joy it was, Lettice thought now, to re-find one's friends. If only Isabella would be a little happier too. Her sister had gone down the alley to the pastrycook's and Lettice was guiltily glad of a respite. Isabella was so tiring. Lettice wished for the thousandth time that her sister could care a little about the theatre. Since the fire, Isabella's indifference—no, it was dislike—of her work was more marked. What she talked about was the gentry. She had an almost religious reverence for the "polite world", and her mother's distant relationship to it. When Lettice wanted to discuss plays and actors, Isabella talked of the titled people her mother had or had not met, those now-forgotten Bagots in Sussex, or of some Lord This or Lady That in the audience the previous evening.

Lettice was pleased when well-born people attended the play, but only if they behaved with propriety and raised the tone of the audience. All Lettice hoped was that there would be no fighting or shouting.

The attic door opened and Isabella came in carrying a plate covered with a piece of muslin. She wore her shabby brown frock and her mother's old black bonnet. The dingy colours did not suit her but her eyes were brighter than usual.

"Letty, Pa has a visitor. He is waiting downstairs."

Lettice looked alarmed.

"Is he someone Papa owes money—"

"Oh no, I am sure he is an actor."

When their father had gone down to meet the visitor, the girls went into their mother's bedroom, the next-door attic, slightly larger than their own.

The lodgings were in a back street fifteen minutes' walk from the theatre. The house was Elizabethan, with bulging walls, blackened beams and creaking stairs, and stood in an alley of houses huddled together like old women gossiping. The alley was so narrow that women strung their washing from one side to the other, like flags.

There was a pastrycook's, a cobbler's, a saddler's, small-windowed cottages smelly and dark, and a dame's school filled during the day with shouting children who poured out in the evening like water through a dam. Ellen Winter did not like the lodgings and liked their owner less, a Mrs. Gunn who had been an actress. The woman dyed her hair and wore rouge, had eyes like flints and was inquisitive. Mrs. Gunn disliked Ellen in return, particularly when she boasted.

"Your father fetched the tea from the kitchen. That woman would not bring it up," Ellen said. "Isabella, your back hair is coming down. Lettice, why are you wearing a ribbon round your neck?"

"I thought it pretty."

"If you don't own a necklace, it is preferable to wear nothing."

"Some of the actors would enjoy it if she did that!" giggled Isabella.

"Isabella, I do not allow impropriety," said her mother coldly.

Lettice caught her sister's eye and they exchanged a grin, something rare nowadays.

Isabella sprawled on her parents' bed, Lettice sat by her mother's side. She took her hand and gave it a kiss and Ellen, who never showed affection, looked pleased.

"A bun, Isabella?"

Isabella took a large one and was biting into it, her lips covered with sugar, when the door opened.

There was a small commotion as Thomas and a tall young man came into the room. Ellen, who could not bear being taken by surprise, put down the dish. Isabella tried to swallow a mouthful. Only Lettice, unselfconsciously holding a bun in one hand, bowed pleasantly.

"My dear, may I present Buckley Vernon? He is to join our company and has done us the honour of calling—"

"Charmed. Delighted."

Buckley Vernon bowed and smiled and Ellen, recovering her poise, graciously offered him tea.

"We prefer our own tea, Mr. Vernon. In lodgings the tea that is served is really a little—"

"I agree, Mrs. Winter. Horrid stuff as black as treacle. Thank you very much indeed."

Buckley Vernon sat down and began to talk.

He was a man who knew how to charm. He was tall but somewhat round-shouldered, his face pale, his brownish hair greasy and plentiful, his nose finely shaped. He had a beautiful thick-lipped mouth which curled upwards like a girl's. His manner, noticeably wooing, would have been called ingratiating in a less handsome man. It seemed to say that he knew he was fascinating, and if you thought so (but only then), he would admire you in return.

He divided his attention and his smiles fairly among the Winter family, larding his conversation to Thomas with "Sirs", deferring to Ellen and being gallant to both sisters.

"Your father tells me, Miss Winter," he said to Lettice, "that he is planning to revive *King Charles's Merrie Days*. You, of course, will be pretty, witty Nell?"

"Not necessarily. There are other actresses in the company," Lettice said. She did not say "good" actresses.

"But the part is suited to you, surely?"

"It is not a case of parts 'suiting' my girls, Mr. Vernon," said Thomas. "In a stock company they have learned the important lesson of being useful. They can play anything, tragedy, burlesque, farce, comedy."

"They are both nice little actresses," put in Ellen.

"There is no question which of us is the better, Mama," said Isabella, not very gracefully. "It's Lettice."

Buckley Vernon looked from one girl to the other with an expression of exaggerated languishing and murmured:

"How happy could I be with either
Were t'other dear charmer away!
But while ye thus tease me together,
To neither a word will I say."

The family laughed and he joined them.

(2)

Vernon's arrival in the Newcastle company was greeted with various jealousies. The two leading actresses, Georgiana Coins, a hard-faced forty-five, and Margaret Frognal, sickly, pathetic and nearly thirty, angrily competed for him. Buckley divided himself between them as neatly as a woman cutting a cake. Some of the young male actors were cold to him. Laurie Spindle would not give an opinion. When Lettice asked he said, "Wait and see."

"I wonder why Laurie does not like Mr. Vernon, Mama," said Lettice thoughtfully.

"He is put out because Mr. Vernon admires you," said Ellen, who considered Laurie Spindle beneath contempt.

If the ladies, with the possible exception of Isabella, openly admired Buckley, the man who welcomed him was Thomas Winter. The fire in Sussex was history now and so was Thomas's position as theatre owner. This engagement at Newcastle was a godsend; but could he make it succeed? He had a horror of debt and sometimes imagined that some unpaid creditor from the past might emerge and would take legal steps to have him arrested. Money was short and the Newcastle theatre not full. The players in a previous season had not been popular and Thomas was suffering from the faults of his predecessors.

But Buckley Vernon might be a valuable addition. There was the old favourite *King Charles's Merrie Days*—it still might have some life in it; Buckley Vernon was to play the King. The play could be pushed into the repertory in a couple of days—no need for more than a few rehearsals. All the circuit actors, including Thomas and his daughters, had fifty or sixty roles at their finger-ends. They must be able to act a role at a moment's notice. It was part of the job and demanded by managers, just as a newly engaged actor must bring with him some feathered hats, a good cape with a swing to it and a well-handled rapier.

Thomas had received the news that Davenant, the great Henry Davenant, had consented to play with the company for a few weeks. Davenant, a star, as they called famous actors nowadays, would fill the theatre every night from pit to gallery. In the meantime, the Merry Monarch and Nell Gwyn must do their best.

Buckley Vernon was as good as Thomas hoped. He had the right sensuality for King Charles and a pleasing stage presence. Once again Lettice pinned up her red hair and carried her tray of property oranges.

One spring evening, when *King Charles* ended and Lettice went into the dark little dressing-room to change out of her Court dress, there was no sign of Isabella. Lettice lit the candles and hung up Nell's buckram-stiffened petticoats. The theatre was quiet. The candle threw shadows on the brick walls, distorting the shape of a feathered hat into the fat profile of a child.

Picking up the candle and protecting the flame with her hand she went into the passage. Buckley Vernon, wearing a massive caped coat, was coming towards her.

"Miss Winter, I came looking for you. I asked your father if I might walk you home."

"Are my family already gone?"

"Your father seems to think I might be trusted," he answered, smiling. He stepped back for her to precede him but his coat was so bulky that Lettice had to squeeze against him, far closer than she thought proper.

They set off through the streets. An east wind was blowing, it seemed to hide round every corner waiting to spring. She put her hands into her mother's moth-eaten fur muff.

"The house wasn't full enough," Buckley said.

"Papa says we must wait for Davenant before the theatre is completely full."

"Why can he do it and not us?"

"Because he's a great actor."

Buckley made a dissatisfied sound.

"Perhaps *we* are. He wasn't the idol of the

68

public when he was young either. Success . . . do you want it as much as I do, Miss Winter?"

"I want to be a good actress."

He laughed.

"One has to be one of three things, you know. More famous than the others. Or richer. Or bigger."

The gas lamps at the street corners threw yellowish circles of light, but between one lamp and the next the streets were very dark and Lettice was glad to have a companion who was bigger than other people, as he had just indicated. They were walking through mean streets not far from Mrs. Gunn's alleyway when Buckley said, "Look there."

In one tumbledown house every window was glowing with candles. As they drew nearer Lettice heard a kind of steady roar of many voices all talking at once. The door was open and a man stood outlined by the light. Catching sight of Buckley and Lettice, both respectably dressed in so poor an alleyway, he disappeared indoors, giving the rickety door a violent slam. The men's voices, the slam, the silhouettes through torn curtains, made Lettice quicken her steps.

Buckley gave her his arm.

"Newcastle is not the peaceful place it used to be. When I was playing here three years ago it was quiet as a church. Now there's a thunderstorm rumbling."

Lettice nodded. Everybody kept talking about the price of bread, how hungry people were, and how angry. Sometimes she felt guilty when she sat down to supper with her parents. And her father had said the bad harvest last autumn meant things could only get worse. . . .

"Have you seen the crowds in the market, Mr. Vernon? We went through it on Sunday on our way to church and a man was making a speech. He had a white face and hair and was so thin—he looked like a spirit. All the men in the audience, I mean in the crowd, shouted and cheered. I saw one man weeping."

"Did they frighten you?"

"Oh no," she said, surprised. "They would never harm us. They're poor and hungry and we have been both. When we were children, Isabella and I were sometimes so hungry when we went to bed that we made knots in our handkerchiefs and bit on them. Papa was almost bankrupt last year too, you know," she added unselfconsciously, "and thought he would go to prison."

70

She was silent for a while. He waited.

"Apart from being sorry for them in the Christian way, there is something else. I always worry that real life may interrupt. One has to be very strong as an actor not to be swamped by real life, don't you think? To use it, not to drown in it."

"I am sure it will never drown *you*," he said, with a certain irony.

(3)

Isabella sat on the window-seat overlooking the chimney pots and the cold, bright sky. It was the first week in May but the room was chilly and the fire, a shovelful of smoking coal, would soon be out. It would need a battle with Mrs. Gunn to get the scuttle refilled. Isabella tucked her feet under her for warmth, balancing on the narrow seat with difficulty. In three days it would be her birthday: she would be eighteen. How old that sounded! Georgiana Coins might be well over forty but she had married at sixteen, even if her husband had been killed in the duel in *Hamlet* two years later. Margaret Frognal, who drank too much gin, had been twice married. Isabella's own mother had eloped at eighteen. Isabella sat doing the arithmetic of age and matrimony and getting low-spirited. Her mother was no comfort. One of Ellen's favourite phrases, when talking of any girl planning to marry was "High time. I do dislike seeing an old bride."

Lettice had taken her own nineteenth birthday, celebrated a few months before, quite philosophically.

"How does it feel to be nineteen, Letty?" Isabella had asked.

Lettice had said Isabella was brooding over "the old bride" again.

"I can't help brooding. I wish I was like you."

"You wouldn't choose to be like me *ever*. What? Worry over acting, get discouraged, spend your time bending over a script."

"I suppose not."

"Well, then," Lettice had said shrugging.

It was true Isabella had never envied Lettice until now. Perhaps it was a symptom of getting older. Lettice was doing what she wanted. She even liked playing opposite Buckley Vernon.

Isabella's manner to Buckley Vernon after the first day or two was noticeably cold, which surprised him for he rarely failed with

72

women. "The dark one" as he called her to himself apparently was not interested, and after a few unsuccessful attempts Buckley stopped trying. As she didn't find him attractive, he would persuade himself that she was plain. But it was quite difficult to do that.

Isabella had always discussed her thoughts with her sister, but she avoided the subject of Buckley. He upset her. Or rather her own feelings about him did. Sometimes, seeing him at a distance, she felt slightly faint. Only stupid women fell in love with actors. She did not want to spend all her time imagining what it would be like in Buckley's arms, feel her stomach drop when she saw him, hear her voice sound hoarse when she answered him. She kept away.

Her mother's neat head looked round the door.

"There you are. Lettice said you must have gone for a walk."

"I was thinking."

Ellen gave a sharp laugh. "It is no good sitting about with a face like a fiddle. Come into my room and tidy my dressing-table drawer."

Ellen liked to give her daughters the tasks of a lady's maid. She sewed all day in the

Wardrobe but "simply could not" mend her own gloves. She had a pleasure in being waited on and a satisfaction in being obeyed.

Lettice was by the window, a script in her hand, when Isabella flounced in. Looking at her sister, Isabella thought Lettice's green dress less shabby than her own brown. Hers was fuller than Lettice's, it measured twenty yards round the hem, but she did not own enough petticoats to make it look right and where would the money for cambric come from to make more? Isabella had spent hours with the detested brown dress, sewing on white bobble fringe. It still looked dingy.

"Why can't Letty do your drawer, Ma?"

"Because she is working."

Ellen had rigid ideas about work. She waited on Thomas tenderly because he was weighed down with work, but she would never lift a finger to help anyone enjoy themselves. Work did not include reading anything but plays, and when Isabella read novels she put paper covers over the books and lettered them "Sheridan" or "Vanbrugh". Work was sewing in the Wardrobe but not stitching a fringe on one's own dress.

Isabella sat down at the worm-eaten oak dressing-table. Like every other piece of Mrs.

Gunn's furniture, it was rickety, one leg secured by curl-papers wedged into its socket. The looking-glass was spotted, the bedcover clean but scorched, the walls blackened with candle-smoke. Nothing in the room was fresh except the faces of the young girls.

Isabella placed her mother's possessions in a row on the table. A pot of rouge. A box of rice powder. Some glove stretchers and a shoe horn. A pearl-handled buttonhook, two handkerchiefs embroidered with violets by Lettice. In a box was a pair of seed-pearl earrings, not valuable enough to be sold during the threatened bankruptcy. Isabella put them on and set the circles swinging.

Ellen was watching.

"They suit you."

"Do you think so?"

"Have them."

"But they're the only ones you've got!"

"Young people look better in jewellery. My face is old."

Lettice, still reading, stretched out her hand to her mother.

"Mama, that is not true."

"You can have the earrings for your birthday," said Ellen. "Which reminds me. Have we decided on your birthday treat?"

Lettice closed the play. She knew the part by heart.

"What about a picnic?"

"Papa likes picnics," said Isabella, still looking at her own reflection.

"He could go to the market early and buy us some fruit," said Ellen, who enjoyed sending her husband on shopping errands.

"Did you know there was fighting in the market?" Lettice said suddenly. "Mr. Vernon saw it. Mr. Vernon said—"

"Oh, Mr. Vernon, Mr. Vernon, why must you quote him all the time? He isn't God Almighty," interrupted Isabella irritably.

Ellen's expression turned to stone.

"How *dare* you!" she said, fixing Isabella with dark eyes. "How dare you swear! It is blasphemous, and what is more it is unladylike. I shall not tell you again." Isabella blushed scarlet and Lettice began to talk, drawing her mother's attention away from her miserable sister.

"Mr. Vernon was crossing the Buttermarket. He said it was so cheerful with all the carts and the vegetables and pigeons in cages, there was even a Punch and Judy show. Suddenly a scuffle started and a crowd seemed to come from nowhere, men with cudgels and the stalls were overturned and one man was on the ground. Mr. Vernon got away as quickly as he could."

"Such courage!" muttered Isabella, still crushed.

"But what man of sense would join in a fight he knows nothing about? Besides, how could he play King Charles if some villain had given him a black eye?"

It was agreed in the family that Isabella should have a picnic for her birthday treat. The weather was good, the skies a windswept blue. The picnic would be on the day before her birthday, a Sunday, the only day when there was no performance. They decided to travel to a fishing village some miles away.

The size of the audiences at the theatre had improved. *King Charles's Merrie Days* was popular and Thomas also introduced a burletta into the repertory, a romp based on a story from the *Arabian Nights*. The idea had been Laurie Spindle's.

"The town's unsettled at present," he said to Thomas, with the confidence of someone very small and very hardy. "People are miserable and as for the price of a loaf! Why not give them a chance to laugh?"

Thomas disliked suggestions from other

people but agreed. The piece turned out a success. Laurie played a miniature Lord Chamberlain, Buckley a prince, Lettice an Arabian princess. On the first night there was loud applause and approving whistles.

When the curtain fell, her white painted cheeks glowing with excitement, Lettice came offstage with Isabella and Buckley. They made a strange-looking trio. Lettice wore purple harem trousers, a vaporous veil, huge anklets studded with paste rubies. Isabella was in blue, star-patterned, a wreath of crimson flowers on her head. Buckley wore yellow satin and a turban sewn with diamonds the size of marbles.

"Did you ask your sister about her birthday, Miss Winter?" asked Buckley. He called other actresses familiarly by their Christian names.

"Oh, Bella," exclaimed Lettice, "Mr. Vernon has begged he may hire a carriage to take us to the sea. Papa said we should go in the public coach but Mr. Vernon says it will be crowded and horrid. So—is it not kind of him?"

Buckley smiled easily.

Isabella thanked him and escaped as soon as she decently could. Lettice continued to talk

78

about the performance, sighing, "I could play it all over again!"

Alone in the dressing-room, Isabella lit the candle and sat down. Why must they have that man at her party tomorrow? She did not want to be with him for ten minutes, let alone a whole day.

She nervously clasped her hands. She had the desire, strong and wild as a nymph in mythology, to run, to flee, to escape from the only man who could make her tremble.

4

(1)

THE Winter family trooped out into the sunshine when the carriage arrived. Ellen Winter thought Buckley very smart in his caped coat with the steel clasps and a hat of sporting style. She wished Mrs. Gunn was not standing in the doorway staring at them.

"I am handling the reins, Mrs. Winter. I'm a dab hand. Wait until you see me," said Buckley. Ellen gave her upward-running laugh, like a rising scale of notes. Her small brown face had a trace of the girl who had made a romantic runaway marriage.

Buckley let down the step and handed Ellen into the carriage. He enquired which of the girls would sit beside him on the box. Before anybody could reply Lettice said, "Would you think me selfish if I asked to be the one? Last time Bella sat on a box she felt giddy, did you not, Bella?"

Isabella agreed she had felt giddy and afterwards had a headache. She was relieved as she climbed into the carriage beside her mother; but Lettice's intuition made her uneasy. What else did she guess about her feelings for Buckley Vernon?

The door was closed, Buckley climbed up on the box beside Lettice and away they went.

The grey stone houses were left behind, they trotted into the country, greener and more springlike than Lettice had expected. Buckley pointed interesting sights out to her with his whip.

Isabella, glad to be away from Buckley, enjoyed the unaccustomed luxury of travelling in a private carriage, not squashed in a public coach. She, too, admired the countryside, but as the sun grew warmer the inside of the carriage was soon unpleasantly stuffy. Isabella could not open a window, her mother was always cold, even in summertime.

At last Buckley reined in the horses and drew the carriage to a stop. Thomas had fallen asleep and woke with a start.

"Have we arrived? Good. Let me take the baskets, my dear. Yes, I must fasten that lid. No, I can manage—well—if Isabella could manage one—"

He collected things and forgot things, making the few possessions needed for the picnic seem as numerous as the costumes of a play.

They took a winding path down the cliffs. Sea birds cried in a melancholy way. Isabella thought the sound mournful. Who had told her that gulls were the souls of drowned sailors?

Down on the shore they found a deserted stretch of rocks and sand.

Ellen took command.

"Where shall we sit? No, no, Mr. Vernon, not where there is a rock pool, one of the girls will be sure to drag her dress in it. Here among these rocks is just right."

Buckley spread a rug across a flat granite rock, Lettice unpacked the food, Thomas uncorked the wine. A gull almost as large as a swan swooped down close to Ellen, folded its wings and stood staring at her with yellow eyes. She stretched out her hand fearlessly and gave it some bread.

They ate their meal and sat enjoying the sunshine and the sound of the sea.

"Tell me, sir," Buckley said to Thomas, "why should the theatre not be a gentlemanly profession? My father is a Justice of the Peace and was deeply shocked at my choice of calling. But I told him then and I believe it—one can be a gentleman and an actor."

Thomas's face lit up.

"My dear fellow. That is something I've said for years."

After a while Lettice stood up and said she would like to walk along the shore. Buckley asked if he might go with her.

"Well . . . I was going to say my lines aloud. I wanted to hear what they sounded like with the waves as an accompaniment."

"An excellent idea. I will cue for you."

"Isabella can go too," said Ellen.

Isabella answered ungraciously that she would stay where she was.

The two young people walked away across the sand. Ellen glanced at Isabella, thinking she was tiresomely moody and best left alone.

When it was time to leave, everybody was lulled by the hours spent in the open air. Lettice was again handed up on to the box, Isabella again went inside with her parents. They set off briskly. The fishing village was left behind, the road entered a wood. There was a blur of bluebells. Emerging into the sunshine, they saw a high stone wall surrounding the well-tended lands and great trees of a gentleman's park.

Ellen leaned forward.

"That must be the Fallowfield estate. There is the house. Handsome, is it not? But too old-fashioned."

On a rise of ground stood a huge stone house as grim as a fortress. Ellen talked knowledgeably about "the Fallowfields", whom they had married, what were their titles. She always knew about the aristocracy. She was still talking when the carriage gave a swerve, Buckley tugged at the reins, and Ellen and Isabella were almost thrown from their seats.

"Perhaps we're making way for the public coach," said Ellen calmly sitting back again.

The vehicle passing them was not the crowded dusty public coach. A shining yellow and black carriage went by, drawn by four magnificent chestnut horses. Isabella caught a glimpse of two gentlemen inside and an elaborate coat of arms on the door. The carriage turned through the open gates of the manor.

As the carriage vanished into the distance, Isabella felt that its brightness had shed a light on her and her surroundings as fierce as that which came nightly from the stage. It shone on genteel poverty. Her cloak was shabby, her mother's gloves darned, her father's boots scuffed so that there remained no leather, only polish, on the toes. She put her hand to the ribbons of her bonnet. Those, too, were threadbare from tying and retying. Even the cushions against which she leaned smelled of dust.

(2)

The great actor Henry Davenant was due in Newcastle that week and Thomas waited his arrival in trepidation. Thomas had seen Davenant act many times—like most professionals Thomas attended the play on any and every occasion, comparing performances as a wine-lover might discuss vintages.

"Kean's Hamlet was at its peak in 1814."

"Kemble's Brutus, to my mind, will never be equalled."

He had favourite theatre stories which he liked telling and told well (they bored his daughters). There was the legendary occasion when Nelson had come to see *The Merry Wives of Windsor* at a theatre where Thomas was working. When the hero's carriage arrived the street had rung with the shouts of the crowd, the box office was besieged. At the end of the performance crowds of sailors from Nelson's ship were waiting outside the theatre to greet him.

"I never saw such a thing. I shall never forget it."

Thomas always ended the story in the same way.

Ellen was as worried as Thomas at the prospect of Henry Davenant's arrival. The man was a great actor but he was a bully. Stories of Davenant were much repeated and laughed over; his despotism had a kind of largeness which suited his huge reputation. But it was one thing to joke about him in the Green Room, another to cope with him in person. Poor Thomas always "caved in" as Ellen privately called it.

A letter arrived from Davenant.

Sir,
I expect to be at the theatre the afternoon of Thursday. I will perform *Lear* and *Hamlet*. *Lear* shall be first. Choose the Cordelia with attention, if you please. She has importance to me. I do not require rehearsals for my

plays but wish to see the young lady on the matter of Scene One. Mind she is young. Not above 30.

Yours obediently.

Thomas looked fussed.

"I must put up the playbills immediately."

"And no rehearsals at all," said Lettice. "Cordelia is difficult. I have always found it so."

She was as anxious as her father.

"Famous actors never rehearse, Lettice," said Ellen. "He knows the great parts as you do your own name. We simply have to fit in."

"Is he as fierce as they say?"

"Of course not," snapped Thomas.

Five minutes after Davenant arrived in the town, before his boxes were taken to his lodgings, he marched into Thomas's office without knocking and demanded that the actors be "mustered forthwith".

The company knew about the great man's arrival and were waiting in the Green Room when the message arrived. Making grimaces and jokes, they trooped on to the stage. Lettice was excited and curious. She had never worked with a great actor before or even seen one at close quarters.

Davenant was standing onstage, his back to the empty auditorium. He was a stocky man with broad shoulders and brown hair worn brushed upwards and curling in the outdated manner of King William. He had heavy whiskers. He was perhaps forty years old but his face, though lined, could look considerably younger. His cheekbones were high, his nose strong but irregular, his eyes large and a burning blue.

He glared at the actors who froze into stillness. Georgiana Coins, usually the first to draw attention to herself, looked quite glassy; even Buckley was nervous.

"This is the company, Mr. Davenant," said Thomas deferentially.

"I can see that, man! Gentlemen, we play *Lear* tonight," said Davenant in a powerful voice with a curious edge to it. "Who is Kent? Gloucester? Goneril? Oswald?"

He ran through the parts like a father checking the presence of a large ill-behaved family. As each actor stepped forward he looked him up and down and said nothing. Finally the call came: "Cordelia."

Lettice took a pace forward.

"And who may you be?"

"Lettice Winter, sir."

"Any relation to the manager fellow?" demanded Davenant as if Thomas were not present, let alone standing at his elbow.

"His daughter."

"Are you, by God?"

Lettice said nothing. Davenant looked at her.

"I wish a word with you," he said at last. "The rest of you," glancing at the silent actors, "can go. I do not rehearse my plays. The performance is at seven, but I wish it to start five minutes later to avoid shuffling from the audience. I trust you know your business. That is all."

The actors melted away until, out of earshot, they all began to talk at once.

Lettice remained where she was. Davenant continued to stare at her.

"You are small, miss."

"Not so very, sir."

Her father looked up as if only just noticing his daughter's height.

"What do you wish me to do?" enquired Lettice respectfully.

Davenant folded his arms.

"Not much. In the Rejection scene:

Peace, Kent!
Come not between the dragon and his wrath . . .

you stand with your back to the audience all the while, then you sink very gradually to your knees. While I am cursing you, mind you stay with your eyes fixed on mine. All the speech through."

"Is that all, sir?"

"Yes. You may go, Miss—"

"Winter."

"How could I forget?" he said with wonderful sarcasm.

Everyone in the theatre was talking about Davenant. In the dusty Green Room, sitting on benches, thumbing scripts, darning their costumes, they discussed Davenant's rudeness and expensive clothes, his bullying manners—and his art. Even actors travelling the circuits, treated as scarcely better than the vagabonds of the past, were awe-struck by great talent. The man who had that possessed a talisman. It was as if they were visited by some kind of ill-behaved angelic presence. It had arrived from above and would return later to paradise. It could never be treated as mortal.

Lettice was sent for during the afternoon. Davenant said he would run through the Rejection scene with her.

"It's the only scene I rehearse," he said,

regarding her again with penetrating blue eyes.

He had shed the greatcoat he'd worn that morning, and was wearing a full-skirted dark blue coat and white trousers. He looked more like a wealthy farmer than an actor. What he could never be taken for was an aristocrat; his body was too stocky, his neck too thick, his whole appearance almost coarse.

They took their places in the centre of the stage; he faced her and began to speak. Everything changed. His face swam, his eyes reflected kingly anger, when he moved he was old yet infinitely graceful . . .

The theatre had never been so full as it was for the first Davenant performance. Thomas was red in the face and excited. He hurried in to see the actor in his dressing-room. Davenant did not turn round when Thomas came respectfully into the room. He was slowly drawing lines on his face, as if on a canvas.

"There's not a seat to be had, sir."

"So I should damned well think."

Lettice, too, was excited when the performance began. Rehearsing with Davenant had been extraordinary. Now, actually playing with him in front of an audience, she felt she had never acted in her life until now.

When the play ended the audience rose and cheered. Davenant, long white hair round his shoulders, face streaked with paint and real tears, bowed his head. Lettice, a halter round her neck, her face grey to simulate her death of a minute before, curtsied deeply. Davenant kissed her hand. The applause poured over them like golden rain.

The curtains finally bounced together, shutting off the love which had surged over the footlights.

Davenant dropped her hand.

"Winter."

Thomas, who had played Gloucester, hurried forward.

"The lighting is bad. The storm is too loud and she"—pointing to Lettice—"speaks too low. One of the walking gentlemen has squeaking boots. Either the boots or the actor must go."

(3)

Returning home, Thomas talked to his wife philosophically. Most great actors had some vice or other which had to be borne. They drank. They were bullies. They were sweet as pie to a manager's face and black as pitch behind his back. There was always a flaw, "a vicious mole in nature" in them; it seemed an inevitable result of fame. Davenant was worse offstage, infinitely better onstage, than others called great whom Thomas had known.

Anxious about so much, Thomas never worried over his daughters. He had coached them since they were small children, their voices were beautiful, they could hold their own with anybody on a stage. But if Thomas had taught them to act, Ellen had brought them up to be ladies. It had been no easy task in a world where there was much drunkenness, language was Rabelaisian and many of the actors and actresses loose-living.

The Winters had strict rules for their girls. Thomas returned from the theatre each night before the evening performance to collect them, while Ellen remained at work in the Wardrobe. The girls were never allowed to walk to the theatre alone.

One evening Lettice sat at the attic window on the lookout for her father. He was usually punctual and his lateness worried her.

"I do wish he would come."

"Oh, Letty, don't fuss."

"But he is always on time, Bella."

"Well, he isn't this evening."

How cross she is, thought Lettice. She loved her sister dearly, but found her moods hard to bear. She opened the window again and hung out.

"Goodness. There's Laurie."

"What do you mean?" said Isabella impatiently.

"Laurie Spindle is coming to the house. Do you suppose Papa sent him for us?"

"I trust not. I cannot bear him."

"Bella, he is a dear little man. Yes, I'm sure he has come to collect us." Lettice snatched up cloak and bonnet and darted down the stairs. Isabella followed slowly. She disliked Lettice's admirer with his stories of being a fiddler, a harlequin, dancing the toe-and-heel, his days of starvation, his brief triumphs. She didn't even see why audiences liked him.

Laurie Spindle was leaning against the open door. He was hopelessly drunk.

"Guvnor says I'm to 'company you ladies."

"Laurie, dear, you are not very well," said Lettice with a sympathy which filled Isabella with scorn.

"P'fctly well," said Laurie, clinging to the door. "Gotter see you get t'theatre—"

"He's *drunk*," said Isabella in contempt.

94

"Leave him to fall into the gutter. I will not be seen walking with him."

She swept by and Lettice looked at Laurie, sighed and followed her. Laurie began to stagger after them.

"Don't walk so fast, Bella. We will lose the poor man, he is in a dreadful state."

"I hope he breaks his neck."

"You are so hard. He cannot help his weaknesses. He has had an unhappy life."

Isabella gave a snort and walked on. Soon the little unsteady figure was left behind.

It was broad daylight but Lettice murmured that their father would not like them to walk alone like this. Isabella tossed her head at such stupidity. She had longer legs than her sister, and Lettice had almost to run to keep up.

Lettice thought there was a curious atmosphere in the streets this evening. Was it because they'd never been alone before? Women at open doorways stared at them. Groups of women—no men seemed to be about—at street corners looked with hostile faces at the girls. One big woman in a sacking apron suddenly shouted, "Dinna go by Market Street."

"Bella—we'd better not."

"For goodness' sake!" exclaimed Isabella. "That's the quickest way."

"But she said—"

"Don't be a cake," jeered Isabella. It was their mother's phrase for a coward.

They crossed a deserted courtyard and came into the long cobbled stretch of Market Street. Suddenly they saw something flowing towards them. It was, quite literally, like a great swollen river. A river of men. For one minute the street was empty, in the next it was filled by a vast moving mass of men walking and talking in a sound like a long unending growl. The girls were too far along the street to turn back and before they could run to avoid it the river engulfed them by sheer force of movement.

None of the men took the least notice of the girls. They looked blindly ahead. They were filthy, in reeking clothes and tattered caps, their faces dark from dirt or exposure. Lettice gripped her sister's arm and managed to keep beside her. Her bonnet was knocked off, her red hair fell down, she let her slight body be swept along, supported by the crowd as if she were indeed swimming in a river. When Isabella looked at her she saw with astonishment that her sister was excited.

"It's all right," gasped Lettice. "Go as they go. Keep calm. We may be able to get out in a little while." Her small hand gripped Isabella's arm. She knew Isabella was terrified by crowds. When they had been children their father had taken them to the races and Isabella had been so frightened by the press of people that Thomas had been forced to carry her on his shoulders.

Desperately clutching Lettice's arm, Isabella was filled with panic. They were being dragged God knew where by this mob of angry men in rags, they were at the crowd's mercy, helpless. She saw her sister's reassuring face under the cap of red hair; then the crowd surged round a corner and Isabella tottered, scarcely able to keep on her feet. The crowd slowed down, there was a sudden roar. They had halted outside a corn-chandler's. Above their heads was the chute used for pushing down the fat corn sacks to wagons waiting below.

"The door, lads! The door!"

Voices yelled, there was a noise of splitting wood, Isabella wrenched herself round and saw—with terror—that Lettice had disappeared. Sobbing and screaming, she tried to fight her way through the bodies to where she'd last seen her. She jumped up for a moment and across a sea of caps saw Lettice's red head at a distance.

The crowd burst into a wild cheer. At the top of the chute the figure of a man appeared, then another, clutching bulging sacks of corn which they pushed into the chute. Down they came and the crowd broke like a huge wave. The sacks fell to the ground, there was a surge of bodies, and just when Isabella thought she could no longer keep on her feet and would be trampled to death, there were cries of, "No more. All gone! No more!"

"Bakers, t'bakers!" shouted the crowd, beginning to move again, chanting and yelling, "We want bread and we'll tak it, we'll tak it."

Half mad with fear, nearly fainting, Isabella was swept down the street past houses where shutters were slammed against the mob. In the distance was the solid façade of the coaching inn, its windows full of people. If only she could get towards the inn . . . with all her strength she pushed against a huge man on her left. He took no more notice of her than if she were a fly. A greyness began at the edges of her eyes, a feeling of giddiness, more shouts. Suddenly

98

she was gripped in two arms, lifted sheer out of the struggling mass and borne, as if flying, out of the noise and stink, into silence . . .

"Give her air, if you please. Stand back. Look, she is reviving."

She heard a low voice and felt her hand clasped. Someone put a cloth on her forehead; it smelled of eau-de-cologne.

She lay without moving, her face smeared with dirt, her clothes torn, her hair a tangled mass on her shoulders. Slowly, she opened her heavy eyes. Two young men were looking down at her. The one who still held her hand gave a smile.

"Ah. You have come back to us. Do not try to speak. You are safe now."

Isabella looked at him drowsily. At first she could not believe it . . . then she was sure. It was the young man she had met what seemed a century ago at Bagot Park. It was Viscount Carteret.

5

(1)

LETTICE had not fared as badly as her
sister in the riot because she managed to
use her wits. When the mob pressed
towards the corn-chandler's she saw, for a
split second, a gap between two men rushing
at the first sack of corn; she darted through it,
stretching out her hand to Isabella too late.
Her sister vanished in the struggling mass,
and Lettice was somehow tossed to the edge
of the crowd like flotsam thrown on to a
beach.

There was a passageway between the buildings. She slipped into it, climbed on a ledge
and tried to catch a glimpse of Isabella. There
was no sign of her. When it looked as if the
crowd would come surging in, Lettice ran to
the end of the passage, then through a maze
of back streets. Five minutes later, trembling
but not hysterical, she was at the theatre
getting what help she could. She insisted on
accompanying her father to search for

Isabella, and it was not until a groom from *The Bull* arrived with a message from the landlord to say Isabella was safe that Lettice burst into tears.

The riot had risen out of nowhere, terrified the town, and vanished as if it had never been. It dissolved into frightened separate men, hiding, skulking, hurrying home to swear they'd never been part of it. In the town it was said men had been arrested and would be hanged. A mounted patrol of militia rode nightly through the streets, bringing a sense of fear rather than safety.

The men who had marched out, half-starved, to steal bread feared the militia. Other people feared the rioters. Less than two years ago the Chartists, instigating riots, had preached physical force. Stephen, a Methodist Minister, no less, had made a speech in Manchester urging just that. "You have only to take a couple of matches and a bundle of straw dipped in pitch, and I will see what the Government and its hundreds of thousands of soldiers will do against this one weapon—if it is used boldly." Farmers still found their ricks blazing. And worse fires, possibly revolutionary fires, smouldered in men's minds. Everybody seemed afraid.

Thomas and Ellen were horrified at what had happened. It was a miracle neither of the girls had been hurt. To Isabella's disgust and Lettice's sympathy, Laurie Spindle grew even drunker after the riot; he drank from remorse.

Both girls soon recovered their health and spirits and Isabella seemed more cheerful than she had been for weeks. She was kind and obliging to her mother, kissed her father good night, and hummed tunelessly (she had no ear) when dressing for the performances. Lettice sometimes quite longed for Isabella's previous gloom, to be spared that voice, always off-key.

Lettice did not comment to her mother, but she was well aware that Isabella's bright face was due to the reappearance of Viscount Carteret. He and his cousin Robert Bagot had called at the theatre to enquire after Isabella's recovery, and later sent her a magnificent bouquet of roses.

Isabella gave the flowers to her mother. Ellen was always given the tokens of admiration offered to her daughters, it was a kind of toll. Lettice won the heart of an actor, the flowers went to Ellen. An admirer left a pair of fine gloves at the Stage Door for Isabella:

Ellen wore them to church on Sundays.

The roses bloomed on Ellen's dressing-table, to the disgust of Mrs. Gunn. Isabella pressed one in a book of poetry.

"Tell me about Lord Carteret, I scarcely saw him when he called at the theatre," Lettice said. They were in their poky little dressing-room before the evening performance; it was two weeks since the riot. The roses were long since dead.

"I know very little of the Viscount. But he seems to me to be very gentle and kind," Isabella said, untying her bonnet. For once she did not scowl at its frayed strings.

"I imagine the nobility arrogant. They're always so in an audience. Quite rude, sometimes."

"You only think of people as an audience."

"Of course. How else would I think of them?"

Lettice smiled, and then looked at her sister and gave a sentimental sigh.

"Is it not strange, Bella, that the Viscount should be here and actually rescue you? I have forgotten why he and that other gentleman—"

"Mr. Robert Bagot. He is Lord Carteret's cousin."

"But why are they here? Mama says something about property in Northumberland."

"They own half the county," said Isabella carelessly. "They have shipyards, you know, and so much land—miles and miles of it. They came to see things are in order."

"You mean because of the riot?"

"No, thank goodness, that was nothing to do with the Bagots," said Isabella, with a happy know-all air. "The cousin told me they are determined to see nobody of *theirs* wants a livelihood. It worries the Earl that they live so far from here."

"They have so much, I suppose."

"They are very rich. You know how it is."

"No, I don't," said Lettice. "Shall they be in Newcastle long?"

"I think they have already left," Isabella said indifferently.

"They should at least have come to see Davenant play," said Lettice, shocked. "And I would have liked your Viscount to see *Lear* because I have a good role in it."

"Egoist. And he isn't my Viscount, alas and alack."

Tunelessly humming, Isabella took off her clothes and began to tie on a series of padded petticoats, fasten a bodice which pushed her small breasts together and dress in a costume sewn with false ermine.

(2)

Isabella was concealing from her family that she'd seen the Viscount and his cousin every day since the riot. It was the first time in her life she was grateful that she knew how to act.

From the moment she had drifted back to consciousness, Isabella knew the two young noblemen were people entirely different from any she'd ever known. She would not have believed it possible for men to treat her with such delicacy. Had an actor rescued her he would have exaggerated his gallantry, loudly repeated that she owed him her life. The Viscount and his cousin did the reverse. When she had been at *The Bull* after the rescue, they treated her with such exquisite politeness that she forgot her clothes were in tatters and that she was bedraggled and dirty. They persuaded her to drink a glass of hot negus, sat quietly with her until she regained her self-possession. When she was stronger, they drove her to the theatre in a private carriage and politely pressed her grubby gloveless hand.

The following day the gentlemen called at the theatre to enquire after the young lady's health. They met both sisters and their parents and asked permission to invite the family to luncheon. But all the family were working except Isabella, so it happened that a seeming impossibility came about; with Ellen's permission she had luncheon in the Bagots' private suite alone with the Viscount and his cousin.

Lord Carteret had been faintly interested when Thomas Winter reminded him that he and his family "had once had the honour to play at Bagot Park". He remembered then that he had spent some time that evening with the younger of the sisters. He remembered no more than that.

When Isabella arrived for luncheon he scarcely recognised her. Ellen had lent her the only real silk gown in the family wardrobe, plain silver-grey which suited Isabella's dark looks perfectly. Why, she was delightful, he thought, surprised.

During the meal Isabella was charming, spirited and remarkably pretty and the gentlemen showed her that they thought so. She interested them. There was an aura of romance about this girl, they thought, it must be the curious life she led, of paint and make-believe.

Sitting between two attractive men, Isabella compared them. They were physically rather alike, dark, with straight noses and grey eyes. But the Viscount, taller than his cousin and with long well-shaped legs, had a round face, a fascinatingly indolent manner and slow voice. "The cousin" was a quicker person in every way. He spoke abruptly as if there were so many ideas crowding into his head that he only had time to select a few. He had a restless way of springing up and walking about. He had a longish handsome face and curling, glossy black hair.

It was clear the two Bagots liked each other.

"Are we going to see you perform in a play, Miss Isabella?" enquired Lord Carteret. "My cousin assures me you are not on the playbills this week. I shall be deuced disappointed if I do not see you act, you know."

Isabella explained that she was not in every play, although her sister was. The famous Davenant was acting with them at present. They must, of course, have seen him? They assured her they had never done so. It was incredible to Isabella that the Bagot gentlemen had never seen Davenant upon a stage and were not going to make the effort to do so. They seemed more interested in her.

She knew they both admired her but she found it easier to talk to Lord Carteret. He had such a sweet lazy manner, he looked at her charmingly, laughed easily. His grey eyes were full of good nature.

When they drove her back to the theatre, Lord Carteret said, "May we have the honour of seeing you again?"

The week that followed was full of amusing subterfuges. Isabella explained to the Bagot gentlemen that her family must not be told she was meeting them. She knew this was not as it should be but her father was a taskmaster about her work. They accepted what she said; everything connected with the actor's life was mystifying to them. As Robert Bagot said to his cousin later, "Possibly her Papa disapproves of her having acquaintances outside her own class. There are many different snobberies."

"Is it not absurd to think of that delicious creature *working* for her living?" said Carteret. "But perhaps acting is not really work, d'you think?"

"From what I remember of our theatricals

last winter, it's deuced hard work," said Robert, laughing.

It was difficult for Isabella to get to *The Bull* to meet them, but by fibs and inventions she managed to do so. Lord Carteret never asked to see her alone, his cousin was always present. Nothing could have been more proper than the time she spent in their private saloon, talking to them as if they were friends. Compared to the pinches and kisses between men and girls backstage, she might have been at Court.

She liked both men very much but it was Lord Carteret she preferred. Not because he was the son of an earl (this thought filled her with awe) but because she knew he considered her beautiful. He called her "the wittiest creature": her smallest joke made him laugh. When he looked at her, she felt as if she were standing in sunshine after months of winter.

"The cousin" also liked her, but she knew *he* remembered she was an actress.

"I fear it is time you left us, Miss Isabella," Robert Bagot said one evening, looking at his fob watch.

"Davenant plays King Lear tonight, does he not?" said Lord Carteret. "Do you have a large role?"

"I do nothing in the play tonight," Isabella said, laughing. "I am just a walking-on lady attendant to Cordelia. That is Lettice. Poor Lettice quakes in her shoes, but she says Davenant is a genius so I daresay he is."

"You have great faith in your sister's opinion," said Lord Carteret, looking pleased for some reason.

"About the theatre—always. Lettice calls us 'children of the arts'. That is what *she* is. For Lettice everything must be about the theatre. It is her passion."

"You are very fond of her."

Isabella put her hand under her chin in an unstudied, careless gesture. Carteret thought he had never met a woman so alluring. The well-bred girls in society paled beside her. She was like a fire. A new-lit fire.

"One couldn't be anything but devoted to Lettice," she said. "She is so sweet and clever and kind. Except when she's acting and then she's strong and rather horrid sometimes! We had happy days when we were children. Mama bundled us into shawls and left us in dressing-rooms when she and Papa were working. Lettice invented wonderful games. Some went on for weeks."

She talked about her sister, exclaiming how

much better an actress, how much kinder a person Lettice was than herself. Carteret watched and listened.

(3)

Isabella had been let off lightly as far as her acting was concerned; she thought Davenant had decided not to use her. Any leading part which required a young girl had gone to Lettice, to Isabella's intense relief.

Thomas called the company to assemble one morning when the weather outside the theatre was the freshest, sweetest kind of May. The actors, creatures of the dark, crowded on the stage.

Davenant was seated on a property throne, Thomas, flushed with nervousness, was consulting the list of players. There was a tenseness in the air.

Isabella took her place as far back as possible. She had slept badly and woken miserable: the Viscount and his cousin were leaving today or tomorrow. She thought Davenant alarming, so stood out of the way, hidden by the tallest actors in the company. Lettice, a bunch of violets pinned under her chin, was in the front row.

"All present then?" enquired Davenant.

Thomas nodded.

"I should think so, too. *I* have been here this half hour."

Davenant regarded them.

"I have consented to remain for a few more weeks," he said. "Thomas Winter earnestly requested me to play in *The Welsh Girl*. Deafening my ears to my own good sense, I agreed. Now I have reread the play. It is trash. I shall play *Othello*."

Even Isabella, absorbed in her own selfish thoughts, knew what a blow this was to Lettice. *The Welsh Girl* was a part in which Lettice had always shone. Looking through the crowd she saw her sister's face was white.

"*Othello* casting is arranged by Winter," continued Davenant indifferently, "but there is the matter of Desdemona."

As with *Lear*, the only role other than his own which interested him was that of his leading actress.

He *must* give it to Letty! thought Isabella, Georgiana is an old bat and Margaret Frognal is ugly. That beast is too clever not to know what a beautiful actress Letty is.

"Miss Isabella Winter, please."

She didn't move.

The actor beside her gave her a push.

"He wants you."

Isabella stepped forward. Davenant made a gesture as if to say "Closer". She came closer. She looked across at Lettice for reassurance: her sister's eyes were fixed on the ground.

"Winter informs me you have played Desdemona."

"I did play it two years ago."

"Speak up. I am not deaf and neither is the audience. You know the role, then?"

"I was not right for it." She was scarlet.

"Not right for it?" he repeated. "What does that mean? Not good enough? Were you not good enough? Winter, I thought you told me the girl could act."

Thomas looked as if he were in the dock facing a hanging judge.

"She is a good actress. Perhaps a little sub-dued, but when she acted Desdemona the Othello was not strong. The newspaper critic was most encouraging about her. She had grace, he said."

"Is that what you've got?" demanded Davenant.

She met the implacable eyes and knew she had no hope of dissuading him. With as much self-possession as she could manage she said, "I will do my best, sir."

"Hm," was the reply. "Winter. See the girl wears a flaxen wig and white powder. I can't have all that black hair on the stage when the Moor is black."

He made a shooing gesture and the actors began to leave. As Isabella walked away she heard Davenant say, "Winter. I require her for rehearsal with wig at two o'clock, if you please."

Feeling she could bear to speak to nobody, she snatched up her cloak and bonnet and fled to the Stage Door. The sunshine outside was bright, in the cobbled yard an old horse was eating from his nosebag, birds pecking round him. There was a cart full of painted scenery, its colours as tawdry as booths at a fair.

"If my family ask for me, I have gone to the milliner," Isabella said to the Stage Door-keeper. He scarcely listened, returning to a mug of beer.

She hurried into the street. Like the sunshine, it had a cheerful air. A man went by on a grey horse. A milk cart had halted and people crowded round with their basins.

She walked as fast as she could towards *The*

Bull. At least I'll say goodbye to them if they are there or leave a letter if they are at the shipyard, she thought, she was miserable and angry by turns. How she hated this acting life. She hated her father's humility in front of that bully sprawled on the throne, hated the fact that Davenant had her father in his power. He did not even dare to answer back.

And if she detested seeing her father in that position, what about herself? Her father had lied. She had not even been passable as Desdemona. She was not like Lettice, able to merge her personality into a role, change magically, pearling over the differences, drawing out the likeness, between a character and herself. Isabella despised Desdemona. *She* believed in struggling against an unkind fate, not meekly submitting.

At the thought of playing opposite "that beast" she felt sick.

The yard of *The Bull* was crowded with arrivals for the races, travellers were climbing from a coach, horses steaming. People greeted each other, the young men in dazzling boots, the old men in heavy coats. Servant girls giggled and eyed the men.

Isabella went into the hallway. The porter,

sitting in a hooded leather chair in the corner, stood up and bowed.

"Is his lordship in just now?" Isabella asked.

The porter had been present when this girl had been dramatically rescued by the two young gentlemen. A shabby little thing, he thought. Pretty, though.

"The Viscount is in the back parlour, miss, shall I announce you?"

"Oh no. I can find my way, thank you."

The parlour was small, dark and two hundred years old, full of mouldering books read by nobody. There was a worm-eaten desk which nobody used and on the wall a pair of pistols inhabited by spiders. The room was damply cold.

As she opened the door, it creaked. Lord Carteret was sitting at the desk and at the sound he turned, then sprang up.

"You! I was this moment—"

"Writing to tell me goodbye."

Everything about her just then, her beauty, her poor attire, her slender figure, her desolate face, went to his heart. He felt as if he had been stabbed.

He came to her and took her hand. Something was very unfamiliar: they were alone.

"You are leaving, are you not?" she said, and began to cry.

"Ah, don't weep, I cannot bear it if you do!"

He took her hands and pressed them, then kissed them, closing his eyes. She stood looking at his bent head, trying to stop her tears. When he opened his eyes he gave her the tenderest look she had seen in her life.

"You must know that I love you," he said.

"My lord . . ."

She began to tremble violently, moved and excited, knowing what he was going to ask. He would ask her to go away with him, perhaps to London, offer her a rich disgraced life as his mistress. Longing to be in his arms, sure now that he loved her, she was as sure she would refuse. The hard-sounding voice of common sense told her so.

"Please don't ask me," she said in a low voice. "I could never go away with you, my lord. Never."

"But I want you to be my wife."

"That is impossible!"

"Isabella—"

"No, no, it's impossible, it cannot be!" She was quite distraught now and crying harder. "How *could* you marry me, with your high rank? Don't say such a thing, it would never, never be allowed. Oh, I am so unhappy!"

"I do say it. I beg you to accept."

She continued to sob.

"Isabella," he said quietly, "I was writing to propose marriage to you. You must know I love you with all my heart. My cousin knows it. You cannot be unaware of it. I beg you to be my wife."

"It's impossible," she said again, rubbing her eyes and looking away. "How could *you*, a nobleman, marry an actress! The Earl would forbid it."

"Certainly he would," he said, "which is why we must be married secretly. My dearest, dearest . . ."

He drew her close and began to kiss her passionately. Her cheeks were wet and the kisses tasted salt.

"Dear, lovely, haunting, irreplaceable girl. I can think of nothing but you. May I speak to your father—ask him—"

"No, no! He would never allow it!"

She started away, and he looked at the shabby woebegone figure in astonishment.

Isabella said, the words tumbling out, "I know I am not your equal and never shall be, but my father doesn't think of that. He would never let me go! I am part of his work. He's afraid of that horrible Davenant and I must work for him. Why are we even talking of it? We must say goodbye. Kiss me just once again."

He kissed her and she clung to him.

"Denys," she said, calling him by his name for the first time. "Oh, Denys. We are both prisoners in different ways."

He smiled at that.

"Of course we are not. We will leave now, and drive to Gretna Green. Robert understands it must be so. We can be there by nightfall. We will write a word to your parents and send it to the theatre. By the time your father reads it, we will be gone."

"But my boxes—my packing—"

He tied the bonnet under her chin by its threadbare strings.

"I would so much rather you came to me just as you are."

Part Two

Part Two

6

(1)

IT was less than a month since Isabella had disappeared, but to Lettice the time could not be measured in days, it was an epoch, a kind of drastic change, like being a child and growing up overnight. Her sister's elopement had hurt her bitterly. They were unalike, yet there had never been secrets between them, they had shared everything. Now they were separated for the first time in their lives not only by the miles between Newcastle and wherever Isabella had gone, but by Isabella's duplicity.

Ellen became pinched and silent when the news came in a letter delivered from *The Bull*. She did not believe Isabella was to be married and from the moment she heard her daughter was gone she scarcely spoke, sat for hours looking out of the window. Lettice was alarmed by her mother's state, remembering an actor who had lost his wits. He, too, had sat without speaking for long periods.

But four days after the disappearance a letter arrived on crested writing paper. It was from both Lord Carteret and Isabella, gave details of the Gretna Green wedding, and enclosed a banker's draft from the Viscount "to buy a memento of a joyful day which alas you could not be with us to share". The banker's draft was for a hundred pounds.

Ellen recovered as if by magic. She became altogether, rather pathetically, happy. She gossiped at the theatre, patronised Mrs. Gunn and was more talkative than Lettice ever remembered, repeating time and again, "Of course, the Bagots are distant relatives of my own."

Lettice had been miserable and Ellen shocked at the time of Isabella's elopement, but Thomas was furious. He shouted at Ellen. He was frightened of telling Davenant that the actress chosen for Desdemona had run away.

But Davenant, never predictable, took the news sardonically, pointed at Margaret Frognal and said, "She'll do." Margaret Frognal was afraid of him and when she first made her entrance she was shaking so much that she could scarcely hold the famous handkerchief.

With Isabella "safely" married, as Ellen called it, life at the theatre continued. Davenant thought of new demands every day. His name was not large enough on the bills. More lamps were needed in the footlights. The actresses all reminded him of elephants and must be given lessons in "the art of walking". Planks were extended the length of the stage and Davenant watched while the actresses were made to walk, slowly at first, then faster, until they could walk right along the planks without deviating once from a straight line. Lettice, fired by the challenge, soon became very nimble; Margaret Frognal fell off.

There were few rehearsals but Lettice went to the theatre each morning. She spent her time in the Green Room facing a courtyard where the spare scenery was stacked. Here she studied her parts and thought about the plays. Sometimes, looking from the window, she saw a small mass of rats which lived above a stable coming down a rope to nibble the paint off the canvases.

Laurie Spindle liked to sit with her.

"Shall I teach you a harlequin trick, Beauty?" Agile as a gnat he would spring up, illustrate a new way of jumping, spinning, almost flying.

Buckley Vernon also came to sit beside her and together they ran through scenes from many different plays. Both wished to have as many parts as possible at their fingers' ends and Buckley was always eager to learn a new one.

One morning when she went into her dressing-room Lettice found a message scrawled on the back of a handbill, saying would Miss Winter do Mr. Davenant the honour of calling at his lodgings. Three o'clock and no later.

Lettice, mystified, found her father in the wings arguing with one of the stage carpenters, a red-faced man called Pick.

Pick was loudly denying responsibility for an unsteady pillar in *Othello* which the previous night had swayed when Davenant leaned against it, making the audience laugh.

"You are speaking of *Mister* Davenant. An actor whose name is known the length and breadth of the country. It is outrageous that the scenery should not be correctly secured."

"Do me best," said Pick, unimpressed. He lounged away.

Thomas, aware Lettice was waiting, said abruptly, "What is it?"

Since Isabella's flight his manner had been markedly cold to Lettice, as if it had been her fault. Lettice was hurt, but refused to be upset about it. Sooner or later her father would have to stop thinking of his daughters as commodities offered for hire with himself and his wife. She gave him the handbill.

He read it and frowned.

"It is clear enough."

"I wondered, Papa, if you knew what Mr. Davenant wanted?"

"Something to do with your acting, no doubt. You are very uneven. Never the same performance two nights running."

"Did he say that?"

"Not in so many words, but I can read his expression. Mind you wear a good frock when you visit him."

He hurried away in search of Pick again.

A minor advantage for Lettice after Davenant's arrival had been a few shillings extra in her payment. She had bought some muslin for a new dress. It was white with a pattern of copper-coloured sprigs of barley. Ellen made the dress for her, sewing every night after she returned from the theatre. The dress had a tiny waist, sleeves full from the elbow, and graceful, fashionable skirts. Ellen also retrimmed Lettice's bonnet with new flowers and a silk frill on the nape of the neck.

While Lettice was dressing for the Davenant visit, her mother came into the bedroom and watched her critically.

"No, the belt is not setting correctly. Let me do it." Ellen fastened the belt, and regarded her daughter with a sharp eye.

"Let me look at you. Yes. You do me credit. But gracious, child, you cannot use that worn-out reticule! Take mine. And my best gloves as well."

Her mother took the precious gloves, which she always kept wrapped in paper, and gave them to Lettice who in turn gave her a kiss.

The square where Davenant lodged was in the "good" part of Newcastle. It had been built in the 1750s and was a pleasant place of terraced Georgian houses. In the centre of the square was a well-kept lawn and a bronze fountain. Everything, Lettice thought, looked so clean. The curtains at the windows, the children in tartan frocks going by with a nursemaid, the very pavement. Nobody shouted from attics or strung up washing like flags.

She rang the bell of Number 27 and a neatly-dressed maid ushered her into a parlour overlooking the back garden. The room had sprigged wallpaper and watercolour paintings of the countryside.

"The Master will be with you directly."

Lettice sat down in a straight-backed chair and looked round. This was no place to be reprimanded about acting. It was genteel. Theatre talk belonged in dusty stretches of backstage or actually onstage. Not here.

When Davenant strode in, she wondered for a moment if it would be suitable for her to stand up. Somehow, she remained seated.

"Good afternoon, miss."

"Good afternoon, sir."

He stood contemplating her, his hands behind his back. Her life was spent being looked at and Lettice was not embarrassed. She gazed back, thinking his eyes a very extraordinary blue, his face much lined. She was sure he noticed everything about her, even her new-trimmed bonnet.

"So your sister galloped off with a lord, is that it?" he said.

"She is a viscountess now."

"That impresses you."

"I am sure she finds it very pleasant."

"Sorry you missed the chance?"

"Good gracious, no!"

He gave a roar of laughter, throwing back his head as if he had been looking, not at a girl in ribbons and muslin, but at a Punch and Judy show.

"Miss Winter, I like you. What do you say to that?"

"I am glad, sir."

"Now, now," he said. "No sarcasm, if you please. I won't hear a word against myself. I daresay you thought I should have given you Desdemona. Were you mortified because I gave it to Frognal? What a bad actress, eh? A drab. You shall have the role for Saturday. Who says I am not a man with a great heart? But that's not why I asked you to do me the honour of calling. There is another matter to discuss."

He had been walking about while he talked but now he sat down facing her. When he was close, not onstage where his art altered his mystifying face, but here in real life, she thought those burning eyes had a calculating look.

"How would you like to come to London with me?"

Silence.

"Did you hear me, miss?"

"I am not sure I understood you, sir," said Lettice faintly.

"That is odd, for I consider you a sharp young lady."

"You mean I could come to London to act—"

"Exactly so."

He looked pleased as he watched her blush. The blush spread across her freckled face.

"Now we're getting results," he said. "The idea appeals, I see. Then with your permission I will have a word about you with your father."

"Oh no!"

His expression of good humour vanished. He looked at her as if not hearing aright.

"What's that?" he said almost angrily. "Are you refusing my offer?"

"Of course not! Of course I want to come!" she cried, so far forgetting herself as to lean forward and grip his arm. "Mr. Davenant, what I mean is please do *not* speak to my father, but allow me to do it. It will be much, much better if I may break the news to him. Please!"

At her entreating voice, her beseeching expression, Davenant's manner changed back to its former jocularity.

"That is a good daughterly attitude. I like that. Yes, I like that."

(2)

During the first days after Isabella's flight, Buckley Vernon had been a great comfort to the Winter family. He had been concerned, understanding, soothing Ellen's fears that her younger daughter was ruined, and assuring her that Isabella was not only virtuous but had a sound head on her shoulders. Buckley had been the only person Ellen was willing to listen to. Later, when news of the marriage arrived, it was Buckley who had pointed out to Thomas that a marriage of such eminence could do him nothing but good.

Lettice had grown fond of Buckley. She liked to be with him, enjoyed his easy companionship. She looked on him as a friend. He never gave the impression of wanting anything more than a brother-and-sister relationship. This was a relief to Lettice who since her early teens knew how tiresome and importunate some actors could be, clasping her suddenly, kissing her hotly and becoming furious when she refused them.

On her return from visiting Davenant the

first person she saw at the theatre was Buckley. He came towards her along the passageway near her dressing-room.

"I am so glad to see you, Mr. Vernon," said Lettice. "Could we talk?"

Margaret Frognal and the sharp-faced Georgiana Coins went by, looking at Lettice with hostility. There were few secrets in theatres.

"Come into my dressing-room," he said.

Buckley's dressing-room, coveted by other actors because of its nearness to the stage, was in disarray. His costumes, brown holland, painted satin, lay on chairs or on the floor. Lettice nearly tripped over a rapier. Pots of powder and shreds of orange peel were in a dish on the dressing-table.

"You cannot imagine what has happened!" exclaimed Lettice, when he had closed the door. Usually quiet, she spoke in a torrent of excitement brought on by anxiety about her father and uncertainty about the great offer. Was it too soon for her? What did Mr. Vernon think?

Buckley would not have been human if he had not felt a pang of envy. It was true that Lettice was gifted: but so was he. She was young and handsome: so was he. She was ambitious: he was more so. To be taken to London by Davenant was the dream which every actor severely dismissed from his mind. Yet here was this slip of a girl, with her red hair and white face, telling him it had happened.

"It's wonderful," he said. "Of course you are ready. Let me congratulate you. With admiration."

He bent to kiss her cheek, still in the elder-brother role. She gave him a radiant smile. Quite suddenly he saw her not as a fellow actor, but as a beautiful woman. He stared.

The call boy knocked, crying monotonously: "Curtain up in half an hour! Curtain up in half an hour!"

Lettice ran out.

(3)

The news that Davenant had offered Lettice an engagement was broken to Thomas Winter when the family returned for supper to their lodgings.

Mrs. Gunn served the usual unappetising meal. She slammed down half-cold plates of herrings fried in oatmeal, the fish too small and bony to nourish the family who had

134

worked until midnight, then she left them to themselves.

Ellen buttered her husband a piece of bread.

"Lettice has something to tell you, Tom."

"What is that?" asked Thomas absently.

It was an effort for Lettice to speak. She drew a deep breath and began, punctuating her story with, "As you have often said, Papa." Her father's face went first white, then red. Before she could finish he interrupted:

"Do you realise that if I do not meet my commitments I could be arrested for debt?"

Lettice's eyes widened.

"But you said things were better since we have been here and—"

"Ingratitude!" exclaimed Thomas in the very tone Davenant used as *King Lear*.

"Please don't be angry with me, Papa," she said, her voice quavering. "I do not think I could bear it if—"

"*You* cannot bear it!" he shouted. "*You* cannot bear it! You have not been almost bankrupt, seen the theatre you owned go up in flames, lost your wife's inheritance, seen her . . . a woman of birth and breeding, brought down to doing a seamstress's work!

135

You are the fortunate one. Go off with that scoundrel! See where that will get you!"

He had never used such a bitter tone to Lettice before in her life, and bursting into sobs she ran from the room.

Ellen looked at her husband for a moment, then poured him a cup of tea.

"Drink it, Tom. It will calm you down."

She went out, quietly closing the door as if Thomas were ill.

He sat looking with unseeing eyes at the smoke-stained walls, the empty fireplace, the dirty plates in front of him. His head ached from his fit of anger, he felt old. He remembered himself at Lettice's age, handsome, lively, flirting with actresses and ballet dancers. He had thought the theatre with its gimcrack finery the most exciting place in the world. He recalled the first time he had met Ellen, a slip of a girl in white wearing long gloves edged with ruffles. He thought of her as she had been, sprightly, mischievous, and as in a dream recalled their violent passion for each other. He remembered the day of their elopement. Their life until now. He and Ellen had given everything to the theatre, their youth, strength, hope, dedication. What had they got from such devotion? Debts.

Disaster. Rudeness from actors like Davenant. One daughter running off to marry some titled fellow they didn't know—he supposed she *was* married—and now Lettice leaving too. And she would get the very things that he and Ellen had toiled for. The theatre owes me something, he thought. For my life. The thought made him bitter against Lettice for being paid when she was owed nothing.

Ellen found Lettice sitting on her bed. The girl had stopped crying, and sat knotting a torn handkerchief.

She looked up.

"I could tell Mr. Davenant I will not go."

Her mother gave a downward smile.

"You know you do not mean that. You of all people. Your father will get over it. Leave him to me."

"I thought he would be pleased."

"No, you didn't. You knew exactly how it would be. He has had a hard life."

Lettice gave a pathetic sniff. Ellen saw in her face all the non-comprehension of the young. They paid lip-service to the sufferings of the old, she thought, but they could not understand them. Lettice was like a sparrow, hopping beside an old imprisoned lion.

Could the sparrow help being cheerful, as it pecked up a crumb and fluttered off to liberty?

7

(1)

ISABELLA, Viscountess Carteret, lay in a four-poster bed, languorously waiting for her husband to finish dressing in the next room, and listening to his voice and the discreet replies of his valet.

Every morning Isabella woke, wrapped in Denys's arms, sleepily thought she must go to the theatre and then remembered where and with whom she now was. She was still in the state of taking nothing for granted. Wonder and gratefulness came to her every time she nestled close to her husband and luxuriously thought of all the things she need not do any more. Her old brown dress need not be darned. Gone was the detested bonnet with its threadbare green strings. She need not walk to a stupid theatre, rehearse a stupid play, see her father fussing, listen to her mother's sour comments about the landlady, eat burned herrings, bear the rudeness of men like Davenant. She looked back at her bondage without a shred of loyalty. Her family, of course, she loved tenderly—when she remembered them. But the theatre had vanished with her shabby clothes.

She jumped out of bed and ran to her dressing-table. A leather case there was open, necklace and earrings lay in their bed of blue velvet. Seed pearls and gold, the necklace in the shape of a string of gold vine leaves, the pearls as bunches of grapes. A bunch for each earring. Three larger bunches on the necklace fell in the centre of her throat. She held the necklace up, then put the pearls between her teeth, scraping them along the uneven surface.

Denys was so generous, she thought, so princely. Since the long enthralling journey from Scotland they had moved into fashionable lodgings in Clarges Street, and her husband had spent all his time seeing she had everything she needed. So many clothes. Morning dresses. Walking dresses. Carriage dresses. Ball dresses. Bonnets. Gloves. Pelisses. Furs. Fans. Jewellery. Everything, Isabella found, opening her brown eyes, could be arranged when you were rich.

"Isabella."

Denys had come through the curtained alcove of his dressing-room.

"You startled me," she said, laughing. "I was admiring my necklace. Shall I wear it when we go to Bagot House? Shall your sisters approve of me?"

He had told her again and again that his family would forgive the marriage, be reconciled to him and receive her.

"But so much is due to high rank and I was an actress!" she always answered, waiting to be contradicted. And he always embraced her in reply.

Now, as he came into the room, she looked at him admiringly. There was a speckless elegance about Denys. It took him hours to look like that—she marvelled at how long a gentleman took to dress. But the look stayed until he changed for dinner when, again after a long, leisurely hour, he emerged as beautifully elegant as in the morning. He wore his clothes carelessly, sprawled rather than sat, leaned rather than stood, yet his silk cravat, dark silver-buttoned coat, exquisite boots, were perfection.

He stood looking at her, the pearls still in her hands.

"I have received a letter from my father."

"But that is good news."

"No, it is not, Isabella."

His tone, his face, were blank and she said uneasily, "May I read the letter?"

He had been holding it in his hand and he folded it decidedly and put it in his pocket.

"I would prefer you did not."

He turned away and walked to the window. Isabella climbed back into bed and pulled up the covers.

"Are you not getting up, Isabella?"

She stayed, only her nose and dark eyes showing, hoping to make him laugh. He did not. She pushed back the covers crossly.

"Just because the Earl will not accept us yet," she said, "it isn't the end of the world. I suppose your horrid father has said something unkind about me."

"He has not met you, Isabella, and is in no position to say anything about you."

"Then why are you so cross?"

"It is no use behaving as if this does not matter to us," he said. "It matters a great deal."

She sat up in bed.

"Do you mean we might be poor?"

He sat down beside the bed and took her hand.

"Dearest one. You must surely see it would not be possible for us to be happy if the family will not accept us. One cannot live like that. Of course, we would not be poor, I came into an inheritance when I was twenty-one. The trouble has nothing to do with money. It is with family. You must take your rightful place. And I love my family and wish always to be close to them. As it should be."

He had never looked so serious before.

Isabella made a sulky grimace. Using her trick of saying things so that he should contradict her, liking to see him change and melt, she said, "Perhaps the Earl will never accept me."

But this time Denys's face did not change.

There was a knock at the door.

"Wait, if you please."

He handed her a flimsy shawl to cover her bare shoulders. How modest he is, she thought, draping the shawl round her, it will only be my maid.

But when the door quietly opened, it was Mr. Locking. He was the owner of the Clarges Street lodgings, and had been—long ago—butler to the Bagots. Isabella thought her husband rather absurdly devoted to Locking, a steely-haired old man with thin lips and a cold manner. She felt he disapproved of her as the wife of Viscount Carteret, but the old man was far too practised in the ways of the great world for her to be sure.

"Two ladies have called to see your Lordship. They are downstairs in the parlour."

Denys's grave face suddenly shone.

"Locking! Is it—"

"I fear not, your Lordship. The ladies are of her young ladyship's family, I am given to believe."

Isabella did not see the bitter disappointment on Denys's face or the compassionate look the old man gave him. She burst out laughing.

"Ma and Lettice! What in the world are they doing here?"

(2)

Isabella would have rushed down at once in a shawl but Denys rang for her maid and told the girl to help her ladyship to dress as quickly as possible.

He went downstairs to greet the visitors.

Isabella could scarcely wait as her maid, a shy little creature, pinned her hair, fastened

144

her skirts, helped her with her lacy stockings and shoes. "Quick, quick, Rivers, my Mama is waiting!"

Rivers thought it very proper that the young lady should be so pleased, but refused to allow Isabella to leave until everything was as it should be. Rivers had been trained by Mr. Locking.

Isabella pelted down the stairs and rushed into the parlour, throwing herself into her mother's arms. Denys, Ellen and Lettice had been seated, exchanging somewhat strained compliments when Isabella came flying in, a vision of blue and white striped satin and lace, her face blazing with pleasure. She hugged her mother, kissed Lettice, burst into laughter like a fifteen-year-old. Denys watched, smiling. When there was a lull he said, "Your mother has done me the honour to say that she and Miss Winter will stay for luncheon. I will now leave you, if I may. I have an appointment to see my cousin at Tattersall's." He took graceful leave. When he had gone Isabella grinned.

"He thinks we would prefer to be alone. Oh! I have so much to tell you both!"

After briefly enquiring why they were in London, and being unsurprised at Lettice's news of a London engagement—Isabella already took good fortune for granted—she talked uninterruptedly. She told them the whole story of her elopement, reliving each detail, describing everything in the actor's manner with mimicry, jokes, dramatic effect. She told of the journey, the village of Gretna, the blacksmith with ginger whiskers who said, "It's to my mind that ye'er safely wed at last!"

She took her mother and sister upstairs into her bedroom, showed them wardrobes full of clothes, opened leather cases to display her jewels, held the bunches of pearls to her ears, asking for, getting, their admiration.

"I have a title now, imagine! Does not Viscountess Carteret sound exactly right?"

Lettice, listening and marvelling, finally glanced at the carriage clock on the chimney piece.

"Surely Lord Carteret will be back soon?"

"I daresay. Then we will have a delicious luncheon. You know the old man who showed you into the house? He is Locking and used to be the Bagot butler. His wife does the cooking, she is *very* good. Wait until you sample her chicken with truffles, Mama. Not one bit like Mrs. Gunn's herrings!"

"Bella," Lettice said thoughtfully, "you haven't spoken about Lord Carteret's family."

"You will have to start calling him Denys."

"Have you not met them?" asked Lettice, ignoring that.

Isabella fiddled with a turquoise bracelet on her wrist.

"Denys says they will come round eventually."

Her mother started. All the morning she had been bemused at seeing her daughter so beautiful, rich and happy.

"The Earl of Bagot refuses to see you?"

"For the present but—"

"He must have been furiously angry when the Viscount married an actress," said Lettice. "Society still thinks we players inferior creatures. Slaves of the public." She smiled.

Isabella didn't smile back. She did not want her triumph spoiled, her family's admiration lost.

"They will come round," she said sharply, "Denys says so."

Her sister and mother knew that mulish look.

The three women made a curious contrast,

Isabella gleaming in satin, Ellen and Lettice poorly and neatly dressed in old darned dresses.

"You know, it's possible they never will accept you," Ellen said, examining the thought. "It often happens with a misalliance in a family as high as the Bagots. They are not only proud, they're adamant. I came merely from small gentry but you both know my parents never forgave me for marrying your father. When my own father lay dying I was not permitted to return home."

"Oh, Mama!" exclaimed Isabella, stung by the often-told story. "That was twenty years ago. Things are different now. I *know* the Bagots will accept us. Denys has told me so."

She glared at her mother, her chin set.

Lettice went over to the window and gazed down. The street was bright and prosperous, pavements swept, windows full of costly objects. Passers-by were rich-looking. Carriages and horses too. As she watched she saw Lord Carteret walking slowly down the street towards the house. He looked tall and very elegant and for a moment she merely admired him. Then a lady and gentleman passed. Lord Carteret bowed gracefully, raising his hat. The gentleman bowed in reply and then hesitated, about to speak to Lord Carteret. But the lady, with the merest stiff nod, swept by, and her companion had to go with her. Is that because of the marriage, Lettice wondered sadly. She went back and sat beside her mother.

Ellen was still thoughtful.

"How much, exactly, have you told the Viscount about us, Isabella?"

Isabella had become nervous. She started up at her mother's question, went to a vase of roses and began crossly pushing the flowers about.

"Very little, of course."

"I have often seen a gentleman soldier and a gentleman sailor, and other sorts of gentlemen, but I have never yet seen a gentleman player!" quoted Lettice. "The less said about us the better."

Ellen raised her eyebrows.

"I mean, Isabella, did you mention to the Viscount that I am related to him?"

"Oh, Mama, of course not! He is the son of the Earl of Bagot, his family had titles four hundred years ago. What would he care for cousins ten times removed? Please don't mention such a thing. I know we're proud of being gentry. Somebody like Denys never thinks of it."

Her mother gave Isabella a look very different from her previous spellbound admiration.

Denys arrived after that and Locking announced luncheon.

During the meal Isabella recovered her spirits. Ellen sat on Lord Carteret's right and he paid a great deal of attention to her. In a way she was a shy person and treated so, she blossomed. Lord Carteret also asked Lettice about her London engagement and talked more about her career than her sister had done.

But when the meal was over and the family had returned to the Carterets' private drawing-room, Ellen's words gave Isabella a chill of dismay.

"Lord Carteret, my daughter tells me your family refuse to receive you both?"

He was taken aback by the directness of the question. Far too polite to show this, he murmured he was sure the reconciliation was a matter of time. Lettice, watching, was convinced Lord Carteret was now looking for some gentlemanly excuse to leave so that further conversation on the matter could be avoided.

Ellen said matter-of-factly, "My daughter also tells me you are unaware that my family and yours are distantly related."

He looked astounded. How naïve of Mama, thought Isabella angrily, she has made us look perfect fools. She was about to try to make it into a joke when Denys said, "My dear Mrs. Winter, in what way are we related? Isabella has never mentioned this."

"Through your third cousins, my lord," said Ellen settling down to a favourite conversation, "the Marchmonts of Ware."

"The Marchmonts? They were with us at Bagot Park last autumn. How very interesting. Wait a moment, Mrs. Winter, I beg—"

He went to a desk in the corner of the room. Rummaging through some documents, he took out a large folded paper which he spread on the table. Isabella had never seen the paper before, it was a family tree going back to 1450, a long complicated, spidery-written pattern of dates and names. Denys and Ellen pored over it.

"There are the Marchmonts," said Ellen, pointing with a small brown hand wearing a small diamond, often pawned, often retrieved. "Anthony Delaval Marchmont was my mother's second cousin. My mother's maiden name was Capell. I believe they were Italian, they came over in the seventeenth century, Mama used to say . . .'"

The talk turned to technicalities.

Isabella looked at the absorbed faces of her husband and her mother and then glanced automatically in Lettice's direction. Lettice met her eyes. Across the table, the sisters gave mystified shrugs. Their mother and the Viscount were mad.

"Extraordinary," Denys said at last. "So I must greet you as a cousin, ma'am."

To Isabella's amazement he bent forward and kissed her mother's cheek. Ellen, shy as a girl, laughed in the way she did when she was very pleased, a laugh like a little ascending trill of music.

"I am very proud of the connection, my lord."

"And Isabella knew this all the time," said Denys, taking his wife's hand. "What a noodle you are, my dearest, for not telling me."

"About what? Being a cousin ten times removed?"

Ellen shook her head. "I thought I had

152

taught you the importance of birth, my child. Do not show your ignorance."

"You are pleased Mama is a kind of relative, then, Lord Carteret?" put in Lettice, seeing that her sister, who detested to be put down by her mother, had blushed an angry pink.

"More than pleased, Miss Winter, relieved. I am not sure, but it is possible that the Earl may be willing to accept our marriage, when this is made known to him. I will write to him at once. Ladies, if you will excuse me?"

He bowed, and left them.

Carteret was more affected by what Ellen had told him than good manners allowed him to show. Even the faintest hope of healing the breach with his family was what he desperately longed for. He had written to the Earl from Scotland, telling him of the marriage and begging his forgiveness. It had been an impulsive letter, simple and direct, an appeal to a father's affection. Given his father's character it had been certain to fail, but Carteret continued to hope for the impossible. Isabella was totally unacceptable, yet he believed the Earl would receive her. The old man was as hard as iron, yet Carteret thought he might soften. He loved his father, and went on hoping without reason that he would be loved in return.

Carteret was nervous during the evening after his letter to his father had been taken to Berkeley Square but Isabella didn't notice and chattered happily about her own affairs. Her pretty voice, her laughter seemed pathetic to him just then.

The Earl's reply was brought by Locking the next morning. It was written in the third person and consisted of three lines. The Earl of Bagot presented his compliments to Viscount Carteret and would receive him and the Viscountess at five o'clock.

Denys gave a sigh of pure happiness.

He put his arms tenderly round Isabella and kissed her, saying how wonderful it was that her mother should have brought them such a blessing yesterday, he could scarce believe it.

(3)

Bagot House, a great mansion consisting of a central house and two large wings, stood back from the road near Berkeley Square in a wide courtyard into which carriages could comfortably drive. It had been built in the late

154

seventeenth century, four storeys high of brick sombrely faced with stone, its windows tall, its roof as square as a Florentine palace, each corner decorated with a kind of stone cannon-ball on a plinth. The Bagot arms were on either side of the heavy gates which stood open permanently during the London season.

For many months of the year Bagot House was empty. The family lived in their favourite house in Sussex where the Earl, although in his sixties, hunted regularly and where his lands were looked after and his tenants cared for. The Bagots had strong country roots and came to London during the season for rather shorter periods than most society families.

When the family left London at the end of the summer Bagot House was silent. The chandeliers hung in huge cotton bags as if containing swarms of bees. The furniture was ghostly under sheeting, carpets were rolled up, doors barred. For months the house was inhabited only by mice.

But at last the hunting season would end, the London plane trees begin to bud, and Bagot House come alive again.

Feet hurried in, windows opened to the light and air. Down the long passages came pails of soapy water, mops, brushes, the sound of voices. Hooves echoed on the court-yard stones, coaches opened their doors and the Earl, his daughters and their personal servants rustled into the newly-burnished house for the season. The mice retired to their holes in the wainscots and bided their time.

It was already late in the season when Denys and Isabella travelled to Berkeley Square in the elegant carriage he had hired for their London stay. Isabella wore a new gown of creamy silk, patterned with pink daisies, and there were daisies bunched inside her bonnet brim. She looked pretty and com-posed. Denys seemed to prefer her not to talk about the theatre, so she didn't tell him she felt as if she were about to go on in a difficult role in a brand new play. She had the same taut nerves, the same dry feeling in the roof of her mouth. The Earl, in her mind, had become a sort of Davenant.

The carriage drew up at Bagot House. The butler was waiting to receive them. Isabella distinctly remembered him. Swayne was elderly, high-shouldered, with great dignity and an ironic face. He bowed low. "My Lord and Lady!"

It was the first time except for that far-off occasion at Bagot Park that Isabella had seen Denys in his own home. Everybody greeted him, everybody was glad to see him. There were dozens of servants in the marble-floored hall and the long corridors. They bowed or bobbed curtsies. As he and Isabella walked down a corridor lined with mirrors, he said in a low voice, "You know who *they* have been looking out for."

"Do you mean me?"

"You must have been the only topic of conversation since Gretna."

They arrived at two enormous doors and Denys took her gloved hand.

"Now, my dearest. Stand your straightest and be your bravest."

The Earl stood up as they came into the room. He was a big broad-shouldered handsome man of sixty with a misshapen back due to a hunting accident. Seated, he looked younger. Standing and bent sideways, he looked old. Something about him reminded Isabella of a bird she had seen on the Sussex downs; her father had told her it was called a Montagu's harrier. Hunched, its powerful dark wings folded, it had a fiercely curved beak and hooded eyes. The old Earl's nose was beaked, his clothes dark, his eyes thick-lidded and very sharp.

"Father, may I present Isabella? My wife."

Denys's voice sounded forced.

"How do you do, Lord Bagot."

Isabella sank into the curtsy she had learned for *King Charles's Merrie Days*.

The old man put out a hand as well-shaped as his son's, the Bagot seal ring showing up the thin fingers, and raised her.

"So you're the hussy who ran away with my son."

"No, sir, it was I who did the wooing," said Denys, with a laugh as strained as his voice.

"Let the girl speak for herself."

Isabella noticed the Earl's eyebrows, tufted and whiter than his hair, met in the middle when he scowled.

"Surely the Bagots always do the wooing," she murmured. The old man looked at her sardonically.

"Hm. Well, I suppose I must drag you round the rest of them. Come along. Put the girls out of their misery. Their eyes are on stalks."

He marched her round the room, presenting her to two young women and then to

Robert Bagot, whose pleasant grin was a distinct relief.

The first lady to whom she was presented was Denys's elder sister, Lady Frances, a slim young woman with a prim manner. Lady Frances had a face which reminded Isabella of engravings in Shakespeare's *Henry VIII*. She was pale and plain, her eyes narrow, the Tudor impression strengthened by her stiff manner, not exactly unfriendly, but guarded. She faintly pressed Isabella's hand.

Sitting by the window, wearing apple green and white silk, was the youngest of the Bagot children, Lady Clare. Isabella saw she was beautiful and felt a pang of jealousy.

"This is the baby of the family," the Earl said. "She likes to keep us in order, don't you, miss?"

Lady Clare gave her father the smile of a girl who knows her power and held out her hand to Isabella, giving the impression that she wished to do no such thing. When Isabella took the hand she received no answering pressure, it was like shaking hands with a wax image. Lady Clare was beautiful, yet it was difficult to know why, for her nose was too large and her mouth too wide, her cheeks too thin, her fair hair almost colourless. In a way, she was like a sulky-looking boy. But there was something feline as well as female about her.

Robert Bagot gave Isabella the first real smile she had received since she entered the room.

"Here's my nephew Robert. I gather you have already made his acquaintance. I've told him I hold him entirely responsible for this marriage of yours. He is supposed to see Carteret behaves himself."

Robert laughed. Apart from his uncle he was the most self-possessed person in the room, for Lady Frances looked uneasy and Lady Clare like a stone.

Denys had spoken a great deal about his cousin to Isabella since their marriage and she knew how much Denys loved and admired him. Meeting him now, she felt he was an ally. Yet in Newcastle he had seemed the contrary. She envied his easy assurance with the Earl, while poor Denys stood by looking at a loss.

Tea was brought on a silver tray; the silver tea-pot with a silver acorn on the lid was so huge that Isabella wondered how Lady Frances managed to lift it. Conversation was commanded by the Earl, consisting of anecdotes which he told well, and at which he expected his family to laugh. Isabella knew he'd told those stories before; he spoke them too skilfully for them to be new. His children and his nephew laughed dutifully. After that he became silent, now and again shooting looks at Isabella from heavy-lidded eyes. There was no way of knowing what he was thinking.

When tea was over he put his tea cup down with a clatter.

"Got to be off," he said. "Robert, that damned fool of an agent Wreford will be here directly. You had best come, for if I'm left alone with the fellow I shall most certainly shoot him."

Standing up with his sideways stoop, he gave Isabella and his son a frowning glance.

"Swayne will send round for your boxes. Fanny will arrange your rooms. Fanny?"

"Of course, Papa."

"In this house we dine at seven," he added, glaring at Isabella.

She gave him an almost roguish smile. It did not appear to surprise him. He continued to look at her appraisingly, then, calling Robert to heel as if whistling a hunting dog, he went out.

8

(1)

WHEN Ellen and Lettice left Clarges Street, they walked through the crowded streets on their way to the lodgings which were to be Lettice's future home. They had spent the previous night at a coaching inn in Holborn.

The address of the lodgings had been given to Ellen by Mrs. Gunn. It had "ground into Ellen's soul" as she confessed to Lettice to ask her old enemy for help, but neither Ellen nor Thomas had stayed in London longer than a night and finding lodgings in the metropolis was an alarming prospect.

"Mrs. Hastings keeps a house in which many of my actors have stayed," said Mrs. Gunn. "I played with her in *Henry Four*. She says she was once Lady Macbeth opposite Kean but I hae ma doots about *that*."

Ellen had her doubts about lodgings recommended by Mrs. Gunn. She also had doubts about leaving Lettice in London.

There was much to ponder over. She was satisfied with Isabella's "great" marriage, thought the young Viscount a pleasant man and congratulated herself on informing him of Isabella's gentle birth. It was satisfying to think that her own ancestry might be instrumental in Isabella taking her place in society.

"Every act re-acts," she thought.

When her mother glanced at her, Lettice was staring at the pavement, lost in thought. Farley Street, not far from Oxford Street, was reached at last. It was not encouraging. The houses were shabby, the railings peeling, there was an air of neglect and dirt. Number 33 was a tall house which had seen better days, its windowsills were dusty, the area steps had a broken handrail. The maid who opened the door, a haggard child of fourteen, had a none-too-clean apron.

"Mrs. Hastings says to take you in 'ere."

She took them into a stuffy room of the kind Ellen knew only too well. The walls were hung with flyblown engravings of famous actors of the past—the Kembles, the Keans. The carpet was threadbare, the heavy curtains looked thick with dust. A canary in a

163

cage hopped monotonously from one perch to another.

"Dicky, dicky," said Ellen, who loved all creatures. She put her brown face close to the cage. The bird immediately began to sing.

"A bird fancier!" cried a powerful voice. Framed in the doorway was a tall figure in black. The lady could have been in mourning except that in place of jet she wore coral earrings and a coral-coloured ribbon in a white cap too youthful for her. The sleeves of the dress billowed like wings. The effect was of a giantess.

"I am Mrs. Hastings," she said. "And this must be Miss Winter about whom my dear friend Hester Gunn has written."

Lettice curtsied politely. She did not like the look of Mrs. Hastings. A tray of tea was brought in by the haggard child who put it down with a clatter. She had forgotten the muffins.

"Sybil, you have a head on your shoulders. Use it!" cried Mrs. Hastings in a voice for filling theatres. When the girl had slopped out she sighed.

"Mrs. Winter, ma'am, I'm sure you agree that servants are not what they were. If I ring this bell for her to hurry, will she do so? But I

164

shall continue. I have always been a bell-ringer."

During tea Mrs. Hastings talked of "the profession". Had Mrs. Winter seen this? Had she liked that? She enjoyed discussing the theatre, opening her painted eyes, laughing in her big low-toned voice. After tea she showed them up a creaking staircase to a back bedroom. It was as small as the Newcastle attic and the view was similar except that the London sky was dark with smoke. My life, thought Lettice, seems spent looking at chimney pots.

"Everything is for your comfort," said Mrs. Hastings, gesturing at the rickety washstand. "And remember, Miss Winter, if you need anything, Sybil is here to serve."

She left them.

Lettice began to unknot the cord on her box. When the footsteps had receded, Ellen said quietly, "If you don't like it, child, you must not stay."

"It is perfectly adequate, Mama."

"Not very clean, I'm afraid."

"We are used to that, Mama."

"Yes," Ellen said and sighed. "I suppose we are. Promise me if you are not happy you will ask someone to help you to move? Mr. Davenant, I feel sure . . ."

"I promise," Lettice said calmly.

Her mother helped her to unpack and they left the house together so that Ellen should be in good time to catch the night coach.

Ellen was flustered by the size of London and anxious at leaving Lettice. Isabella's glory slipped from her mind.

(2)

Lettice arrived at the theatre next morning after a long walk through both shabby and fashionable streets crowded with horses, carriages and jostling crowds. She was awed at the theatre façade. It had the air of a temple, with Shakespeare's statue on the roof over the portico and other statues, Garrick among them, along the walls in niches. Imposing, dazzlingly white, it was far removed from the theatres Lettice was used to, most of which looked like warehouses. But when she went down a passage to the Stage Door she felt at home. It was in a dull alleyway at the back of the theatre, exactly like every Stage Door she had known, ill-lit, dark and confined. The doorkeeper was like all the other doorkeepers, small and brusque with a peremptory manner. Lettice knew one of his duties was to keep out the duns, as her father called them. The duns . . . creditors . . . bailiffs . . . haunted every Stage Door in England. The doorkeepers were the actors' friends, their shields against the outside world. They alone knew their secrets, and told lies for them.

"Morning, miss. Name's Jack."

"Good morning, Jack. Lettice Winter."

"Good egg," said Jack surprisingly.

Lettice found her way, using her instinct, into the auditorium. The place was lit and seemed enormous, a landscape of plush seats, draped boxes, a heaven full of chandeliers, a crimson hoop of circle above which gold cherubs held bunches of gas globes.

She stared for a while, then slipped through the pass door and went on to the stage to join the actors assembling there. There were far more of them than she was accustomed to. But everything today was on a huge scale . . .

A timid little woman with a knob of dyed black hair came up to her.

"Miss Winter? I'm Gwynyth. Your dresser."

"I'm glad to meet you, Gwynyth," Lettice

said. "Everything is very strange to me at present, I'm afraid. The only person I know is Mr. Davenant."

"He is the only one you need to know, miss. Mr. Davenant is a great man. I've known him since he was young, you know. When I think of the splendour of his name now!" murmured Gwynyth.

On cue, Davenant strode on to the stage.

He looked, Lettice had to admit, magnificent. His stocky figure was enhanced by a dark green coat with silver buttons and perfectly fitting trousers of dove colour.

He walked to the footlights and turned to face the actors. The crowd became very still.

"The list, Bryson, if you please."

Davenant put out a hand without looking at the man at his side who reverently placed a paper in it.

Lettice guessed that the man addressed as "Bryson" must be the manager. He was tall, towering over Davenant, but stooped as if apologising for his height. He was foppishly elegant in lavender-coloured clothes with velvet cuffs and black frogging, his hair dressed in a fashion too young for him. Lettice thought he looked fussed: just like her poor father.

"Well, friends, I am here to talk about the programme," said Davenant, in a voice which could have been heard in the farthest seats of the stalls. "Bryson wished me to do one of those French fal-lals which he says are all the rage. They are not the rage with me. Today we start rehearsing *The Iron Chest*."

Lettice drew a breath. She knew the play, which both Kemble and Kean had made famous. It was a curious mixture of domestic comedy, melodrama and songs. What made Lettice's heart beat faster was that there were two main roles for young girls—Barbara, the child of a poor family in the New Forest, and Helen who lives in the house of Sir Edward Mortimer, the Kemble/Kean role.

Perhaps, oh, perhaps, Davenant planned to give her one of those.

He called out the names of the characters, as he had done in Newcastle. At each name, an actor or actress stood in front of him.

"Barbara?" called Davenant.

A blonde actress, considerably older than Lettice, with a pert face and a tilted nose, came to the centre of the stage.

"See you behave yourself this time, Violet."

"Get on with you," said Violet. Davenant laughed.

More roles were called. Then, "Madam Helen?"

This *must* be it, thought Lettice, blushing with expectancy.

A tall young woman with copper hair stepped out of the line of actors. She had an expressionless pale face.

"Well, Jessie?"

"Well, Mr. Davenant?"

"I hope you're going to work hard and show your paces."

"Oh yes," said the girl with a condescending smile.

The rest of the roles were called. Then a list of "New Forest countryfolk". Lettice was one of these.

When Davenant dismissed the company Lettice was so nervous and disappointed that at first she did not hear Gwynyth speaking to her.

"Shall I take you up to your dressing-room, dear?"

Lettice thanked her and followed her up a flight of stone steps. Gwynyth explained that the "big dressing-rooms", in which four or five of the young actresses dressed together, were full and Lettice was very lucky, she had a dressing-room on her own.

In silence, Lettice followed Gwynyth along the chilly corridors. They went through rooms hung with costumes, stiffened, fantastic, seeming to be inhabited. At the end of a passage longer and narrower than the rest, Gwynyth opened a door into a stone-floored room the size of a large cupboard.

"This is yours, Miss Winter. Nice, isn't it?"

"It is very nice. Thank you."

Lettice was too miserable to smile, either at the hideous little room or the kind old woman.

"Just you settle in, then," said Gwynyth, looking round as if expecting to see a costume hanging there. "Then Mr. Davenant wishes to see you."

"Oh."

"Yes. He spoke to me this morning," said Gwynyth, with her look of adoration again.

She took Lettice on another long journey, and while they made their way through a honeycomb of passages, Lettice's spirits rose. Davenant must have news for her. He was going to explain that there was another play, another role he had in mind for her.

Gwynyth left her, after tapping on a pair of lofty doors.

Lettice had thought today was on a large scale, but had never seen anything like the suite which was called Davenant's "dressing-room", two high-ceilinged rooms divided by a door thrown open to make a chamber large enough for a banquet. The rooms were carpeted in white garlanded with roses. The curtains were royal blue velvet, the furniture large and heavy, polished so that it glittered.

Davenant was sitting in a high-backed chair with an air of weariness, while Augustus Bryson talked in a complaining voice as if he would never stop.

As Lettice came into the room Bryson gave a polite smile and continued to talk. Davenant gestured her to sit down.

"The problem, sir," said Bryson, "is that the public requires novelty. Novelty is what they want."

"You have told me that four times."

"Novelty," repeated Bryson. "It is my duty to point out to you, sir, how many times *The Iron Chest* has been seen. And over so many years."

"Kemble. Kean. That is the point," said

Davenant, sighing. "It worked then and it will work again. *I* am playing in it."

"But the public likes spectacle, sir. In my experience—"

"Your experience! If you are referring to what was allowed on this stage recently, Bryson, all I can say is I pity you. An elephant. Serpents writhing to Hindoo music. Are you saying you wish me to share my stage with them? Go away, Bryson, and make the arrangements and stop bothering me with your serpents."

He waved Bryson, who looked offended, out of the room.

When the door closed he turned to Lettice, sitting quietly some distance away, her hands folded. Her dress was fresh but much faded, her green slippers scuffed.

"*The Iron Chest* is a wonderful play," ventured Lettice. "I have acted in it a number of times."

"I daresay," he said absently. "Do you remember an actor who played Romeo in Newcastle? A friend of yours, I believe. A lot of hair and a good conceit of himself."

"Do you mean Buckley Vernon?"

"That's the man," he said. He scribbled the name on a piece of paper and then nodded

173

to her, rather in the way he had dismissed Bryson.

Lettice waited. Surely he would tell her now!

He looked up.

"Well? What are you waiting for?"

Suddenly, she couldn't do it. She couldn't ask what her parts were going to be. Perhaps it was the trepidation of coming to a vast, strange theatre, having no friends, missing the confidence of knowing her parents were there to help her. Perhaps it was something challenging in Davenant's face. She must trust him.

"I wanted to thank you for engaging me," was all she said.

He raised an eyebrow, but did not reply.

When she was gone, he scratched his nose. She was slightly on his conscience at present. Not much, but slightly. Had the chit been sarcastic just now? Difficult to tell, with a face like that.

9

(1)

THE theatre was Lettice's passion, but she never deceived herself about it. She knew it was all work, study, practice and many disappointments, whether one played in a converted malt-house or in Drury Lane. But Isabella had invented a fantasy for herself about the aristocracy. She had thought their ordered ceremonious life could never be anything but happy. She had imagined that living in a sumptuous mansion, meeting the rank and fashion, spending the season in a round of balls and soirées, must be a state of bliss.

Lord Carteret and his bride moved from Clarges Street into a suite in Bagot House for the last weeks of the season.

The rooms given to the Viscount and his wife were very fine. Tall windows overlooked the garden, where a bronze statue of a Roman emperor stood on a lawn surrounded by lilac trees. The Carterets had a lofty-ceilinged bedroom with a huge ancient four-poster hung with embroidered curtains. There were dressing-rooms for the Viscount and his lady, a private drawing-room also with a garden view. Lord Carteret's valet, a Scot called Robertson, quiet and neat-handed, returned to his master's service. Denys treated him as he had treated Locking, as a friend.

But Isabella lost the kindly little Rivers, the girl who had maided her at Clarges Street, and was given instead the Bagot's retired family nurse, Hopton.

Isabella disliked Hopton on sight, a big slow-moving woman with a pinched mouth and expressionless hazel eyes. She had the powerful look of a peasant. Hopton did everything well; she ironed beautifully, did Isabella's hair to perfection (but hurt her when she washed it, her fingers were like steel). She scarcely replied if Isabella made a pleasant remark, bringing an atmosphere almost of dislike. You may be "My Lady" but you are not so to me, she seemed to say. It was useless for Isabella to complain to her husband, he had known Hopton since he was born. He was devotedly fond of the servants and they served him with smiles. It was vexing; but Isabella had to put up with it.

There were other things to put up with. The strict formality of the manners; the meals at the Earl's table at which he talked solely of his own affairs; the many things Isabella was supposed to know. No lady could go shopping in Bond Street in the afternoon, for example, it was not proper.

Lady Frances, "Fanny" as the family called her, soon became a friend. Lady Fanny loved clothes and she and Isabella discovered this interest in common. They went shopping together in the Bagot carriage.

"Lady Quenington was telling me the Queen is changing the way she does her hair." Isabella was an entranced audience to remarks like that.

Paradoxically, the most considerable member of the Bagot family was the one with whom Isabella was a complete success. Denys was surprised and impressed by Isabella's way with the Earl. He was afraid of his father, or it was more true to say he was afraid his father would hurt him by the brusque impatience of an unloving heart. Isabella saw the Earl as a man—and therefore to be managed.

He was difficult, but she had been expecting that. He looked at anybody who spoke to him from under hooded eyelids, as if to pounce. He was usually rude.

"There's a damn fool thing to talk about!" he exclaimed, when Lady Fanny spoke to Isabella about a new gown.

The worst of Isabella's troubles came from Lady Clare. And since Denys was devoted to his young sister, as to his family, the servants, and everybody in the world it seemed to Isabella, she had to wage this domestic war alone.

It had never occurred to her, naïve, spirited, and eighteen years old, that when she stepped through the doors of Bagot House and made her curtsy to the Earl she was also about to meet an enemy. Lady Clare proved to be exactly that.

Lady Clare was the traditionally spoiled child, and the fact that her mother had died when she was born made her all the more precious and petted. She had inherited her looks, ugly and fascinating by turn, from a Scottish great-grandmother Melisant, daughter of a duke, a lady of strong will, imperious and difficult. Melisant was talked of when Lady Clare was at her worst. Isabella never saw her at anything but her worst, since Lady Clare either ignored her or made disagreeable remarks aimed at her.

"Why do you allow Clare to be so absurd?" asked Isabella when she and Denys were dressing for a ball. "When we went in the carriage today she wrapped her skirts round her so that they would not touch mine. I longed to ask if she thought her sister-in-law had the smallpox."

"Clare is only a child, my dearest," said Denys, rearranging his white silk cravat.

Isabella rustled over in her petticoat and wound her arms round his waist.

"She is not a child, she is seventeen years old. When I was seventeen—"

"Ah, yes. We all know about that."

"You mean I must hold my tongue."

He merely smiled, turning to press a kiss on her lips. Looking at his face, so sweet, so reserved, she wished he did not imply—he was too tender to do more—that he preferred her not to speak of her past life. How could that be anything but uncomfortable?

"Anyway, you must defend me against your younger sister. She is very ill-natured."

"I will talk to her. Clare is a dear girl *au fond*. All my friends want to marry her, you know. She's clever, too."

179

There was no answer to that.

The news that Bagot and his son were reconciled and the new bride installed at Bagot House soon spread. Streams of visitors drove up, and Lady Fanny did the honours when her father was absent. Invitation cards arrived, far more than could be accepted for any single day. Isabella was greeted (not without great curiosity) by London society. Being launched into the great world turned out to be as hard work, she thought, as being an actress. It was like playing a matinée and an evening performance every day of the week.

Denys was always beside her except when he "rode out" as he called it, each morning in the Park, or sometimes when he and Robert went to their club, Brooks's in St. James's.

It was generally agreed in society that although Carteret had made a *mésalliance*, the girl was beautiful and seemed to have a head on her shoulders. The Earl had put it firmly about that Isabella was related to the Bagots and this interesting fact took on a life of its own. From being a distant relative Isabella soon became closely related to a ducal family in Northumberland. Her father had fallen on hard times and she, daughter of a noble

180

house, had been forced for a while to earn her bread as an actress. The days before the season's end went by in luncheons, garden parties, dinners and splendid balls.

"You are bidden to a drawing-room next week, my dearest," Denys said one morning as he came in from riding in the Row, fresh-faced and handsome in black and white.

"To make my curtsy?" exclaimed Isabella. She knew something of the Queen's drawing-rooms from Lady Fanny, but had never asked when she herself was to be presented.

"To be kissed by Her Majesty," said Denys, sitting beside her and stretching out his long indolent legs.

"I thought the ladies kissed the Queen's hand."

"Not the daughters of dukes, marquises or earls." Denys always knew things like that. "Her Majesty will kiss your forehead or your cheek."

Looking at her sparkling face he added, "Now you can enjoy planning your presentation frock."

"I do think of other things besides attire," said Isabella shortly.

He looked at her, genuinely surprised.

"But why should a lady not think of attire?"

That afternoon the Earl said, "Glad to be making your bob to Her Majesty?" He had condescended to come into the long drawing-room to take tea. Everybody was expected to be there as a consequence, including Lady Clare.

"It was good of you, my lord, to arrange such an honour," said Isabella in the right tone.

"Melbourne gave your name to the Lord Chamberlain," he said. "Told me he liked the look of you. 'She doesn't fidget,' he said, 'I detest a fidgety woman.' Always liked Melbourne. He makes me laugh." He gave her a glance. "My mother will present you, by the by." He relapsed into silence.

"I suppose you should have a lesson, Isabella," murmured Lady Fanny, from behind the giant silver tea-pot. "Making your curtsy to the Queen is not the usual obeisance, you know."

"Will this do?"

Isabella stood up, faced her father-in-law and gracefully fell into the lowest curtsy, then magically rose without effort in a movement of exquisite slowness. It was the curtsy she

182

and Lettice had perfected when playing ladies-in-waiting to Anne Boleyn in *Henry VIII*.

Lady Fanny looked amazed, Lady Clare furious.

"Hm," said the Earl. "I daresay it will serve."

(2)

There were strict rules for Royal drawing-rooms. Isabella must wear white, her head-dress of three white plumes must be set off with a lace veil (only unmarried girls wore tulle). Her train, jewelled and embroidered, must be at least three and a half yards long. When nearing the Presence Isabella must drop her train, which would then be spread out by the Court officer.

"Drawing-rooms are in the early afternoon. You will have to begin dressing after breakfast," Lady Fanny said.

The dressmaker and two assistants were summoned to Bagot House with books full of pictures of the newest styles from Paris. Isabella was entranced.

"Do you like this one, Fanny?"

Her sister-in-law had recently asked her to drop the "Lady".

"Oh, no, Isabella. It is much too—well, it is too much."

"And this one?"

"That is quite impossible," said Lady Fanny, looking at the design, an elaborate affair of flounces, with far too low a neckline. The style was finally approved and Isabella stood for hours while yards of white Spitalfields silk were pinned round her. It reminded her of the days when her mother had made her costume for *The Smuggler's Bride*.

Three days before the drawing-room presentation, she was sent for by the Earl. A footman took her to the study, which Isabella had never visited before.

The room was sunny and smelled of leather, from books, from furniture. Isabella was conscious that she looked her best. She wore a black silk dress patterned with brilliant crimson flowers; it was a new fashion, a dramatic change from the old pale muslins of the past. She had changed her hair in imitation of the young Queen, and it was plaited and looped to leave her ears bare. A thick chignon was knotted in the centre of her head at the back.

The Earl looked at her. She never knew

what he was thinking. Faces like his, she thought, have no discernible expression, they are just handsome and wicked. But Robert gave her an admiring glance and a grin.

The Earl gestured for her to wait a moment while he settled something in his mind. Isabella sat, upright, unselfconscious, in respectful silence.

Robert sorted through a heap of letters. Before Isabella had come in, his uncle had been discussing the embarrassing matter of the Bagot diamonds. By rights, for the Queen's drawing-room, Isabella should wear the diamonds. She was the wife of the Bagot heir. It was true the tiara and necklace were very old-fashioned and she might not like them much but she had every right to wear them. However, there was the little matter of Clare. "She'll not stand it," said the Earl, with mixed amusement and relish. "If she sees the girl wearing the things, Clare will raise the roof."

"Like Melisant?"

"As you say, my boy."

"Is there any possible solution, sir?" enquired Robert, who had thought of one and guessed that his uncle had done the same.

"I believe so."

Now the Earl roused himself from his thoughts and told his nephew to be off.

"I am taking my daughter-in-law to buy her a few diamonds."

"When, sir?" said Isabella. Perhaps a shade too quickly.

"Now, of course. Off and get your bonnet."

Returning briskly to her own rooms, Isabella grinned to herself. Like Lettice, she knew how to deal with men. It was an art taught to her daughters by Ellen who believed the male sex should be managed. Managing meant coaxing, deferring, treating men as superiors. And enslaving them.

Denys's feelings about his father irritated Isabella. Nobody must hold sway over Denys but herself; she did not like to see her elegant, lazy, sweet-natured lover unmanned when he was with that ill-tempered old man. Why was Denys afraid of him? What was there to fear?

Sitting next to the Earl in the carriage, Isabella was enchanted at the thought of her destination. He did not bother to speak and when she glanced at him he reminded her more than ever of the Montagu's harrier, with curved beak and hooded eyes. This bird of prey was taking her to buy her something very expensive indeed. Surely that must mean she had tamed it?

The carriage halted at a small eighteenth-century house in South Audley Street.

"The Frenchman who owns this place has taste," said the Earl.

The footman coming to the carriage door recognised the Earl and when Isabella and he were ushered into the house, a well-dressed man, short, dark, and with a crooked nose, greeted the Earl with respect and a kind of gleam.

"Gautry, this is Viscountess Carteret," said the Earl, seating his bulky crooked frame on a small chair. "She needs diamonds."

"A necklace, my lord?"

"Necklace, parure, tiara, bracelets, the whole shooting match."

Gautry disappeared, returning with his hands full of morocco leather cases.

Isabella was requested to remove her bonnet and close-fitting jacket. She sat at a table with a looking-glass in front of her, and Monsieur Gautry placed a diamond tiara on her glossy hair. Earrings larger than pear-drops followed. There were necklaces which cunningly took to pieces, bracelets made like chains of flowers.

187

The Earl talked weights and carats, using mystifying phrases. He held pieces to the light, narrowing his eyes. Some of the jewels he pushed aside as "vulgar", others as "unimportant". He picked the jewels up in his beautiful hands, swinging them between his fingers, muttering, "Try these," and looking at Isabella with his grizzled head to one side.

Finally, without asking which she preferred, he chose a magnificent tiara; the rose in its centre, set on wire, slightly trembled when the tiara was worn. There was a matching necklace, earrings and bracelets. There was also the parure, a smaller necklace, to be worn with a brooch and earrings.

"Bring them round tomorrow."

Gautry bowed deeply. And so he should, thought Isabella, wondering at the fortune the Earl had just spent on her.

During the journey homewards she looked over at her father-in-law slumped in the corner of the carriage, deep in his own thoughts.

She leaned forward and lightly touched his sleeve.

"How do I say thank you, my lord?"

"How would you like to?" he said sardonically.

"Like this."

She kissed his wrinkled cheek lightly.

"You women think that pays the piper, don't you?"

There were many answers to that. She could have replied teasingly, or with affectionate propriety. She could, actress-like, have been as ladylike as Fanny, as farouche as Clare.

She said, "If I am the most beautiful woman at the drawing-room, it will be thanks to you."

"Certainly it will," he said, very drily indeed.

10

(1)

FOR all her hope, all her ambition, Lettice had been afraid of living in London. She had been happy with her parents even if "home" had been lodgings in dreary towns and half-filled theatres, except during the glorious year in Sussex when they had owned the North Street theatre. As an artist, she'd been free from responsibility when she lived with her parents. All she had to do was act. Everyday things were left to Ellen, who gladly exclaimed if Lettice was tired or her boots were wet. Mothering her (though never admiring or petting her) made Ellen happy. Thomas, too, for all his fuss, gave her roles which stretched her talents. She had encouragement, the company of beloved parents and safety. Why had she been mad enough to leave?

Davenant had offered her what every actress burned for, a chance to conquer London. Or so she had thought when she left her parents. Now a year had gone by since she'd arrived at the Royalty and Davenant had given her nothing but parts of a few lines. Violet, the pert fair-skinned woman with blonde hair, was given every comedy part. She was good enough, but Lettice knew she herself was better. It was Jessie Ramsey whom Davenant cast in every important dramatic role. Why? Jessie Ramsey was conceited and of questionable talent. Onstage she was a nobody though offstage she gave herself airs. Gwynyth told Lettice that Jessie Ramsey was wealthy, and Lettice had seen her leaving the theatre in a smart-looking phaeton.

Perhaps, wondered Lettice, Jessie Ramsey was more than an actress to Davenant?

"Gracious no! Her father is one of Davenant's best friends. Jessie is his *goddaughter!*" was the innocent, perhaps true reply from Gwynyth.

Lettice knew she should have faced Davenant long ago, made a scene, angrily demanded why he'd brought her to London if all she was to be was a walking-on lady. But it was too late. The months had gone by and a kind of miserable lethargy had come over her. Perhaps he believed she had no talent? *She* knew that she had, but was too crushed to think how to prove it.

She was lonely, unhappy over her work, and she was poor. It was difficult even to pay for her laundry. In the early summer, she received a letter saying her parents were taking a ship for Ireland for a tour. They were taking ten actors with them, many of whom were old friends, and a number of plays Lettice knew well, even the dear old *Welsh Girl*.

Reading her mother's letter from Liverpool, Lettice felt homesick, and guilty too. She was not there to share her parents' discomforts, support her mother in small affectionate plots to save Thomas from worrying. Ellen wrote that "your father is very pleased about the Irish engagement. He has collected such a satisfactory company. They are so cheerful and gifted and your father is more sanguine."

Lettice didn't believe a word.

The letter brought back strongly the higgledy-piggledy, bedraggled, on-the-edge-of-debt life she and Isabella had known since they were born. Why did I long to come to London? she thought miserably. Why did Davenant bring me here? He had tempted her with false promises implying (though never saying) that he would give her good parts. She thought of him now with the greatest bitterness.

She took her mother's letter downstairs to show it to Mrs. Hastings, not because she was fond of her landlady but because Mrs. Hastings would be offended if she did not.

The landlady was in the dingy parlour. She spent most of her time there, drinking tea, doing her accounts, quarrelling with her husband and grumbling at the servant Sybil. In between times she read plays. She never read books.

It was a rainy, chilly London day of the kind that comes in early summer. Mrs. Hastings put down a dog-eared prompt copy of *Hamlet*.

"Good afternoon, child."

"I have had a letter from my Mama, Mrs. Hastings," said Lettice, "I wondered if you might like to see it."

"Thank you, dear. I would be most interested," said the landlady.

Lettice was not offered tea.

"Irish touring is very tiresome," remarked Mrs. Hastings, returning the letter and fixing eyes of surprising brilliance on the girl. "I was in a fire at Dublin and a riot in Londonderry. They threw turnips," she added, her voice at its deepest.

"In Sussex when we played *King Charles's Merrie Days* a man threw a firecracker on the stage."

"Of course, of course," said Mrs. Hastings with the disinterest of one actress in another's career. "Did Mr. Hastings remember to tell you we cannot provide supper on Sunday? It is his birthday and we are giving a collation for a few friends. I should ask Sybil to buy you a pie if I were you. Imagine, dear," she added, lowering her voice although they were alone and the door closed. "Mr. Hastings is fifty."

"Indeed, Mrs. Hastings."

"Fifty," echoed Mrs. Hastings. She gave Lettice the look of one young girl to another. "I'm told one has to expect, when a man reaches that age, that there is a decline in his powers of enjoyment. I remember my poor Papa . . ."

When she was leaving for the theatre, Lettice met Mr. Hastings coming up the front steps, under a large umbrella. He was a small neat man with a youthfully thin figure, far more energetic than his spouse. His face reminded Lettice of a turnip lantern, with holes for eyes and mouth, circular and white. One had no idea what he thought of his life, his wife or the actors who clattered in and out of his house. His turnip face never looked pleased. He gave her a cold smile and disappeared indoors.

Lettice walked to the theatre, picking her way through the cobbled streets covered in mud. She went down a street full of shawl and fan shops, along Drury Lane with its windows full of ballet shoes and to the back of Covent Garden past inns and lodging-houses. Horses steamed in the chill air. Windows were gas-lit although it was June. The road widened as she approached the theatre.

A slight figure in a grey cloak, she slipped through the Stage Door. Two or three members of the orchestra went by, carrying clarinet and violin cases, their coats spangled with rain.

As Lettice glanced through the doorkeeper's window she saw a figure she thought she recognised. Surely it could not be—yes, it was! Buckley Vernon.

"You'd best take the filly, sir," the stage doorkeeper was saying with his country accent imitated by scores of actors. "A pretty little goer she is. You choose Delicate Lass."

"Put me down for a guinea. And here's another delicate lass," exclaimed Buckley, striding out to greet Lettice. "Isn't this the best moment of the week?"

"I am glad to see you after all this time, Mr. Vernon."

He burst out laughing.

"Don't sound so formal, Miss Winter! You can't be surprised at seeing me since I have you to thank for my engagement."

"Me?"

"You told Davenant where to find me."

"That was months ago."

"Yes, it was, and he offered me something but it wasn't big or interesting enough."

"Did you refuse him?" she said in a small voice.

"Of course. I waited for a better offer," he said with the look she remembered, waiting for applause. He little knew the pang his boast gave her. *She* hadn't such courage.

They met again during the first act interval in the Green Room. Buckley was spirited and cheerful; he knew a number of the actors in the company and Lettice, sitting alone, was grateful when he came to join her.

"We can't have you sitting there like a

mouse," he said, with his flattering boyish smile. "Is this the girl who set them by the ears in Newcastle? Tell me about yourself. Are you a little *triste*, or do I imagine it?"

"Perhaps a little," she said. "I had a letter from my parents today. They have left for Ireland."

"So?"

"How hard-hearted you are," she said, laughing in spite of herself. "I miss them very much. As they must miss Bella and me. They lost both their daughters."

"Do you seriously expect me to be sorry for them when one daughter is a full-blown coroneted countess or whatever she is and the other is at a London theatre?"

"Since I have been here I have only been a walking-on lady."

It was difficult to confess it and when he scoffed she was pleased.

"What does it matter if you have no speaking part yet? You are here. That pretty little foot is in the door. Great things will follow."

"Do you truly think so?"

"I truly do," he said, with the inward-looking expression he wore when talking about work. "For us both."

"I suppose you know that Mr. Davenant is

197

reviving *The Iron Chest* again," she said. "We played it when I first came to London and he wants to do it again. I think it a stupid play. But Gwynyth, who's my dresser and knows everything, says Mr. Davenant loves it."

"Anything Kemble and Kean succeeded in," said Buckley, grinning at her.

"Mr. Vernon!" exclaimed Lettice scornfully. "It is almost sixty years since Kemble played in it. That was in 1780! Even when Kean was in the play I was *eight* years old!"

He laughed at her vehemence.

"I have to confess I find the play interesting."

"Then you must have a leading role in it."

"It is not quite settled," he said, with the actor's caution and superstition. "The piece has a great deal to offer, you know. Comedy, drama."

"I call it melodrama."

"Perhaps so. But Davenant is always extraordinary. And there is music and songs. What more can one ask for?"

"Shakespeare."

"*Macbeth*?" he said. "Our audiences want to enjoy themselves. It is very natural. Don't look sad," he added in a tone of a man to whom good fortune is so close that he can afford a kindness.

The bells rang for the next act and Lettice stood up. She did so automatically, with no feeling of excitement or danger. All she did was to be a "walking lady", sing a song with the other girls, stand about. She thought of her mother's old phrase, "It grinds into my soul."

To have worked all her life with dedication and to achieve *nothing*. She had made the wrong decision in accepting Davenant's offer, she could not forgive herself or him. She was poor and disappointed, living in the teeming capital, and despite Buckley Vernon's kind company, alone. It was true she was too busy to notice loneliness much of the time but there were hours when she passionately wished to be with her parents in the old rattle-trap life.

Another thing which saddened her was that she had lost Isabella. Her sister had been away from London for months at Bagot Park with the family. Since her return for the season, weeks ago, Lettice had received one short letter. "I'm at Bagot House again. Come and take tea tomorrow. Do!"

But there had been a rehearsal on that day

and after Lettice had written saying she could not come, she had not received another word.

Unhappy over her work, anxious at her lack of money, disillusioned in Davenant, she remembered her sister's companionship painfully. The separation would soon be something neither of them could cross. Years ago Lettice had seen two people skating. There had been a thin crack across the ice and suddenly, with a strange sound, it began to widen so that the couple were left on separate stretches of ice. They had managed to scramble to safety but it had been terrifying to see them one moment close, the next separated by a path of black water . . .

She was not called for the first rehearsal of *The Iron Chest*, she had a mere four lines at the end of the play. The rain had stopped, and she made up her mind suddenly to walk to Bagot House and leave a message for her sister. Isabella might be at home. How absurd, how hurtful, to live so close, scarcely a mile from each other, and never meet.

She had never visited Bagot House and asked the way of a bored-looking footman standing on the steps of a house in Conduit Street. Two minutes later she walked through the gates of Isabella's home. It was very mag-

200

nificent. The front door up a flight of steps reminded her of the studded doors of a patrician mansion in *Julius Caesar*.

A footman in livery said non-committally, "Yes, ma'am?"

"If Lady Carteret is at home would you inform her, please, that her sister is here. Miss Winter."

"I will ascertain," said the footman, ushering her into the hallway.

It was a great spacious place, the floor patterned in black and white like a chessboard. Marble statues stood in alcoves. I was right about *Julius Caesar*, thought Lettice. He and Cassius should make their entrance from the OP side.

The house was silent. Lettice sat and looked at her worn slippers. How different it is here, she thought, to the rustle of a theatre, the snatches of song as actors go to their dressing-rooms, the hammering, slam of doors, bars of music as the orchestra rehearses, bursts of laughter . . .

"Lady Carteret is taking tea with Lady Frances. Would you be good enough to join them," said the footman, returning. Lettice followed him up the staircase, along corridors hung with paintings, to a pair of double doors. The footman announced, "Miss Winter, my lady."

Isabella started up, hands outstretched.

"Letty, how delightful to see you!"

She kissed her fondly, took her hand. "Lady Frances, may I present my sister. Lady Clare, my sister Lettice."

Lettice curtsied politely and was answered by a kindly pressure of the hand from one lady and a stiff bow from the other.

Isabella, to her sister's eyes, had changed again and looked quite different from the girl she had seen almost a year ago in Clarges Street.

She wore a silky silvery dress with myriads of little tucks, and sleeves with lilac-coloured bows at the elbows. Her hair, plaited at the back, was dressed to show her ears. She wore amethysts. She was quite at her ease.

Lettice, watching the Earl's two daughters, thought Lady Frances very missish with a stately air that would suit a lady twenty years older, but she seemed kindly. Lady Clare was another matter. Here was that recognisable character, the jealous foe. Every actress sooner or later met one in her career and Lettice knew this lady was Isabella's enemy. When Lettice curtsied, Lady Clare raised her eyebrows as if to say, "What, pray, are *you* doing in *this* house?" Actress-like, jackdaw-like, Lettice noticed the expression. She might use it sometime.

Isabella made Lettice sit beside her and they drank tea. Lady Frances, having poured a cup for Lettice, waited for the footman to carry it across the six feet of carpet which separated them.

"My sister tells me," Lady Frances said (she meant Isabella), "that you are performing at the Royalty Theatre."

"Yes, Lady Frances."

"I think my grandfather saw Kemble once," said Lady Frances, looking for a subject to interest her guest. "I don't exactly recall what he thought of him. Wooden, would it be?"

Both the Winter sisters burst out laughing. There was an astonished pause from the Bagot ladies. Lettice did not dare look to see if Lady Clare's eyebrows had gone up again.

Conversation was stilted and although Lady Frances made an effort it was a relief to them all when tea ended and Isabella extricated Lettice from the drawing-room.

"I will take my sister to show her our apartments, Fanny. You shall not mind?" said

Isabella, whisking Lettice out of the room.

When they were in the corridor Isabella whispered, "Thank goodness that's over. We had to stay to tea, or it would have been talked about. Is not Clare a gorgon?"

She bustled Lettice into a different wing of the house.

"The relief to go through this door!" said Isabella. "This is all Denys's and mine. We can make as much noise as we like." She gave the door a slam.

The sisters spent an hour in Isabella's drawing-room. It seemed Denys was gone to Richmond to visit his grandmother, who had asked that he should come alone.

"The old lady doesn't like me very much. She's the image of Clare so Denys will have a horrid time," said Isabella, laughing. "Oh! It is lovely to see you! But you do look a little thin."

"*You* look beautiful."

"The dress is pretty, is it not?" was the careless reply. "But wait until I show you what the Earl bought me last season when I was presented. Diamonds, Letty. My own diamonds. A sack full! He is a frightening man, everybody is afraid of him. Even Clare, who is his pet. Cousin Robert understands him but treats him with kid gloves."

"Does he frighten you?"

"Not one bit," said Isabella, smiling. "He does not like anybody. I mean he does not love them. He is cold and clever and strong. He makes my dear Denys so unhappy. Do you know why? Because it is so evident that he despises him."

"How could anybody despise Lord Carteret?" exclaimed Lettice, shocked.

"He doesn't stand up to his father. How I wish he would. Denys is too kind. I tell him that so often. And then, you know, Letty, if your mama had died when you were a child, perhaps you would *wish* to love your father much more. Oh, don't let us talk about the Earl and Denys, it only makes me cross. What do you think of Fanny?"

"The tinkling one in pink?"

"She is my favourite. She takes me shopping."

There was a picture of Lord Carteret over the chimney piece, a pencil drawing which exactly caught a look of indolence and kindness in his face. Something in its expression gave Lettice a stab of the heart.

"How is your husband?"

"Oh, Denys is a dear, dear man and I shall

love him for ever. Shall we ring and get the diamonds? They have to be kept in a safe. Imagine. Don't take any notice of my maid, Hopton. One has to put up with her. Ah, Hopton," as a stout old woman in a dark grey dress came into the room. "This is Miss Winter, my sister. She wishes to see the diamonds Lord Bagot bought for me. Could you ask Mr. Robert if they may be removed from the safe, please?"

When the woman had gone Isabella made a grimace.

"Can you imagine her playing the witch in *Hansel and Gretel?*—Oh, Letty, the things one must endure. What with Lady Clare looking as if she would willingly kill me. Why? I don't do the creature any harm. We never speak. And as if Lady Clare were not enough, there is Hopton who brought her up and is now my maid. She and Lady Clare hobnob like an old witch and a young one. And then—" continued Isabella, gesturing, "there is not being allowed to do things."

"What sort of things?" Lettice asked curiously.

Isabella giggled.

"The other evening I began to fold up a card table, Fanny nearly swooned. 'The footman does that' she gasped. Then last week when I was talking to Robert I pulled one of the chairs closer to him. Lady Clare looked at me as if I were the crossing sweeper. 'What do you imagine servants are for?'"

With the actress's gift of mimicry, she caught the drawl and the stare.

She shrugged helplessly.

"One has to remember not to do anything. Not to undress oneself. Not to fasten a belt or button a glove. I must hold out my hands— so. I must not do my own hair. Nor pass a cup and saucer. Nor open a carriage door. It is like being a doll. Or too ill to move. Yet there is a sort of fascination about just standing and watching people spring forward to wait on you."

"Don't you feel guilty?"

"Oh Letty, don't be so holy! If I did things for myself, the servants would be offended, they would be much, much more shocked than horrid Lady Clare. One has to get used to *not* doing anything."

"It is a very odd world you've strayed into," said Lettice drily.

(2)

Robert Bagot had a natural authority he had

been born with, as he had been born with dark springy hair. He was a cousin of the Bagots, his parents had died and the old Earl taken him into his house when the boy was a handsome twelve-year-old. From that time Robert had shown himself to be what old Locking used to call "a born leader".

Carteret was the heir and three years older, but it was Robert who led and Carteret who followed. Robert's pranks were more daring, he studied harder, he made the decisions, he was the one Carteret turned to. Carteret, it was true, excelled in physical things; he rode better, was a more accurate shot, could box and fence and win at any kind of game, which he picked up without effort.

When the boys grew up, the Viscount went into the Army for a while. The Earl considered a year or two in the Army would be good for the heir; it was an alternative to university where Robert did well.

Robert grew up to be the Earl's right hand. He managed the complex matters of the great estate, the shipyards, coalfields, thousands of acres, tenant farmers. Everybody in the Bagot household consulted Robert. He had scarcely any property of his own, his father had gambled it away. But to possess wealth genuinely did not interest him. He enjoyed the challenges, responsibilities, the weight of management. When Carteret left the Army, Robert constantly suggested he should be consulted in the matter of running the estates. But it was clear to the Earl, to Robert and to Carteret himself, that such things bored the Viscount and that he did them badly.

The affection between the two young men had no trace of jealousy. Carteret admired his cousin's quickness and sureness, his thoughtful intelligence, tact, authority. Carteret went too far in his admiration and, "Robert's a wonderful fellow" was always the answer. Robert must be consulted about everything but Carteret's own provinces . . . horses, guns, clothes, sport and . . . the matter of choosing a wife.

The old Earl had been very bitter against Robert after the runaway marriage. Carteret was a fool and his cousin knew it, why had he not stopped such a disaster? Robert stood up to the Earl with a coolness Lord Bagot found it impossible to crack.

"I know, sir. It could not please you. But Deno—" Robert's nickname for his cousin since childhood—"Deno would not listen.

Might as well tell the north wind not to blow as stop a Bagot when he's made his mind up."

"Marry an *actress*."

"I had an idea, perhaps I have it wrong, that the fourth Earl . . ."

Robert knew, and so did his uncle and the rest of the family, that the fourth Earl had wedded an actress in James II's time, that the lady had been much respected and one of their sons had become an ambassador.

The storm had been over for months as far as the Earl was concerned. Robert saw Carteret's wife managing his uncle, and approved. But she had not won over Clare and probably never would. Robert sighed over a character as tough-fibred as his own.

Returning from seeing his grandmother, Carteret came to the study where Robert worked for some part of each day.

The room was kept in severe order. The old-fashioned desk, by Sheraton, held papers tied with coloured tape, the silver ink-well was refilled every morning, there were leather chairs and, for reading matter, any books from the Earl's collection which Robert considered useful. Law books, peerages of England and the Continent, agricultural books, English history, Bagot history.

Robert glanced up as his cousin came into the room.

"How was the old lady?"

"Not very agreeable. Very sharp about Isabella."

"Did you get a little angry?"

"How could I? Her back is painful."

"Sometimes I find myself wondering about the Dowager's painful back," said Robert. But when he looked at Denys, his cousin did not smile.

Denys's round sweet-natured face no longer had the lazy contentment of the past. Robert was sorry, but not surprised. He had been moved by Denys's fierce romantic gesture at marrying Isabella. He envied its rashness, but knew what it entailed.

"Why are you looking anxious, Deno? Surely not after drinking tea with one arrogant old lady on Richmond Green."

"My grandmother is part of it. Clare listens to her. Even Fanny does sometimes. Family troubles are upsetting, Robert. I do not seem to have the knack of settling them."

"Or ignoring them?"

Carteret sighed.

"How can they *not* like Isabella? After a

year of knowing her, too. She's handsome and getting handsomer every day. As for manners, she can give points to Clare any day of the week. Besides, she is related to us, ain't she?"

"What did your grandmother say?"

"What else but that she is making another will, that I was a grief to her in her old age. At one time she wept," Carteret added, in a low voice. He had not liked to see the old lady with her eyes full of tears.

"Poor Deno. Is there anything I can do, dear fellow?"

Carteret had been contemplating the toes of his brightly shining boots. He looked up.

"Could you perhaps speak to Clare? I tried but she was hurtful. Most hurtful. See if you can persuade her to be more pleasant to Isabella. Clare is so stubborn. She gets it from my father. But she listens to you."

"When it suits her."

"You could think of a way of making her believe it did suit her."

"I can try. What does Isabella feel about Clare?"

"She is an extraordinary girl. One moment she is angry, the next minute she bursts out laughing. I don't understand her. I never have understood women. But I am sure you do."

Before the gong warned that it was time to dress for dinner Robert went in search of Clare, and found her alone in the upstairs drawing-room. She wore white, which did not suit her pale hair and skin, and frowned as he came into the room.

Robert rather admired Clare, but then so did every man. There was something teasing and sulky about her, something which demanded a challenge. She was like a young lioness whose colouring she resembled; one felt compelled to stroke, rather hoping the animal would scratch.

"Deno and I are riding out tomorrow morning. Shall you come with us, Clare?"

"I don't expect so."

"Why not? You like to ride. And we like you with us."

"She will be there."

"Isabella, you mean?"

No reply.

"Isabella never rides out, as you know."

"I don't expect she can ride, except perhaps a donkey."

He laughed and sat down near her. Clare looked out of the window. He found her attractive; her farouche manner added to it.

"Why don't you give it up?"

No reply again.

"Clare. I spoke to you."

She turned, then, full-face towards him, her large, long eyes glittering.

"Carteret sent you as peacemaker, I suppose. Why can't he fight his own battles? Does he think I'd eat her? No, Robert, I will not accept that woman as one of us. She painted her face and strutted about for show—everybody knows actresses are harlots. My father took her into the family because of some trumped-up story about being related to us. To the Bagots! That creature is no more related to me than I am to a scullery-maid. Do you know what happened yesterday? Her sister had the impertinence to come here. Another actress, sitting here with Fanny, bold as brass. Don't you expect me to change my tune, Robert Bagot, because I shall not. I shall do everything to persuade my father to come round to my way of thinking."

"You're very hard, Clare."

She closed her eyes in contempt at that.

"And very pretty," he added and laughed.

11

(1)

DENYS'S affectionate heart told him he ought not to spoil his wife so absurdly, but he simply couldn't help it. As their marriage progressed, he was more under her spell than ever, he treated her more tenderly, indulged and protected her.

Isabella had developed a dazzling self-assurance and seemed to grow more beautiful; she was certainly not more sweet-tempered. But if she was sometimes jaded, Denys perfectly understood it. When the season ended she would welcome, as they all did, the refreshment of the country.

Isabella now belonged in this close-knit world walled with privilege, where she was expected to be always at her beautiful best. Wearing a bonnet heaped with roses, she ate strawberries at a duchess's garden party with admiring friends; she returned home to change into a satin balldress, put round her hair a wreath of cornstalks made of gold and leave for a soirée or a ball. Across a lofty room full of people wearing diamonds, orders, Garter ribbons, she sometimes saw the little figure of the young Queen on the arm of her handsome Consort.

Isabella danced more lightly, answered more wittily than almost any other lady. Men were captivated by her. A visiting foreign prince enquired, "Who is the enchantress in white?"

It was very late, very quiet, when the Carterets' carriage trotted home through squares still lit by the wavering light of flambeaux. Most of the nobility in May Fair resisted gas-lighting, and preferred the torches their ancestors had known.

Sweeping into Bagot House, Isabella knew the next day would be as demanding. Her best would be expected of her and she would give it. She was a success.

She slept late in the hot summer mornings, and woke to the noise of the fountain in the garden. But one morning when her old maid and enemy Hopton pulled the curtains, Isabella heard Denys's voice. He was talking to Hopton, who answered in a gruff friendly way. Hopton never used a tone like that with Isabella.

The curtains were looped back and the sun pounced fiercely into the room.

"Gracious, what time is it? Dawn?"

Isabella burrowed under a pillow.

"It is eight-thirty, my lady," said Hopton. She left the room and Denys sat down, gently pulling Isabella out into the sunlight. He had the fresh look of a man who has been out of doors for hours.

"I want to go back to sleep."

"But I have something to tell you, my dearest."

"It can wait," said Isabella, beginning a long yawn.

"I fear not. I have been in the Row with Robert and we have had a long talk. It has been decided that we will be travelling to Northumberland."

Isabella, who had begun another yawn, shut her mouth with a snap like a dog catching a fly.

"To *Northumberland*? Do you suppose I am strong enough to travel—"

"Isabella, don't be foolish. Of course you will not go. My cousin even suggested that he would make the journey alone, but I won't hear of that. He needs my help. We must visit the estates and there's some matters about mining rights. Robert received a letter from the agent this morning. I won't trouble you about it but it is more urgent than we thought. We must go in two days' time."

She gave a furious frown. Such an expression, which her sister and mother used to know only too well, was rare nowadays. The Carterets never quarrelled, since she always had her own way.

"Robert can go alone," she said sulkily. "He works for your father, doesn't he?"

She knew she had hurt him.

"You must not say things like that, Isabella. It's the greatest good fortune Robert is in the family. He's the best and kindest of men. And such a clever fellow. He does all the things I should do."

"Why don't you do them then?"

He did not reply. Her eyes brimmed with angry tears.

"Oh, you're *stupid*! You've spoiled everything. Had you forgotten we are to go to the Royalty on Friday to see Lettice playing? It's months since I saw her and I thought it would be so amusing to give her a surprise. I told you. Fanny and I have new gowns. Now it's all spoiled and I shan't go."

He leaned forward and took her in his

arms, kissing her, saying of course she must go, and should he invite someone to escort her? What about James Fane, Isabella liked him? He didn't scold her for ill-temper or say that he would be travelling hundreds of miles on the family's business. He had been taught, and deeply believed, that women were despots—in a way. In return for the embraces of this beautiful girl he must pay with love, indulgence and generosity.

Isabella crossly refused the company of James Fane. She did not wish to be with "strangers", as she called the attractive man with whom she often mildly flirted.

"If you are going away, I shall not go to the play at all."

"But my father has taken a box, Isabella."

"Then I shall go as a member of the family," conceded Isabella. "But nobody will notice my gown."

It was a final arrow to wound her kind husband's heart.

Lord Carteret and his cousin left two days later for the long northward journey. It would take days to reach Northumberland but the young men liked to be together, and although he would never admit it to himself, Lord Carteret often missed the careless pleasures of masculine company. He took a remarkable number of boxes, guns and fishing tackle with him. He regretted that he could not take his own horses but Robert said the Northumberland cousins would "find something ridable".

Isabella came into the courtyard to see them off and allowed her husband to give her a tender embrace. She had not exactly forgiven him. But Lady Clare's eye was on her, she wasn't giving her the satisfaction of looking vexed.

(2)

Before the opening night of the new play at the Royalty Lettice received a card, heavily coroneted, from Isabella.

"I thought I would surprise you, Letty, by coming to the first night. You are always so quiet about your work, and this time I can't keep away. It will be delightful to see you play again, dear Letty. The family have taken Box D, so do not forget to look up! Denys has gone North, which is very vexing. I will come round to see you afterwards, but I do not imagine the others will!"

220

Lettice frowned and tore up the card. She wished she had had the courage to see her sister, and confess that her career was going badly. But when they did meet, which was rarely, Isabella was so full of her own affairs, and Lettice so glad not to talk about hers. Like every actor she detested failure and had the superstitious belief that if she did not speak of it, it would stop.

Since her marriage, Isabella had not once visited the theatre. The Bagot family had never been play-goers although they went to the opera on Royal occasions. Isabella sometimes thought their marked disinterest in play-going was a silent agreement between the family to avoid a world where she might recognise some undesirable friend.

When the Bagot family arrived at the Royalty and were shown into their box, Isabella was quite excited. She and Fanny were at the front, the old Earl and Lady Fanny's dull escort, a fair young man in the Guards, sat in armchairs behind them. The Earl ordered his chair to be pushed well back and Isabella guessed it was because he would go to sleep.

Lady Fanny glanced round interestedly. She looked, Isabella thought, quite pretty

221

tonight in her embroidered net gown, with a wreath of rosebuds in her hair. Lady Fanny smiled and bowed, raising her gloved hand to acknowledge the salutes of friends.

Isabella stared round. How elaborate this theatre was. The gas-lights covered in soft rainbow shades, the front of the boxes festooned with crimson silk, chandeliers held by gilded cupids. It was strange, rich, yet familiar. The audience made that curious noise, like bees, there was the feeling of expectancy, the rustle, the figures making their way to their seats. Isabella, absorbed, quite forgot to look at her programme. When the vast curtains flew up, she didn't know which role Lettice was playing.

The play began. Scene after scene went by, marvellously played by Davenant, but there wasn't a sign of Lettice. After the first act she began to suspect her sister had no part worth playing. Isabella was shocked. Poor Letty, how disgusting of that beast Davenant! Her opinion of him so long ago had been right.

Why give Lettice nothing when she was so clever? For the first time since her marriage, Isabella mentally travelled back, sat in Green Rooms, joined in arguments over who should play which role. She watched, disliked, the actress playing the lead, a pudding-faced girl with an inferior voice. And when Lettice finally appeared, so pretty and remarkable with her white face and red hair, Isabella felt quite a pang of love and indignation.

Then a man came on to the stage. A strong broad-shouldered man, with the figure of a soldier and a voice with a caress in it. It was Buckley Vernon. She'd known he was in the Royalty company, Lettice had told her so, but seeing him gave her a shock.

She had not thought of Buckley Vernon since the day Denys had taken her from Newcastle. He had belonged to a time when money was short and lodgings cold, when parents worried and food was sparse, and nothing was beautiful or luxurious.

Seated in the box, a posy of scented gardenias in her lap, she thought of Buckley. The curtains flew up for the second act and her spirits flew with them. I shall go round and see Letty and speak to him, she thought. I am a viscountess now.

The play was long and the old Earl slept. Lady Fanny heard him snore, turned to look at him and pursed her lips. But the dramatic climax of the piece woke him with a series of pistol shots and he applauded vigorously when the curtain fell.

The applause rose almost to a roar. Aware he had the audience in the palm of his hand, Davenant bowed, indicating with the very angle of his body that he was their servant.

"Humbug!" thought Isabella, discovering as she clapped that gloved hands did not make a satisfactory sound.

"We should come to the play more often, Isabella," said Lady Fanny. Her little face was quite vivacious with enjoyment.

As they were leaving the box Isabella said, "Would you like to come round, Fan?"

Her sister-in-law looked mystified.

"Come round backstage. To congratulate my sister," translated Isabella impatiently.

Lady Fanny, intrigued, wondered if it would be allowed. She spoke to her father who was fastening the buckle of his cloak.

"Isabella wishes to congratulate Miss Winter. May we go, Papa?"

"If Coterill goes with you," grunted the Earl. "Where's the fellow got to?"

"He is in the next box," said Isabella who had no idea where Fanny's escort had gone.

The Earl took out a gold hunter and consulted it.

"You can have five minutes. By rights I should come with you but I am not going to. Coterill will have to serve. Off you go. I suppose," he added, glancing at Isabella, "you know the way to get behind the scenery?"

"I think I can manage, my lord."

"Tell Coterill to keep you both close, then."

Isabella and Lady Fanny sped down the staircase. Lady Fanny looked vainly, in a harassed way, for her escort.

"Oh, come on, Fanny, or we won't be able to get into the Stage Door at all. Mr. Coterill will find us. Stop fussing," Isabella said. Leaving the crowded foyer, the girls walked down the side of the theatre. Scores of carriages were waiting, and footmen on the lookout for their masters. Isabella took Lady Fanny through the Stage Door. She made her practised way past crowds of admirers, actors, writers, men of fashion, women of dubious reputation, dancers and footmen pouring towards the dressing-rooms.

Lady Fanny looked dazed as Isabella walked indifferently through the mass of people and arrived at two open doors.

She guessed they belonged to the star dressing-room and was sure Buckley Vernon would be there (but not Lettice). Buckley, she faintly remembered, was a man who would always try to be where the important people were.

"Where is your sister? Can you see her?" asked Lady Fanny, pink with excitement and shyness as she looked at the actors and actresses, talking and loudly laughing with Davenant. These were people she had never seen in real life, unfamiliar as rare animals. Their faces were haggard and full of life, there was something dangerous about them, something laid bare, not hidden, not controlled. They frightened her.

"Lettice must be somewhere here," said Isabella coolly. She had seen Buckley.

He gave a very deliberate smile and began to walk towards her. It fascinated him to see this woman, her bare shoulders rising from an exquisite evening dress, diamond stars in her hair, and remember the girl he'd known.

He gave a bow.

"Mr. Vernon," said Isabella, using a manner borrowed from Lady Clare. "I am glad to see you. Lady Frances, may I present Mr. Buckley Vernon whom you saw in the play just now."

"I trust we pleased you, ma'am."

Lady Fanny murmured something. She wore a look of delight and shyness at actually talking to an actor.

Buckley, self-conscious and determined to look the reverse, said to Isabella, "I scarcely recognised you."

He did not use her title.

"Indeed, Mr. Vernon? I recognised you at once!"

They both laughed, Buckley because he liked to be with women as dazzling as these, Isabella because she thought she would faint with pleasure.

(3)

On the morning following the first night, Lady Fanny sent a message to her sister-in-law saying she would be paying calls and did Isabella wish to accompany her? The carriage was ordered for eleven.

"Her ladyship is waiting for your reply, my lady," said Hopton, standing by the bed while Isabella languidly drank her coffee.

Isabella remained silent to annoy her. How the woman disliked her, and how she showed it while staying perfectly correct. Hopton did everything well. She was a fine needle-woman, ironed to perfection, dressed her skilfully, never forgot a pin or a button. It was she who chose Isabella's bonnets, gloves, boots, slippers, fans, parasols to go with whatever dress Isabella's whim decided upon. Hopton was a treasure. And a foe. She had a great broad body and muscular hands and narrow eyes. Isabella had seen that peasant's face melt with Denys and his sisters.

"Tell Lady Frances I will be glad to go," she said coldly. "And hurry back since it seems I have to be ready shortly."

She leaned against her pillows, incapable of dressing without help.

The calls took most of the morning. Lady Fanny enjoyed them, and enjoyed gossiping with Isabella. Did Isabella know Lady Quenington had the migraine for a whole day? The Nicholls heir had lost heavily at cards and his papa refused to pay his debts. People said Lady Sarah was in love with Cousin Robert, but he only danced with her once, had Isabella noticed?

Isabella answered automatically, smiling and scarcely hearing a word. The carriage trotted from Park Lane to Belgrave Square, the girls descended, were received, paid and received compliments, rustled back into the carriage and were trotted off to another great house. Lady Fanny, precise in social matters, sat beside Isabella, looking satisfied at the morning's achievements from under the shade of her pink parasol.

"We have only two calls tomorrow. By the way, have you sent your sister some flowers since we did not manage to find her last night?"

"I thought I might go to the Royalty this afternoon."

"Would Carteret not mind?" asked Lady Fanny, shocked at the idea of Isabella going behind the scenes again. It had been a place she did not approve, alluring though it was.

"Denys encourages me to see my family," Isabella said. She did not say that Denys was almost stern on the matter of her connection with the theatre.

After luncheon, Bagot House sank into its afternoon trance. Isabella rang for Hopton to dress her. The old maid-servant, disagreeable but neat-fingered, dressed Isabella in frilled russet and white silk. The carriage set off through sleepy streets emptied of carriages and riders. Nobody was allowed to trade or sell things in the quiet acres of May Fair, except the women who sold lavender and the men who sold muffins, whose parents and grandparents had done the same. The tall plane trees shed a grateful shade, but nobody played or sprawled under them.

Isabella's heart was thudding as the carriage began to cross shabbier streets. It drew up at the front of the theatre.

"Edwards, tell the coachman to take me to the Stage Door where he collected Lady Frances and myself last night," Isabella said. The footman looked slightly surprised.

Isabella sat straight. She believed for the moment in her role of a lady of quality visiting a sister who was a poor player.

Edwards opened the door again and respectfully asked if he should leave Her Ladyship's card?

"No, I will speak to the doorkeeper."

She picked her way across a pavement littered with straw. Jack jumped up at once. He knew a lady when he saw one.

Isabella graciously enquired if Mr. Vernon was perhaps in the theatre?

"As it happens, madam, he's this minute stepped out on a matter of business," said Jack. He had seen Buckley go into *The Cross Keys* with two actors half an hour ago.

Isabella was so disappointed she felt slightly sick. Her gamble had failed. Remaining cool, she enquired for her sister. It seemed prudent to do that.

"Miss Winter won't be in until six for the evening performance, madam. Sorry," said Jack sympathetically.

A tall man, elaborately dressed, had swung into the Stage Door. He bowed with affable formality.

"Surely it is Viscountess Carteret? Did I not see you in Mr. Davenant's dressing-room last night? Buckley Vernon said you had done us the honour of calling. I am the manager, my lady. Bryson is the name."

Isabella was gracious, Bryson bland. They talked a little. Something in Bryson's way of speaking about Lettice penetrated Isabella's disappointed self-absorption. This man with the foxy face and vulgar clothes was patronising Lettice.

"The young lady has a pleasing little talent," he drawled.

There was a pause.

"Mr. Bryson," Isabella said slowly, "I am glad of this opportunity of speaking to you. My family, the Bagots, as you must know, have always been patrons of your theatre." It

231

was pure invention but Bryson did not know it and the name worked.

"I was deeply shocked to see how my sister has been overlooked," continued Isabella. "Surely you could speak to Mr. Davenant? Use your influence in some way. I assure you it is a grave waste of talent."

"Yes, yes, I understand. Just so," said Bryson, taken aback by the request.

"Ask Mr. Davenant to reconsider. I'm sure you could insist that my sister is given her chance," said Isabella.

She gave him her coolest smile.

There was no sign of Buckley and Isabella had no further excuse for lingering. Bryson, who had not the slightest influence over Davenant, promised that he would speak to the actor and was certain something would be done for Lettice at once.

Isabella allowed him to hand her into her carriage and returned to Bagot House.

She felt extraordinarily tired. The thought of the coming adventure had buoyed her up through the day, from the moment when she woke that morning. All through those interminable calls, during the long luncheon when the Earl was at his most abrupt, on her journey to the theatre, she had been trembling with anticipation—for what? Just to see Buckley again.

Anyway, I did Letty some good, she thought. That over-dressed fool won't dare not to help her now.

She wandered into the upstairs drawing-room. The tall windows were open on to the courtyard, the side windows on to the street. The clip-clop of a single rider went by. Then silence. She sat down in the Earl's chair with carved arms ending in a lion's claws.

She put her hands on the polished claws and pressed hard, thinking of Denys with yearning melancholy. Not of Denys himself but of her own feelings about him until Buckley had walked on to the stage last night. Her affection for her husband had always been as unquestioning as when she had admired him in Newcastle. To be made love to by Denys was as happy as she'd imagined it would be. He was an experienced, ardent, tender lover. He never spoke about love-making. He was passionate, and silent when the loving was over. She could not bear to think about Denys now. It was Buckley who haunted her, Buckley whose figure, face, voice, self-conscious smile, filled her mind.

There was a knock at the door and one of the footmen came into the room.

"A letter for you, my lady."

"Thank you."

"A person is awaiting a reply, my lady."

"A person, Kingsley?" said Isabella, raising her eyebrows.

"A porter from the theatre, my lady."

"It must be from Miss Winter. I will ring when I have written my answer."

He left the room.

The handwriting was not Lettice's and when she tore open the envelope she was trembling.

"How did I miss you? Let us meet. Why not at the theatre for some champagne? Tell *the nobs* you are visiting Lettice.

                    B."

She turned the letter over, scribbled "Yes. At five," and sealed it in a fresh envelope, using the Bagot crest.

When the letter had gone she went back to the chair with the lion's claws and sat down. She shut her eyes. It was as if at that moment she was at the top of a steep hill, almost a precipice, and could choose whether to

234

descend or stay. As if, sitting on a kind of sledge guaranteeing no safety, she hesitated for a second at the slope's top, looking downwards. Then deliberately pushed with both her feet. Down, down went the sledge faster and faster, ripping round corners, hurtling down slopes, every moment the speed quickening, while she gripped its sides, felt its speed, was unconscious of what waited for her at the end of that journey to God knew where . . .

(4)

Robert and Denys had been away a fortnight. Robert wrote regularly to the Earl with news of the shipyards, properties, various problems and successes of the visit.

"We have seen a mort of people," wrote Robert. "But we have also been out sailing, Deno is a dab hand in a boat. We have been riding a great deal and Deno has a good horse but mine is a bad-tempered old woman. We hope to be back with you shortly, but things must be tidied up with Carrisbrook and Browne's. There have been some difficulties over the men's Sunday . . . ." And so on.

The Earl missed his "right hand" as he

called Robert. When Robert was absent he noticed the inadequacy of his London agent, a young man who seemed positively to enjoy pointing out difficulties. The Earl grew very short-tempered. Apart from needing his nephew, he despised a house which was only a nest full of women. He liked women about him, of course, but in their place. Silly women he despised. He had despised his wife Cecilia who died when Clare was born. Cecilia had been of high rank, a duke's daughter, and pretty as a rose when she was a girl. One of those women in whom frivolity and beauty make an irresistible combination, helpless, confiding, lighthearted, full of ribbons and nonsense, innocent, merry. She would probably have been stupid and dull when she was old but she died too soon for him to know that. Poor thing.

He was not at present inclined to seek out Clare's company (Fanny bored him) because, although he admired Clare's spirit, he recognised that she was going through a tiresome period of growing up. Some man, the Earl said to himself, would settle all that soon enough. He must find a man who could cope with Clare and then she'd behave herself.

Robert-less, the Earl looked round for

entertainment at home—courtesy demanded he should be home at least part of every day—and his hooded old eyes rested on his sprightly daughter-in-law. He liked the girl. He knew Clare considered Denys had made a *mésalliance*; he himself was satisfied with Isabella's slender pretension to gentility. It would serve. She was a lass of mettle with eyes that looked at him sometimes with a certain acuteness. She might be clever for all he knew. She was certainly a beauty, he had enjoyed buying her those diamonds. It must be slow for her just now. That minx Clare did not like her, but Clare was a Bagot and a touch of arrogance never came amiss. Carteret's wife was very thick with Fanny but that could not be very amusing for the girl. Fanny bored him as his wife had sometimes done. They were women who never took the trouble—perhaps did not know it was necessary—to interest a man in their talk. At least Clare rode well, read a book or two, came out with intelligent if unkind observations about their friends. Fanny chattered about clothes, servants and other women . . .

His thoughts returned to his daughter-in-law. She must be missing Carteret. That would explain the absent look in her eye, her lack of appetite. Isabella sat at his right when they dined, and he'd noticed recently that she hadn't the appetite of a wren. He had wondered if she was ailing, but she looked perfectly well.

He found her, in white with blue ribbons and lace flounces, sitting at her desk in her own drawing-room, writing a letter.

Walking in his half-crippled way, the Earl came sidling into the room. Isabella gave a violent start. It was afternoon, a time when Bagot House was at its quietest. The Earl had never entered this part of the house since Denys and she had come to live here.

"Startled you, did I?" He gave an abrupt laugh. "Shouldn't leave your door open if you want to keep people out."

He stood, looking at her with his harrier's face.

"Thought I'd pay you a call."

She showed him to the best chair, welcomed him, asked if she should ring to have the blinds lowered. She had no idea why he had come. She had been writing to Buckley and felt so nervous that her heart pounded. The colour in her cheeks only made her prettier.

"The sun does not bother me, brought up

238

in the country. Wish some ladies didn't see fit to keep us in the half dark. Well," he said, falling, more than sitting, into an armchair. He immediately looked younger because he no longer bent sideways. "Missing the Viscount, are you?"

Isabella said of course.

"Writing to tell him so?"

"Denys is a dreadful letter-writer. I count myself lucky if I receive half a page from him," said Isabella, closing the blotter and picking up a letter she had recently received from Northumberland.

"You don't have to show my son's epistles to me. He never could write a letter. Told him so when he was at Eton. Sent one of his letters back, 'Do better,' I wrote on it. Not like Robert—there's a boy who knows how to put a letter together. Or anything else, come to think of it."

"Denys never claims to be clever."

"He'd better not," said the Earl with another laugh. Isabella rearranged a fold of her dress. She thought of defending Denys, but what notice would his iron-willed father take of that? When she glanced up, he was looking at her ruminatively. He's a handsome old devil when sitting down, she thought. I wish he would go.

"You don't like living here, do you?"

Taken aback she blushed a second time, then began a conventionally polite reply. He interrupted with an impatient "Tt-tt". He hadn't come here to listen to such missish stuff.

"Yes, yes, it was very *kind* of me to have you and Carteret to live here," he said satirically. "But who wants to live in a mausoleum?"

"Don't you like this house, sir?"

"Can't stick it. I used to come here when my grandfather was alive, that was 1800 and London was a sight livelier than it is today, but I didn't like the place then. It is too small."

She was excited this afternoon, full of expectation; she gave an enchanting smile. He was delighted.

"What I came to say," he said, "was that it comes into my mind you and Carteret need a house of your own. Not a few rooms in a corner," he said contemptuously, "but a piece of property. Something worth having. Would you like to look at a house or two with me?"

Isabella accepted with more smiles. The Earl, still pleased with her, said he would waste no more of her time (by which he meant his own) and would take her out tomorrow morning to look at houses. Did that suit her? So it should.

When he was gone she finished her letter to Buckley and then calmly began a letter to Denys. "Imagine, dearest Denys! Your papa has decided to buy us a house! I am to go out with him tomorrow to look at some. I hope, dearest Denys, you will not mind I shall look without you. You always say you approve my taste and now it will be the Earl's too. Perhaps by the time you return we will already be the owners of a *house* where we can do as we please and enjoy ourselves and invite all your friends to dine and—for my part— escape your sister Clare!"

The letter was affectionate and so was her expression as she wrote in her sprawling girlish writing. She ended the letter with her love, glad to think how surprised and pleased he would be to know the news. Thinking of her husband, she did not have a single pang of conscience. Twenty-four hours before she had been in Buckley's lodgings, lying in his arms.

12

(1)

SHE simply had no feeling of guilt. Every
time she thought of what she had done
she felt a wave of remembered pleasure.
The days of longing for Buckley had been a
kind of nightmare, sometimes she had felt she
was going mad. When she drove out in the
carriage every male figure riding or walking
looked like Buckley. It seemed in her feverish
state that through the whole of London, in
every street, park, across great reception
rooms, in gardens, ballrooms, she saw
Buckley, Buckley. She would recognise his
swaying walk, the shape of his head, the coat
he wore. Her hunger and desperation woke
her at four every morning. She could eat
nothing, often felt faint. How could she now
regret that Buckley had at last made love to
her? She felt carefree, affectionate to everybody in the world.

And it was she who had done the pursuing,
not Buckley. He had written her one single

letter but after that it was never he who suggested they should meet—which they managed to do many times. She sensed in him from the first a curious kind of immunity to her. Yes, he desired her. But for some reason, vanity, self-satisfaction or sheer perversity, he had decided that *she* must beg, she must show she wanted him. Yet she was the one who risked everything if they were discovered. Perhaps that was why. Buckley never gave her the impression of being strong, though she knew perfectly well that he was ambitious and selfish. Perhaps he would not take the responsibility of wooing her away from her husband. If she were mad enough to do it he would enjoy her. But he was going to make no decision.

The feeling that Buckley, with his marvellous gift of making her desiring and desirable, wouldn't lift a finger to get her into his arms worked on Isabella like a fever. If he would only fall in love with her as Denys had done, give her the feeling that she had him, however little, in her power. They contrived to meet in his dressing-room (Isabella safely used Lettice as an excuse) and they went for a drive in a hired brougham to Kensington village, well away from Berkeley Square. It was always Isabella who said as they parted, "When shall we meet? Tomorrow?"

After half a dozen such meetings, she sighed: "I wish we could be alone."

They had been walking towards the theatre having spent a mere half-hour together; she did not dare to be away longer.

He gave her arm a pinch. He was so different from the men she was accustomed to; it attracted, yet slightly repelled her.

"Come to my lodgings. If you dare."

Safe now in the haven of Bagot House, she thought of what had happened with awe at the risk she had taken. Buckley had hailed a hackney carriage and driven to a street of shabby lodging-houses behind Oxford Street. How crowded and dirty the streets were—it was a London she knew nothing about. Buckley led her through a battered front door into a hallway smelling of dirt and cabbage.

"Not your style, is it?"

He opened the door of a bedroom like a hundred rooms she had seen when her parents were at their poorest, but which her mother had always refused. The curtains were ragged, the bed unmade, the chair had a broken seat, Buckley's clothes, a frilled shirt, a dark blue coat, stockings, a silk cravat, lay anyhow. There had never been a fire in the grate and in winter the room must be as cold as now it was airless and stuffy.

"No locks in this place," he said and pushed the chair under the doorhandle.

Much Isabella cared. She untied her bonnet strings. He moved to her, and began to unbutton the jacket of her dress . . .

When she thought about making love with Buckley, she remembered how wildly she had wanted him, the intense delight of getting just that—Buckley's arms, kisses, Buckley naked and passionately loving her, Buckley's face pressed close, his voice muttering her name, her own thirst and how he slaked it. It was utterly different from her lovemaking with Denys . . . Denys was loving, silent, expert, oddly chaste. Being loved by the two men was like eating a dish full of both their lives, Buckley's disreputable and dirty and strong, Denys's good and wholesome, as things should be.

Other women, the world over, had lovers when they were married. Why not she? I'm nicer, happier, because of Buckley, she thought. She ran to a looking-glass over the chimney piece. "And I'm more beautiful."

Two days later the open carriage stood in the courtyard. Sun sparkled on the chestnut coats of the horses, the brass fittings, the yellow and black doors painted with the Bagot arms.

When Isabella came down the staircase, the Earl was in the hall. His valet, a little spider of a man, was brushing the Earl's crooked shoulders, fussing over him as if he were a baby. The Earl's bent figure, wearing his full-skirted black coat, gave Isabella a faint frisson.

"There you are," he said as she came towards him. She wore pale green and white flounces, a bonnet curled with tiny feathers. He looked her up and down critically.

"I've told William to drive us to Regent's Park again," said the Earl. "Wreford is to meet us there."

She smiled delightedly.

The house in Regent's Park which they had seen the previous day was the one she liked the best. But he had told her it was too expensive.

Trotting through the streets, they talked of the house, or rather Isabella talked because that was what he required; without stirring himself to interest or amuse her, he made it plain he wished to be both interested and amused. The only compliment he paid was that of listening attentively and occasionally giving his abrupt laugh.

When she was with him, Isabella had the sensation of sitting beside some ageing but still ferocious animal whom she must charm by a spell.

Although it was a day of blazing sunshine the air was pleasantly fresh in the open carriage; it had rained in the night. Isabella opened the white lace parasol Denys had given her and held it over her shoulder to shade her face. They trotted into the curves of Regent's Park. The trees were in full leaf. Children ran about with hoops, and nurse-maids sat in the shade.

Beyond a crescent built when the Regent was alive was a house standing in its own garden with wrought-iron gates and a curved carriageway. It was one of the few houses which was not in a terrace and Isabella had liked it immediately. It was spacious but not overlarge, the dark polished staircase was handsome, a long landing opened on to bed-rooms with views of the lake.

"*If* I buy it for you," the Earl said—he

liked to tease her—"it will be my gift to you. Not to Carteret. Your own house. Your property."

As the carriage neared the house, she gave a murmur of pleasure, a kind of sigh. He looked at her from under his eyelids. There was something about her these days. Something sensuous, at times lazy, at times excited. "Mettlesome," thought the Earl.

The front door stood open and the Earl's agent, Tom Wreford, was waiting for them. He was a gloomy young man with rings under his eyes from working late for a despotic master.

"Wreford," said the Earl, "I take it you told Sherington he's asking too much for this place?"

"I have been with Mr. Herriot, my lord."

"Who the devil's he?"

"Lord Sherington's steward, my lord."

"Steward? What do I want with him? The house is Sherington's, ain't it? Tell him I won't pay a penny more than the price I offered. Look at the condition of the place. It's falling down," said the Earl, pointing contemptuously at a carved pearwood fireplace. "My daughter-in-law will cost me a small fortune putting it to rights. You tell

Sherington himself, none of your stewards. Tell him plainly that my offer stands and my daughter-in-law will be moving in as soon as the place is habitable. Are you pleased, young woman? You're costing me a mint of money."

"Denys will be delighted."

"I'm not buying it for Carteret. This is for you. What's that French expression? A *bonne-bouche*. If you want to thank me," he added, seeing Isabella was about to make a speech which would bore him, "take Wreford off my hands."

Wreford had wandered off into the distance and was despondently examining a loose banister. The Earl glowered.

"Gloomy beggar. What's a few repairs? The place only needs a nail knocked in here and there. Tell him what's to be done. He'll look as if you're announcing the date of the Day of Judgement but that's nothing new. I shall go to my club for luncheon. You can drop me there and then take the carriage home. You've worn me out enough for today. Don't ask for another house. I can't afford daughters-in-law like you."

(3)

It was weeks since Denys and Robert had

travelled to the North. To Isabella it seemed a year crammed with subterfuges. It was dreadfully difficult to see Buckley; it was extraordinary that she managed to meet him at all. She was hedged in, protected, practically imprisoned by social conventions, and her constantly-used excuse that she was visiting her sister was not sufficient. Lady Fanny, representing the head of the family in such things, disapproved of Isabella going out alone.

"I am going to see Lettice," Isabella said, light as air as she came down the great staircase.

"You must take Hopton."

"My dear Fanny—"

"Ladies are always accompanied by their maids," Lady Fanny said, lowering her voice so that the servants should not hear her. "Send for Hopton, Isabella."

Isabella's face became set, her brown eyes like stones. Murmuring she would discuss the matter with her sister-in-law later, she swept from the house. Lady Fanny was distressed.

It was only by persuasion and ill-temper in a judicious mixture, at which Isabella became more skilful as she became more desperate, that she managed to escape from Bagot House on her pretended visits to Lettice.

Then something totally unexpected happened. Isabella received a letter from Lettice. It was so angry that she could scarcely believe her gentle sister had written it. Lettice had discovered from Bryson that Isabella had visited the Royalty and interceded for her.

"How *dare* you patronise me! Do you think because you are now married into the nobility you can drive round to the theatre and order them to give me roles as if they—and I—were so many servants? Do you suppose I cannot look after myself? If Mama knew . . ."

And so on for three pages written when Lettice was so furious that had Isabella been present, she would have slapped her face.

The letter upset Isabella, who was out of the habit of quarrels, though she and Lettice had had many spirited, short-lived ones in the past. She refused to admit she had been interfering, she thought Lettice stupid and touchy. She saw no reason to apologise, at present, anyway. What worried her far more than her sister's feelings was that Isabella saw a danger to her passionate, complicated plans. She did not dare use Lettice as an excuse now. Suppose Lettice took it into her head to march round to Bagot House and talk the matter out? One sentence in front of Lady Fanny—"I have not seen my sister for weeks"—and Isabella was lost.

But now when Isabella was wildly thinking how to resolve this, the Earl bought her Finstock Lodge. Here was a new excuse to be alone. She went shopping, carelessly saying she would "probably call to see Letty as well". Taking the carriage, she alighted at Regent Street, five minutes from Buckley's lodgings, and told the footman she would be some time choosing silks, visiting this warehouse or that. She wished to be collected in an hour. She even had time on occasion to collect snippets of silk or news of furniture which she used in conversations with Lady Fanny.

These half hours—they were never more—spent with Buckley gave the days a mounting excitement until the time she threw herself into his arms. All the rest of the day went by in a lazy, purring satisfaction.

She had arranged to see Buckley one afternoon in the "usual" way, after she had visited an India silk warehouse. A short letter arrived as she was leaving Bagot House. "My

dearest. At last we are returning home."
Isabella went pale.

The door of Buckley's lodging was ajar, something he arranged, and Isabella ran up the dark staircase and turned the handle of his bedroom door.

He lay sprawled on the bed, studying a script.

"I've had a key put in the lock of the door," he said, smiling. "Now you can feel safer."

"Thank heaven." She turned the lock and ran to him. He gave her a long, exploring kiss, then looked searchingly into her face. Her bonnet had fallen off. Her eyes were swimming.

"You've been missing me, I see."

"Every minute. Every hour. Every heartbeat."

He pulled her into his arms.

Their lovemaking today seemed to her both more tormenting and more exciting than ever. She knew it would be her last time. Till when?

After they finished making love he never lay in her arms and slept. He always got up, washed in the basin in the corner and put on his shirt and trousers while Isabella, naked, watched him.

253

This afternoon he dressed in silence, then went to the fly-spotted mirror on the wall and began to comb his hair.

"You think you are very handsome, don't you, Buck?"

He grinned and arranged his thick hair.

"You are quite handsome too."

His voice had no meaning at all. The moment he'd made love he became absorbed in his own thoughts, she sometimes thought he scarcely saw her. She'd noticed it many times and it made her suffer—for a while. Then he desired her again and then she forgot it. Every time she was with Buckley she had, at the finish, a sensation of pain which later became forgetting.

"Buck. Come and sit by me."

He came over, willingly enough, and sat down by the girl who lay naked as a conquered Sabine.

"I have something to tell you," she said in a low voice.

He gave his indifferent smile and spoke as if to a child.

"Now what is it?"

Isabella reached for her bodice and covered herself. He made her feel cold.

"Denys has written to me. He and his

cousin will be in London by tomorrow."

She looked at him fixedly, desperately longing to see his face change. To see, in effect, the look she knew in Denys.

"So?"

"Buck, don't you understand? How can we meet when Denys is returned?"

"I daresay you'll think of a way. You're an ingenious creature."

She turned her face away.

He patted her shoulder.

"For heaven's sake get dressed. You'll scarcely have time to get back to that warehouse if you stay much longer."

Longing to burst into sobs, she dressed in hurried silence, putting on her white embroidered stockings and rosetted shoes, tying the tapes of her petticoats. She waited while he buttoned the back of her dress, she did her hair carefully with his dirty comb. She put on her bonnet, arranged her India shawl. Dressed, she was the Viscountess again.

"Don't sulk, Bella," he said, laughing and speaking quite affectionately. "I'll have to be patient until I hear from you, won't I? You're the one who must think how we can manage to meet. You're also the one who finds it difficult."

"But do you *want* to?"

She despised herself for saying that.

She thought her heart would crack. He looked so perfectly cheerful and indifferent, opening the script he had just picked up.

"Buck, for God's sake—"

"Isabella, what a child you are. Do you suppose after the last hour I don't want to see you?"

With this, and only this, she had to be content. They walked down the musty-smelling stairs and out into the street. Buckley usually ordered a hackney carriage, which waited at the door to take her to Regent Street. But that afternoon when they came out of the house there was no sign of the cab. Buckley stared up the street.

"What a damned thing. It hasn't come."

"I cannot wait," she said, suddenly taut with anxiety. "I must go at once."

"I'll walk you to Regent Street."

"But that's impossible! I can't be seen with you. I daren't."

He laughed.

"Would you rather go through these stinking alleys on your own?"

She pulled the lace veil on her bonnet down to cover her face and hurried beside him.

256

Buckley strode along cheerfully while Isabella bent her head, almost fainting with nervousness. She began to imagine she could hear footsteps—she did not dare look back.

"Is there someone behind us, Buckley?"

"About half a hundred," he said, as they passed a filthy doorway crowded with ragged people and made their way through hawkers and rough-looking men. Guessing that she was frightened, he took her arm. She shook him off. There was that step again! This time she could not help glancing over her shoulder. She was convinced she caught sight of a broad, dark-clad figure which vanished into a doorway.

"Look. There's a hackney," Buckley said suddenly. He waved and the driver reined in his horse.

"What a fuss over a little walk," Buckley said, helping her into the carriage. "Off you go. We'll meet soon."

He raised his hat and strode away.

Safe in Regent Street, Isabella paid the driver and walked into a warehouse. She was immediately greeted, bowed to, surrounded by a reverent attention. But as she sat talking to the warehouse manager, her heart was thudding. *Had* that been Hopton following her just now?

When she returned to Bagot House she went to her room. Her head was splitting, and she lay down and tried to sleep. An hour went by. But when the gong for dressing was rung, she was no calmer.

Hopton came quietly into the room, went over to the wardrobe and took out one of Isabella's dinner gowns. Isabella watched as the old servant smoothed its white silk folds and came slowly towards her. Did Isabella discern something new in that stern old face? It's my imagination, she thought, as Hopton began to unpin her hair. I feel guilty because I was in the street with him. So I begin to imagine things . . .

(4)

Lady Fanny took the responsibility of being the eldest in the family seriously, and liked both her sister and Isabella to take tea in the upper drawing-room every afternoon, sometimes with guests, sometimes alone. Lady Fanny was firm on the matter. Even Lady Clare submitted to her sister's ruling, though she never made the meeting anything but

258

uncomfortable if the ladies happened to be alone.

The relationship between Isabella and the youngest of the Bagots was worse rather than better. Lady Clare had established at the first meeting that she resented Isabella's marrying into the family; her manner—sometimes laughably rude—had not changed.

Robert had failed to mend it. Denys did not know how to do so. Lady Fanny, half afraid of her sister, pretended things were as they should be.

The news that "the boys" as she called them were on their way home made Lady Fanny happy, and during tea, with Lady Clare seated as far as possible from Isabella and nobody else present, Lady Fanny kept repeating, "Surely *that* is the carriage?"

"No, Fan, it is not."

"But Clare, dear, do look from the window. The boys might see you and . . ."

Lady Clare shrugged and sent a footman to the window who confirmed there was no sign of it.

Lady Clare began to talk about a ball the Montacutes were giving.

"Violet Montacute hoped the Queen might come, but it seems she and Prince Albert are to be at Windsor. Violet says the Prince enjoys Windsor; she and the family went to a ball there. The Queen was in white but very *décolleté* and a wreath of white roses. I think it odd we are not lately invited," said Lady Clare, staring at her sister. "Why would you suppose we have not had a card?"

Lady Fanny lifted the monstrously heavy silver tea-pot. Isabella rearranged a ruffle at her wrist. The footman took the tea-cup on his salver and walked across the room to give it to Lady Clare. Everybody in the room, including the footman, knew that what Lady Clare actually meant was, "Now there is an actress in the Bagot family, the Palace has decided we are not to be invited."

Lady Fanny had discussed this difficult subject with the Earl, who had told her to stop behaving like an old hen. Melbourne had told him the Queen was cutting down her guests because she was with child and easily tired. Lady Fanny did not consider this a proper subject to discuss at the tea table. Once again she heard carriage wheels.

This time even Lady Clare couldn't deny the clatter and darted to the window. Her face lit with a rare, brilliant smile: "It's *them*!"

All three ladies, Lady Clare the quickest, then Lady Fanny and Isabella more sedately, went to the head of the staircase.

Below in the hall the great double doors were open and servants were bustling in and out with boxes. There was an air of excitement, as if the old house had woken from sleep with a start.

And there, carrying bunches of flowers which made them look charming and absurd, were Denys and Robert. Lady Clare flew down the staircase and rushed to embrace them. She looked so happy that Isabella had a pang of the sharpest envy. Isabella, too, hurried down to Denys who put out both arms. He pressed her to him, then bent to kiss her hands.

"How I've missed you!" he said looking at her as if his eyes were hungry. "Robert and I thought we would never get home!" He still held her hands.

"Are you well, my dearest? Of course you are. More beautiful than ever."

He himself looked tired, pale, transformed with happiness.

Everyone talked at once. Lady Fanny exclaimed over the quantity of luggage which seemed to have grown from the boxes "the boys" had taken away. How lovely the roses were, but where had they come from?

"All the way from the North," said Robert, laughing. "We bought them in the Burlington Arcade."

Swayne and Mrs. Judge, the housekeeper, greeted both young men. The Earl was at Richmond with his mother.

"And did you bring us presents, cousin?" asked Lady Clare, hanging on Robert's arm.

"By thunder, you're the one who slipped our minds!" said Robert.

Lady Clare burst out laughing. It was a sound Isabella did not remember ever having heard before.

They went into the drawing-room where fresh tea was ordered; Robert and Denys told them the news of their weeks away, of the shipbuilding problems, the estates, the week spent with Lord Lennox, the girls Robert had flirted with, the sailing, the shooting. There was a great deal of teasing and nonsense. What a difference, Isabella thought, between now and the weeks gone by. Between a family which included two young men, and a parcel of women on their own, with one elderly male despot usually absent.

She was glad of the noise and talk, glad to

sit and listen, and so nervous that at times she trembled. Denys, long legs stretched out beside her, caught her eye at every moment, gave his lazy smile. Her heart hurt her. Suddenly and for the first time, she wished she had never met Buckley. Never succumbed to that dreadful hunger, that madness. It had been madness. What did she mean "had been"? It still was. Sitting here full of meaningless alarm because Denys was near her, she could still remember Buckley physically with the sensation as if she were falling from a height. Remember his love-making. Want him. And in a way hate him because Denys looked so blissful, indolent, handsome and her own.

He will make love to me tonight, she thought. Will he know, then?

13

(1)

"A VISITOR to see you, Miss Winter," said Mrs. Hastings, panting to indicate the exhaustion of ascending her own staircase.

Lettice, standing by the attic window looking at the chimney-pots, was surprised.

"I am expecting no one, Mrs. Hastings."

"Personally I never had dealings with the circus, Miss Winter. Your visitor has the appearance of a juggler," said Mrs. Hastings, sweeping out.

Not having been invited into the house and philosophically leaning against the front door was the dwarf-like figure of Laurie Spindle. Lettice rushed towards him.

"Laurie! Laurie! Where have you come from? How did you find me?"

The beautiful girl and the little man clung together. Mrs. Hastings, raising her eyes heavenwards, made off to the back parlour.

Laurie and Lettice talked at the same time,

stopped, laughed, continued to talk. Laurie had, it seemed, been engaged by Davenant, wasn't that a stroke of good fortune? He had called at the theatre and met an old friend, Gwynyth, and she had given him Lettice's address.

They set off together to walk to the theatre. Laurie described his adventures since the Newcastle days.

"And what about you, Beauty?" he said, finishing a saga of the circuits.

The smile on her face died.

"Nothing at all. Parts of walking ladies. Some of four lines."

He was shocked.

"After his promises! You've made him a scene, of course?"

"I couldn't."

"But that is ridiculous!" exclaimed Laurie, stopping to shake her fiercely by the arm. "Actors have to speak out for themselves, otherwise who'll help them? Your trouble is you were looked after too long by your father. You must beard Davenant in his den. You're not afraid of him, are you? What worse can he possibly give you than to be a walking lady? Comfort yourself with that."

It was very different advice from Buckley

Vernon, who had counselled a waiting game.

By the end of the walk, which took an hour, she was convinced. If Laurie could confront fate, why so could she.

"You'll have to hang about near his dressing-room," Laurie said. "It's the oldest trick in the profession. Then as he comes along, pounce."

Lettice did as he bid her. After what seemed hours of waiting, she saw the actor swinging cheerfully towards his dressing-room, wearing one of his stylish dark blue coats with silver buttons.

"Could I speak to you, sir?"

He stopped. Did she imagine there was something wary in his face?

"I daresay."

She followed him into the magnificent suite of rooms. He threw some scripts carelessly on a table and folded his arms.

"Well?"

"About my work."

"What about it? I am not complaining."

She looked at him steadily. He frowned.

"That was a jolly little part I gave you in *The Iron Chest*. Plenty of points to it."

"It was four lines, sir."

"I used to make my mark with two."

Lettice's spirits quailed. She could see something which until this moment she'd hoped wasn't true. She did have a genuine complaint against him. He'd brought her to London with promises and then for some reason decided to break them. He felt uncomfortable about her. She saw it in his face. But he'd developed a fine technique for putting any actor asking for advancement into the wrong. Everybody wanted favours. If they didn't like what he gave them, they could leave.

"To do so little work, sir, is very dull."

"Dull? How can that be? Do you know all the parts in *The Iron Chest*?"

"I am not an understudy in the play."

"I never said you were. Whether you're an understudy or not, miss, take your profession seriously, then time won't hang heavy on your hands. Learn the three I's. Imagination, intelligence and industry. Put your mind to industry. It's valuable advice that I am giving you," he added, using a fall of the voice to indicate the interview was over.

How could she stay?

She was walking down the passageway when Augustus Bryson stopped her.

"Miss Winter. I have been thinking about

the Viscountess's visit and the word she had with me about you. She clearly felt that my influence . . . . of course it is not easy." He looked expressively at the door of Davenant's suit.

Lettice was suddenly so angry she could have screamed.

Her voice shook.

"Please do not trouble yourself, Mr. Bryson."

"No trouble, I assure you."

"I do not wish any kind of preference. Please refrain from speaking to Mr. Davenant. Or to anybody else."

Meeting her eyes, which were unusually bright and glittering, he bowed. It was clear the girl resented his help and when it came down to it he didn't want to give it to her. That was a relief.

During the afternoon Lettice was not called for a rehearsal at which both Buckley and Laurie Spindle were needed. She went into the Green Room, sat down and tried to take Davenant's advice. She would learn all the female parts in that favourite play of his, *The Iron Chest*. But her mind would not work. Her career was coming to nothing. Davenant would never help her. And there was Isabella.

She'd tried to forget how angry her sister had made her but Bryson had brought it back with renewed bitterness. Did Isabella remember nothing of their lives together? Did she now look on Lettice as a housemaid, dependent on my lady's recommendation to get employment?

Too miserable and angry to work, and with four hours before the evening performance, she decided to go home. Home. That was a stupid word. Walking down the dusty streets, sometimes jostled into the gutter, she thought of Isabella at Bagot House, of long cool rooms, marble-floored, smelling of roses . . .

When she let herself into the lodgings she heard Mrs. Hastings's voice arguing and now and then a low reply apparently from Mr. Hastings. Then the woman's voice again, declaiming, complaining.

Lettice toiled up the staircase. The voices oppressed her, and the smell of stale food and the dust on the windowsills. She opened her bedroom door.

Sib, the maid of all work, was standing at Lettice's dressing-table rifling through the drawers. When she saw Lettice, she gave a violent start and recoiled as if expecting a blow.

Lettice slowly shut the door.

"What have you taken, Sib?"

"Nothing."

"Please give it back."

The girl looked away, frightened and furious. How thin she is, Lettice thought. Her face looks dirty, but is it dirt? I've seen actors look like that from exhaustion. But Sib is dirty too. That apron is disgusting . . .

Lettice sat down on the bed. Sib stood facing her, terrified and fierce as a wild animal.

"What have you taken of mine?"

"Nothing. Didn't have time," was the vicious answer. "How was I ter know you'd come 'ome this time o' day. Yer never does."

"That's true. And there isn't much to take, is there? The ring my mother gave me. My clothes, I suppose."

A pause.

"Are you in trouble?"

"Whatyermean?"

"I didn't mean a baby. I mean other trouble. Why did you have to steal?"

Not a word.

Lettice sighed.

"Yer'll be off an' tell Missus and she'll

throw me into the street, the old bitch, so off and tell her."

Lettice saw with pity and horror that the girl's eyes, large, dark, the colour of Isabella's, were full of tears.

"Of course I do not mean to tell Mrs. Hastings. Just don't do it again or someone else will catch you and then you'll go to prison. I know you won't tell me what the trouble is," Lettice said, "so get on with your work. We'll forget it ever happened."

The girl went past like a bird released from a net and rushed down the stairs.

Late that night when Lettice returned home she discovered Sib must have found the purse under Ellen's letters. It contained every penny she had.

(2)

She did not know what to do. The money, saved in pence from her meagre wages, was to pay the next month's rent which the landlady insisted on having in advance. It was also money for Lettice's slender meals, bought in cook houses, eaten in the Green Room. For her very existence, living thinly from one week's pay to the next. Sib might have stolen

271

the money for a family nearly starving, a lover, who could say? Lettice could not sleep and rose with the dawn.

In Covent Garden the crowds of carts, horses, men, baskets, was so great that she could scarcely make her way. The pavement was thick with flower petals, crushed oranges, cabbage leaves, the air smelled like the inside of a fruit barrel. She felt bruised and stupid when she finally escaped the shouting carters and shying horses and turned into the Stage Door.

Jack looked up.

"Early bird, Miss Winter."

"You once said Mr. Davenant is always early, Jack."

"Guvnor come in half an hour since."

The door of Davenant's suite was open, and when she knocked, his voice, full-toned, with the edge that gave it its beauty, called, "Come!"

Davenant, sitting at a desk under the high window, turned round to look at her.

"Good grief, you again? What do you want at this ungodly hour, pray? Have you no shame?"

"It is nothing to do with my career, sir."

He gestured to her to sit down but she

remained standing. She made a sober little figure in her shabby cotton dress of grey and white and that unbecoming bonnet. Governessy. Why doesn't she dress like an actress, he thought.

"Someone came to my lodgings during the performance last night and stole all my money. I wonder if you could help me."

"Help you catch the thief, you mean?"

"Oh no."

"Why not? Thieves must be brought to justice. You've informed your lodging-house keeper, I take it?"

"No."

"I don't make much of that," he said. "You don't wish the thief caught. You don't tell your landlady of the crime. What *do* you want?"

"A little money."

"Indeed. For what?"

She had lived too long with poverty to be ashamed of it, and although this man was powerful she had never been afraid of him.

"Mr. Davenant, I cannot pay my rent, which is due today. Neither can I eat or pay for my laundry. I had saved enough to live for a month."

"Yes, yes, all very sad, " he said impatiently. "What is more interesting is why you don't wish thieves apprehended and landladies informed."

"Because I know who did it and the person is in distress."

He dropped his jaw in amazement.

"Beware, Miss Winter. You are turning into one of those milk-sop heroines you played in Newcastle."

"At least I had something to play in Newcastle," she snapped.

He raised his eyebrows.

"Dissatisfied here, are you?"

No answer.

"Well, well, I suppose we can't let poor Nellie starve," he said. "Here are two sovereigns." He pressed them into her hand.

"One sovereign would be quite—"

"Stuff."

Taking the hand which was not holding the money, he lifted her slowly to her feet. His eyes made her feel hot and uncomfortable. She tried to withdraw her hand.

"How are you going to repay me for my munificence?" Before she realised what he was going to do, he put a strong arm round her waist and pressed her mouth with a violent kiss. Lettice struggled, but he kept his mouth on hers. When he finally released her she was so angry that she was crying.

"*How dare you!* How dare you think you can behave in this disgusting way! Take your horrible money if that's what it means!"

She threw the sovereigns violently across the room.

"Now there's a stupid thing!" he exclaimed, "I help you in your hour of need and you throw my money about as if it were so much muck. That won't do at all."

He walked across the room, knelt down and peered along the floor until he found the sovereigns which had rolled under a table. He returned to Lettice.

Her face was scarlet. Not just a mild blush from surprise or self-consciousness but a flood of red which made her cheeks feel as if she had been scalded.

"I must go," she said, looking away.

He began to laugh. It started with a chuckle, then grew louder until he was roaring and mopping his eyes. In between guffaws he gasped, "Lettice, Lettice, you'll be the death of me. Oh dear, you certainly play the virtuous virgin to perfection."

She looked at him with humourless resent

ment and he continued to chuckle. He put the sovereigns back into her hand.

"You have no need to throw my cash about. I shan't demand the kind of payment you're so frightened of," he said. "Take the money and don't waste it. It's hard-earned. Money should be respected, not pitched in the faces of one's friends."

She said coldly, "Thank you. I will pay it back."

"So I should think. Now off and leave me to my work if you please. Any more jokes and I shan't be able to concentrate."

When she was alone, Lettice thought over the matter of Davenant's sovereigns very seriously. She liked to reflect on things before she made up her mind. She decided it was perfectly fair to accept the money and was glad she hadn't been forced to ask Laurie or Buckley Vernon for help. When she had better roles (which must come sometime) she would pay Davenant the money, and she would not do it pleasantly. How cheap a woman must be to him, she thought. Imagine his thinking *I* would be willing to be his kept woman. It shows he knows nothing about me. Nothing.

She despised him for his loose morals. Her

own were rigid. The old bad days in the theatre were changing. She remembered audiences in her early teens, their filthy language and behaviour, the way they regarded actresses as harlots. It was not like that today, and Lettice thanked heaven for it. As for Davenant, he had been in his twenties when George IV was on the throne and everybody knew what morals were like *then*. The way he embraced me, the things he took for granted, are not only wrong, they're out of date, she thought with twenty-one-year-old disdain.

She paid Mrs. Hastings the rent. Her land-lady counted the money and locked it away.

"If one could only have guests and not be forced to take emoluments," said Mrs. Hastings, sighing. "But I regard you, Lettice, as a friend. Will you take tea?"

Lettice also went in search of Sib whom she found on her knees scrubbing the stone-floored basement kitchen.

"Whatyerwant?"

"Sybil, I am not going to eat you. I came to give you this."

Lettice offered her sixpence.

Sib regarded the coin as if it were a serpent.

"Keep yer money."

"Don't be a donkey. You've already had

277

my money, so don't bother to deny it. Why not," said Lettice, without much hope, "at least buy a new apron?"

Sib pocketed the money in silence.

Lettice thought the sixpence had made her an enemy, but Sib did buy an apron, and occasionally washed her face. Meeting Lettice on the stairs, she actually gave a wink.

If things at her lodgings were improved, Lettice had made matters infinitely worse by her refusal of Davenant's embraces. He began to pick her up on the smallest points, declaring he had never seen such a bad performance as she gave in the two sentences allotted to her in the new play.

Lettice found this persecution hard to bear, although she understood it—Davenant was having a male revenge. Her friends were kind to her. Gwynyth made her cups of tea, Laurie Spindle sat on an upturned skip and talked good plain shop.

"Know what I've been trying, Lettice? Rouge applied to the tops of my ears. I have discovered that it is the ears which suggest good health."

Kindest of all was Buckley, who kissed her hand, declaring that Davenant was behaving disgracefully. She warmed to Buckley, who understood her hopes and fears and was part of the pattern of her life. His handsome presence comforted her very much.

As Davenant continued to ridicule her, some of the actresses grew very cheerful. Perhaps Davenant would get rid of her. That would be a mercy, as she was so pretty.

14

(1)

THE leaves of the plane trees had begun to yellow, and the last balls were given before the great houses closed. Society would soon be gone to that infinitely-preferred country life. Denys had been so glad to be reunited with Isabella that he could scarcely bear to let her out of his sight. He approved of everything; the new house, her new gowns, the bright weather, the interminable dinners, the drives in the park by his wife's side, where he lazily saluted the friends who rode past. It was weeks since Isabella had set eyes on Buckley.

One morning just before the season ended, Denys and Robert discussed whether they should go to Sussex ahead of the family, to buy some new carriage horses. Denys, full of apologies to his "dearest", explained that he and Robert did not trust the agent at Bagot Park to buy the horses. "Poor fellow, he has no eye."

Isabella assured him he must not feel guilty and was tenderly kissed for her goodness. Two days later Denys and Robert left London. When they had gone Isabella ordered the carriage to take her to Regent's Park. On her way, she told the coachman, she would leave a word for her sister at the theatre.

It was a letter to Buckley.

"Imperative I see you at once. My new house, Finstock Lodge, Regent's Park, any hour between now and four. Do not fail me, for God's sake. I."

It was sultry and airless as Isabella alighted from the carriage and the footman opened the door.

"Don't wait for me, Edwards. Lady Fanny needs you and I am meeting Mr. Wreford. He will bring me home."

The footman bowed, the horses were whipped up and trotted away. As the sound of hooves faded, Isabella went into the house, leaving the door ajar. Ladders leaned against walls. Furniture was pushed in corners and shrouded in sheets. There were wallpapers, paints, carpets in cotton wrappings. It was like a play before the scene was set.

Despite the thinness of her muslin dress, she felt suffocatingly hot. She pulled off her long gloves; her hands were sweating.

She wandered through the unfinished house like a ghost. Then she heard a sound and rushed into the hall. It was Buckley.

He stood, with the panorama of the deserted park behind him, smiling at her. There was something untidy and rough about him after Denys's immaculate elegance.

"Isabella," he said with the old self-conscious look. "I'm sorry I could not come sooner. Rehearsals."

When Isabella saw him she had the falling sensation in the pit of her stomach.

"Buck."

Answering the note of her voice he strode across and took her into his arms. He gave her a kiss so long, exploring, desirous, that she felt giddy.

"I suppose there's a bed somewhere in this house?"

"No. There's nothing."

"And you're too much the aristocrat to lie on the ground."

He pressed his thin cheek against hers, rocked her to and fro. She scarcely knew what she was doing. She dragged herself out of the swoon of desire.

"Don't kiss me or I'll never be able to talk."

"Why should you talk? Mmmmm."

But she slightly resisted him. The effect was immediate, he let her go and walked away.

"Well?"

"Don't look like that!" she burst out. "I've so longed for you! I thought I'd be sick with want. All these weeks and weeks. But there's something I must tell you. You have to know. I am with child."

Over and over again Isabella had imagined speaking these words. Her thoughts never went further than that. She did not know how he would take them. Rush to her? Love her?

He said, drawling affectedly, "An heir for the Viscount? That will make you popular with the nobs."

She put her hands to her heart.

"Don't joke. I cannot bear it."

With a strained, worldly smile he said, "What do you want me to say, my love?"

"It may be your child. Yours and mine."

"Now why should that be? You're a married woman, Bella, and in cases like this—"

"Buckley," she interrupted, convulsively gripping his arm, "I am nearly two months gone."

There was a pause.

He stared.

"What do you want me to do?"

Isabella sighed. Now he accepted the possibility, now he shared it, she was no longer afraid. A little colour came back into her cheeks and she loosened her tight grasp and took his hand. He pressed it kindly, and a rush of suffocating tenderness came over her. She loved him so intensely that anything, everything was possible. What happiness just to stand here with him knowing that in a while they would make love, that there was a whole hour together. Even bearing what might be his child made her happy.

"Oh Buck, what shall we do?" she said with a wavering smile. "Do you think we might go away together? Wouldn't it be wonderful? I shall not be penniless, you know, there was money settled on me when I was married, and Denys is so generous. Why shouldn't we share our life together, Buck, and have our child? It *may* be ours! And it's what we want, isn't it? Ah, isn't it?"

He kissed her and put his arms round her,

murmuring something. For a while she thought they would go upstairs through the empty house and lie on the floor and make love.

But he said no, not now, not with the child. Wasn't it sometimes dangerous? "Especially as I want you so much. I could never be gentle with you, Bella. Never."

Lulled by his voice, she accepted this and took his hand, and they went out of the house together. She locked the doors. They went down the road under the trees until Buckley saw a hackney which he hailed for her. He stood by while Isabella settled herself, arranging her lacy skirts, putting out a gloved hand.

He pressed it closely.

"You will hear from me."

"Do you promise?"

"I swear," he said, making a little kissing movement with his lips.

She gave him a long look. The carriage trotted away and disappeared through the gates.

Buckley stood for a while staring back at the house, its windows shuttered. Then at the park, where the grass was dying. Whistling absently, he made his way out of the park along the dusty streets. What a mess, he thought, what an unlucky, accursed mess. Isabella was as pretty a piece of flesh as he'd known for years, but did the stupid fool really imagine he'd run off with her? She was mad. Why, his career was only just beginning. It wasn't every actor who had the chance of working with Davenant. Go back to the provinces and live on twopence with a pregnant woman! And she'd be penniless, if he knew anything about the nobility. What would life be with a squawking brat and a woman who'd learned to live rich? There was another thing. The little matter of seducing a viscount's wife. Duelling would soon be against the law, but it was accepted among the nobility. A man had been killed in Battersea Fields only last week. "A matter of honour", settled with revolvers. Buckley despised such claptrap; but Isabella's husband, that viscount, might think differently. He might consider it an excellent thing to kill the man who had broken his marriage and possibly impregnated his wife.

He would kill me, too, thought Buckley. Men like that are prime shots. I've never handled a revolver except a stage prop. God, what a coil. Why didn't I keep my hands off her? But he'd never been able to say no to a beautiful woman who, by her insistent desire, proved how irresistible he was.

He was hot and disagreeable when he arrived at the theatre. The stone-walled building was gratefully cool backstage and he heard the familiar sound of actors arriving for the evening performance, laughter, slamming doors. He went into his dressing-room, wrenched his satin stock loose and threw himself into a chair.

There was a tap at the door.

"Go away."

A freckled face peered in.

"I only called for a moment," said Lettice. "If you are working I won't stay."

"Come in," he said, brightening. He scarcely remembered this shabby little thing was the sister of Isabella. This girl was a professional; he respected her.

"My parents have returned from Ireland," she said. "They will be in London tonight, lodging at Holborn Bars. Would you take supper with us, Mr. Vernon?"

"I would like to very much."

Lettice looked pleased.

"Laurie has accepted too."

"Why do you call Laurie by his first name? You never do that with me."

"Because he is old, I suppose. Like an uncle."

"I could be a cousin, couldn't I?"

"I'm not sure."

"Of course I could. It's not so difficult. Say 'Buckley'."

She laughed and said, "Buckley".

"That's better. I am glad Davenant has stopped harassing you. Poor girl. You had a most unhappy time."

"I knew why he was like that—" Lettice began and blushed.

Always sex-conscious, he understood at once what she meant.

"Did he make advances towards you? Now I understand. What a swine!"

He was full of chivalrous indignation.

Lettice sat down. She looked very young.

"It is sometimes a nuisance, you know, being twenty and unattached and an actress. It was different on the circuits because of Papa. I know he never seemed to pay us much attention, but the men, any men, respected Bella and me because we were with our parents. Now it's as if I am fair game. I do hate it."

"You have Laurie Spindle. And you have me."

"Oh yes." She looked at him in a way which, despite her common sense, was very innocent. "I am grateful."

He liked her very much just then.

An idea came into his mind which by its very simplicity seemed inspired. Could this pretty creature provide an escape from his troubles and from Isabella herself—by actually becoming his wife? It was something he must think about . . .

He took her hand. An hour ago it had been Isabella's hand, hot and damp and heavy with emeralds, lying in his. Lettice's hand was small and cool, ringless and firm.

"It would do me great honour," he said affectionately, "if you would always look on me as your friend."

(2)

The snow lay crisping on the fields for weeks. It was icy cold. Sometimes a thaw began, but then the slush froze and it began to snow again. A freezing wind blew across the whitened fields.

289

The family had been in residence at Bagot Park for months. The visitors' book with the Bagot coronet on the cover, which lay open in the entrance hall, was filled with signatures. Carriages and riders came and went in all weathers, there were never less than a dozen visitors, sometimes the number rose to more than thirty. At night the windows shone, and music was heard faintly across the icy park.

The house was more lively than the old "mausoleum" in London disliked by the Earl. The Earl, his son and nephew all preferred the country, they liked to live among their tenantry, liked the business of the estates, the hard riding and daily hunting, the cold rooms and blazing fires, the visitors, the bustle of a great house full of people. Lady Clare, much in demand, was often away staying with friends, returning with more admirers to dangle after her. She grew prettier, but never more pleasant to Isabella. Lady Fanny was busy with guests from morning until night.

Isabella took little part in the dinners, games, music and winter fun. One evening when she was in the drawing-room she fainted. After that Denys refused to allow her to tire herself, and she kept much in her own rooms, occasionally coming downstairs to see visitors.

She looked haggard during the final months of her pregnancy. She slept badly. Uncomfortable with her growing bulk, she often rose in the middle of the night and sat wrapped in a shawl, looking through the curtains at the fields under the snow. But she never woke without Denys waking at once, as if she had shaken him by the arm.

"How are you, my dearest? Let me ring for Hopton. You need a hot drink. Your feet are cold. Let me wrap this round you."

Tired after a day in the open air, deeply asleep, he was always instantly awake and beside her, sharing everything with his tender company.

The Earl considered his solicitude absurd, and scoffed to Robert: "What a fuss the boy makes. He's like an old hen."

"Deno has a kind heart, sir, and Isabella is not well."

"Pooh. When Denys was born I was out hunting. Remember the day distinctly. We found in Queen's Spinney but the beggar got clean away across the river."

From the first, Isabella's health was not good. She felt continually sick, and sometimes so ill it was as if she'd been poisoned. She was languid and exhausted. But she behaved well, and Denys thought her courage a marvellous thing. That, at least, made her smile. She did not say, because he wouldn't let her talk of the past, that she'd been reared in a world where nobody complained when they were ill. What was the use, when there was a performance to be got through? As a sick child she had been bundled into a shawl in her parents' dressing-room, or in bed in their lodgings, longing for her mother to come home. Now if she gave the slightest grimace of pain, Denys was at her side. She accepted such proof of love. He had always been like that.

She forgot for days that the child leaping inside her, growing so heavy, might not be his. The first weeks when she had known she was pregnant, when she'd had the lunatic hope of running away with Buckley, seemed so long ago she could scarcely remember them. Much, much longer ago than when she had been an actress and come to Bagot Park and first set eyes on Denys.

Sometimes fate, or God, did spare you from ordeals, she once thought. Her mother and Lettice had called at Bagot House to tell her

292

the news of Lettice's coming marriage. By chance Isabella was prostrate with a migraine; it had been Denys who was told the news, who had kissed them kindly and congratulated them, explaining that his Isabella was too sick to see them.

"She will be so disappointed not to see you and so glad for you all."

So Isabella was spared from being told of Buckley's perfidy by Lettice. Denys sent a magnificent wedding present of silver. Isabella wrote her congratulations. The Bagots left London for Sussex the day following her family's visit and she had not seen Lettice, Buckley or her parents since then, although her mother and Lettice both wrote regularly.

Her passion for Buckley, the feverish desire and ecstatic pleasure, had utterly vanished. She remembered those feelings rarely and with wonder. She was now simply the Viscount's lady about to give birth—possibly to a son. She lay in a four-poster bed and watched the fire twinkling and the snow whirling outside the windows. Denys strode in, bringing a sweet smell of the country clinging to his clothes.

Isabella's son was born in March, earlier

than expected, with a long painful labour which she bore with fortitude. The child was a small, perfect boy with a thatch of dark hair and a nose like a miniature beak. He was, declared the entranced Lady Fanny, the image of his grandfather. It was decided by the family and not by his mother that he should be christened Frederick, which was the Earl's first name.

Denys was scarcely interested in the baby for the first day. He had been more frightened than she, had sat with her until the doctor and the monthly nurse drove him from the room, then waited in the outside dressing-room in an agony of mind as sharp as Isabella's birth pains.

Now was a time of the greatest joy. Everywhere in the house, people heard the sound of Carteret's laugh.

Robert was greatly interested by the new baby. He took to calling into the nursery next to Isabella's bedroom, then coming to see her with reports of the baby's progress.

"Young Freddy knows me already. When I stood by his cot he distinctly winked," said Robert, "I have an ally there."

Isabella, finishing her luncheon with little appetite, smiled.

Denys, for the first time since the baby's birth, had been persuaded by his father to go hunting. Isabella's windows were slightly ajar and she had heard the hunt leave, the sound of the horn, the baying of hounds. The snow had long ago melted. Spring was nearly here.

She lay against a pile of pillows, wearing a cap of stiffened lace which Robert amusedly thought looked like a halo. Everything about her was lacy. She reminded him of Herrick's poem, "the liquefaction of her clothes". Now the child was born the haggard look which had made her olive-skinned face so plain was gone. She was like a tea-rose.

"Stay and talk, Robert. It is wearisome in bed. I do so long to get up."

"When shall you do that, Bella?"

He was the only Bagot who called her that.

"Not a foot on the ground until Sunday, Nurse says. You would think nobody in the world had ever had a baby before."

"Ah, but this isn't any old baby, is it?"

He laughed, looking at her with eyes as dark as her own. Robert is very good-looking, she thought idly. She liked his narrow bony face, springy dark hair. He had an air of quickness, impatience, of being in command

295

of life, taking it over. He was as strong as the old Earl, in a way.

"What a devoted father Deno is," he said, burying his nose in a bowl of white narcissi. The air smelled of their heavy scent. There were other presents from Denys. A silver box with a cherub on it, a bracelet of pearls, a piece of porcelain of a child crowned with daisies, an India shawl.

"He is glad Frederick is a boy," she said languidly.

"The Bagot heir."

"But you were the heir until Frederick arrived."

He burst out laughing.

"Is it weighing on your mind, cousin? Certainly I used to come second after Deno. But you and he will have a quiverful. And with every boy, Bella, I shall get pushed further down the ladder. Think how I shall shake in my shoes when the monthly nurse arrives again."

"You don't take anything seriously."

"It looks as if I'll have to take the christening seriously," he said briskly. "My uncle has asked me to help Fanny with it and I fear Fanny makes work rather than simplifies it. Freddy will, of course, be done at St. Mary the Virgin like all the other Bagots who kneel about in marble glaring at us every Sunday. Have you noticed the third Earl under that canopy? I wonder what annoyed him in 1672? The vicar's sermons, I daresay. The reception will be here and we think there'll be about two hundred and fifty. Bagots enjoy christenings."

"Do we have luncheon or will it be dinner afterwards?" asked Isabella.

She had followed her mother's advice after she married Denys, remembering "never to show her ignorance", picking up from Lady Fanny or the Earl anything she did not know, rarely asking questions even of Denys. It was usually easy, and she was quick. But with Robert she never minded showing there were society matters of which she still knew nothing.

"Luncheon first. Then the carriages to the church. Then champagne in the blue drawing-room, and the cake and Freddy to be shown to the admiring ladies—he has to be shown to the staff next morning too, Bella, and they have their own cake, quite as big but with a different recipe, Mrs. Judge informed me. Forty or so are staying at present so we might dance. What do you say?"

She smiled and stretched.

"Lovely to dance again. It all sounds delicious. So important. And all for baby Frederick."

"Yes, Freddy is important," was the matter-of-fact reply.

When he left her Isabella lay back, listening to the distant sounds of the house, to voices on the terrace, to a horse trotting by, a dog barking. Spring was coming, her baby was born, everything was safe and beautiful. She would write to her mother with the news. Lettice too. She faintly smiled at the thought of Buckley learning in such a way that perhaps he had a son. She thought of the little creature in his elaborate cot next door, the Bagot crest in silver holding up the transparent curtains, the nurse seated beside him. Would little "important" Frederick look like Buckley? In her forgetting-yesterday way she was certain he would not. She was filled with dreamy, idle, pleasing, selfish thoughts. It was spring and she was twenty years old.

Part Three

Part Three

15

(1)

LETTICE stood at the window of her Kensington house, slowly brushing her hair. She was thinking about the theatre. It was 1844, and in the last four years it seemed to her that her life had been completely absorbed by family life. The theatre, her great love, had been pushed to one side. She had married Buckley, borne him a daughter and a son, and learned the art needed for living with a difficult man. But now she felt she might, perhaps, think about herself again.

It was a dull spring morning, and she could hear the children romping downstairs. She frowned. How loudly Matilda shouts, she thought, and how I dislike the noise of raised voices in the house. Buckley had left for the theatre and Lettice decided to spend a quiet morning, reading and thinking, while the nurse-maid took the children into Kensington

Gardens, to use up some of those high spirits in the open air.

The London season was beginning again, the social columns of the newspapers announced the return of the Duke of This and the Marchioness of That. There were elegant riders in the Row now, and the great Piccadilly houses behind their high walls had begun to open their shutters like eyes.

Lettice, too, felt she was waking up. She knew she'd changed. The births of her children had given her new energy and a new glow. The men friends whom Buckley brought home to dine were more gallant towards her than they used to be. If only, she thought, I could use my attraction to draw audiences instead of merely friends.

She envied Buckley the progress he had made. Davenant now gave him leading roles. Buckley's good looks and ease upon the stage were "useful"—Davenant's word. London audiences liked Buckley, but Lettice knew that they did not fall in love with him. They still did with Davenant: the moment *he* walked on to a stage, audiences had eyes for nobody else. Perhaps Buckley's lack of magic is why Davenant keeps him in the company, she thought. It is odd how a great actor can still be jealous.

Lettice was fond of her husband, but he had not proved to be the man she believed him when they had married. He was touchy, childish and easy to offend. He had pleasant qualities; he was ardent, he liked to laugh, he was generous with money, and at times was excellent company. But for Lettice's fastidious taste he drank too much, and—despite his ardour towards her—she knew that he was sometimes unfaithful. It was impossible to be involved in a theatre company and not know if one's husband had begun to stray. These infidelities, she thought, did not last. She thinned her lips and pretended that she knew nothing.

Buckley visited the Garrick Club a good deal: he liked to be seen with well-known actors and authors. Moods of gloom and self-pity came over him at times, usually when Davenant had not given him some particular leading role which he coveted. When a gloomy fit was on him he would go to the Garrick, drink too much and arrive home intoxicated and vulgar. Lettice, with a calm face, was silently angry. But it would all blow over and life become pleasant enough again.

The Vernons lived in a not-large house in the village of Kensington, which was less than an hour by carriage from the theatre. But it was a country place, with farms and stretching fields, and the children thrived. Matilda, now three, and William, a sturdy two, went for country walks every day, liked to visit the farmyard down the road, watched the cows being milked. They were handsome children; Matilda much resembled Buckley, with curling hair and grey eyes; William had Lettice's red hair, straight nose and freckles.

There was a knock on her bedroom door.

The nursemaid, Mary Anne, poked her head round the door. She was too pretty, Lettice thought, but staff were hard to find.

"Letter for you, ma'am. And a brougham at the door waiting. I do wonder why!"

"That will do, Mary Anne," said Lettice, in much the repressive voice her mother still used. Mary Anne bounced out and began shouting at the children. Lettice was about to spring up and scold her when she turned the letter over and recognised the writing. It was from Davenant.

She tore open the envelope.

Scrawled across a card with the Royalty

304

Theatre coat of arms at the top were a few words:

"Come to the theatre this morning if you please. Brougham will bring you. Trust not incommoded. H.D."

She stared at the card for a moment. It was the first time since she had left Newcastle as a raw girl that Davenant had shown interest in her as an actress. It must mean something. But what?

She put on her bonnet, rearranged a loop of red hair against her cheek and went down the staircase.

There was a flick of Mary Anne's white apron, a giggle of children's voices from behind the dining-room door.

"Mary Anne."

"Yes, ma'am?" The girl came out as guiltily as one of the children.

"Please take Miss Matilda and Master Billy out for their morning walk. You know I do not wish them to play about the house. Tell Cook I will not be in for luncheon, I shall be at the theatre. And see Miss Matilda eats properly."

Mary Anne said meek yeses and waited

until Lettice left the house. When the front door was closed Matilda put a round face round the dining-room door and made a grimace at her. Mary Anne gave her a slap. Matilda, her mother out of the way, did not bother to cry.

Lettice settled herself in the brougham, and the journey to London began. The winding road under tall old elm trees was deserted except when the mail coach went galloping noisily by. She saw farm carts behind great patient drays, and a man cutting the first crop of early hay. She took the card from her muff and looked at it again. Davenant. How unhappy he had made her, and how she'd longed to understand why.

But her life had dramatically changed. She had married Buckley. Davenant had not been pleased or kind when she broke the news. He'd had the gall to tell her that if she married Buckley she would be "wasting her talent". Lettice had answered sharply that it had been Davenant who had wasted her talent. He hadn't liked that. For a moment, she had thought he was going to explain something to her. But all he'd done was stare at her oddly, and then say nothing.

She had continued to act at the Royalty, her

roles never any more important. Childbearing had meant a great deal of absence; as time went by she knew Davenant had no interest in her at all.

Until now?

At the Stage Door Jack greeted her as a friend.

"Coming back to us then, Miss Winter? Guvnor's expecting you."

Walking along the passage, the first person she saw was Gwynyth.

"Lettice!"

The two women kissed fondly, looking—Lettice in lavender silk, Gwynyth in rusty black—like figures of Youth and Age.

The door of Davenant's suite was open. Lettice tapped lightly and went into the room. He was at his desk, his back to the door and without turning said, "Sit down, my girl. I will be with you shortly."

He went on writing. The quill made a loud scratching sound, then caught the paper and spurted. He swore under his breath.

Lettice studied the back of his head. His plentiful hair was greying and broke into curls on the nape of a neck as thick as a column. Lettice, accustomed to Buckley's grace, thought Davenant's shape though powerful very middle-aged. There was nothing pliant about it.

He finished the letter, sealed it, then swung round.

He looked at the young woman in her discreet, stylish dress of lavender silk with braided epaulettes. She met his eye with interest.

"When is your next lying-in?" he demanded.

She couldn't help laughing.

"Does it matter to you, sir?"

The answer seemed to annoy him.

"That's a damned stupid question, Lettice."

"I was only teasing you."

"Then don't waste my time."

He was making it clear that if in the distant past he had made advances to her he had no such intention now. He looked at her as a sculptor might at a lump of clay.

"You've never played Shakespeare, have you?"

Before she could answer he held up his hand.

"Don't tell me you played every role on the circuits at the ripe old age of sixteen. Are you up to *my* Shakespeare?"

Another actress might have exclaimed that she was waiting, a greyhound in the slips, for any—every—Shakespeare role. Lettice said nothing.

"Know how to make 'em laugh?" said Davenant sharply.

"Oh yes."

"Indeed?"

"Yes," was the firm reply.

He picked up the quill and turned it in his hand.

"I'll tell you something curious, Lettice. The Shakespeare comedies are coming back. Odd, eh? When I was a young nobody managers wouldn't have dared try *Twelfth Night*. People thought it was stuff. What they wanted was *Lear* and *Othello*. Shakespeare's comedies collected dust on top shelves. Now it is all different. Do you know what audiences want? Romance!"

"Do you dislike romance?"

"Me? I am the most romantic man alive," he said savagely. "So what is on the bill of fare today? *As You Like It*."

She was silent again. She had an eloquent way of being so.

"You think I treated you badly in the past, don't you?" he suddenly said.

"Not after I was married."

"And before that?"

309

"Very."

Meeting her eyes fixed on him, he appeared—for Davenant—slightly uncomfortable.

"You are not still holding it against me that I gave you a kiss donkey's years ago? I apologised at the time for succumbing to your beauty. Always thought you a taking little thing."

"Neither of us is referring to that."

He looked at her slyly.

"Oh, very well. I know I promised I'd do something for you when you came to London—don't interrupt, hear me out. The fact is I ran into difficulties. The Royalty was a damned sight more costly than I'd expected."

"I don't understand."

"Use your wits. Jessie Ramsey is the daughter of an old friend. In plain English, Ramsey lent me the money for the lease. And take that religious look off your face; if it were not for Ramsey you and I wouldn't be at the Royalty at all. I like to pay my debts."

"I am sure you do. Why am I here?"

"You're very hard," he said sighing. "Jessie Ramsey has decided to retire from the theatre. The lass is to be married."

Years ago, in another life, Lettice remembered the exit of a marble Venus, one broken hand accusingly pointing. But it was she who had had the Venus removed. I was stronger then, she thought.

"Well," said Davenant, looking at her as if reading her thoughts, "*du courage*."

"Oh, I don't need that," she said involuntarily.

He raised his eyebrows.

"I can see you don't. Here's the matter, then. Thought I'd offer you Rosalind. How does that strike you? Aha. Now that face has a different look on it!"

(2)

The news that "Miss Winter" was back in the company, not in small parts but in the role of Rosalind in Davenant's new production of *As You Like It*, was greeted by the company in various guessable ways. The men were momentarily pleased, since Lettice's glow and ripeness shone upon all. The elder women actresses enjoyed foretelling "disaster, my love". The younger actresses were angry and jealous but too practised to show it.

Buckley was offended. He considered Davenant should have spoken to him before approaching Lettice. Lettice was his wife: he would say whether she could accept the offer. Besides, he wished to be treated as an important member of the company, one with whom Davenant discussed things. However, he was offered Orlando and decided to be magnanimous.

"You're clever, Letty," he said, his mouth full of oyster pie when they were dining at home that evening.

"I hope I can do it, Buckley."

"So do I," he said, with a loud laugh.

She recognised that self-absorbed, glassy look. If she failed, *his* career might be damaged.

(3)

It had been a joke in the Winter family when she was a child that Isabella must have happy ends at all costs. Lettice said that if someone told her sister about a man losing his leg, Isabella would be sure he "walked quite well on his wooden one afterwards". Isabella pearled over anything unhappy.

Her life on the circuits, her passion for Buckley, had disappeared from her mind; the Honourable Frederick Bagot was simply her son and Denys's, doted upon by the family, even by Lady Clare. The old Earl bought him anything he fancied, from a pony to a greyhound. Denys taught him to ride when he was so small he could scarcely balance on a horse; Robert picked him up every time he saw the little boy. Freddy was spoiled. He was a clever child, and the small face which had looked like a new-born bird grew handsome. He had dreamy brown eyes, a proud air. "How like his grandfather he is!" Lady Fanny constantly exclaimed.

Two years after Freddy's birth Isabella was brought to bed of a daughter, a pretty little creature with Denys's smile and grace. She was christened Elizabeth Lucy Effingham Bagot and known only as Betsy. From the moment Betsy could crawl, she made straight towards her brother. She followed him on all fours, then in tottering steps, then with dancing feet, his loving slave. If Denys asked: "Will you come for a walk, Betsy?" the answer was always, "*And* Freddy." Frederick treated his sister with a kindly contempt.

Isabella's life was that of all people of rank, with the liberties of wealth and the restrictions of manners. She took for granted the pattern of the year, ordered as the seasons: the short social time in London, the return to Bagot Park for long months of country life. The Bagots ruled their district like benevolent patriarchs, hunted with the farmers, knew every farmer and labourer. Isabella learned to be interested in the building of cottages, in family dinners at Christmas or harvest-time given for "the neighbourhood" when 500 people sat down to dine in the gardens or the house. She went to village cricket matches, sat under the oak trees and watched Denys hitting a six. At sports Denys was always best of all.

Her parents had not long continued the hard work of the circuits. Denys insisted on settling some money upon them. Thomas accepted this with effusive gratitude when he met the Viscount and private resentment afterwards. But practical Ellen bought a cottage in Richmond and soothed Thomas's ruffled self-respect.

Isabella found Denys's kindness to her parents obscurely annoying, particularly since Denys never spoke of her life in the theatre and she must not do so either.

"Denys, you don't *have* to give my parents money. Papa is quite proud, you know, and has never lacked work."

"Don't be a goose, Isabella. Your father cannot refuse a small gift from his own child."

"But I did not give it."

"I said it was from you."

Oh Denys, Denys, she thought. There was something disturbing in living with anybody so good and so kind. At times his goodness was stifling. Robert, for all his manners, had moments of being rather heartless, and shocking Denys very much.

After six years of marriage, she knew her husband like the back of her hand. There was an immovable quality in him. He always knew without hesitating the choice between right and wrong. It was this adamant quality in his son, together with his lack of intellect, which the old Earl despised. *He* did not see life as black and white and nor did anybody with brains or a pair of eyes, he thought. It wasn't possible to continue to be such a simpleton, yet Carteret managed it. The Earl had grown up in the disreputable days of the Prince Regent, spent a raffish youth and enjoyed it. He knew which side his bread should be buttered and was damned well going to see that's how it was. His son never seemed to be conscious of such a thing. "I'll swear he wouldn't stretch out his hand if the butter was in front of him," said the Earl to Robert. Carteret was curiously free of the arrogance one would expect from a Bagot with immense properties and power to match. It was true he was rather a lazy man. He was also unselfish, affectionate, and too straightforward for his father's taste. The old Earl turned, as always, to his more worldly nephew.

Denys's attitude towards Isabella's family was kindly but distant. Isabella had seen to it that she and Denys never met Buckley. It was not difficult. She sometimes visited Lettice and her children when Buckley was at the theatre, and Denys out with Robert. But the sisters did not meet very much. Lettice and her mother accepted this state of things and spoke of it philosophically.

"It is the way of the great world," Ellen said.

"Of course, you are right, Mama."

"The fact is your sister is too good for us now," put in Thomas shortly. But the women refused to admit that.

Lettice wrote to Isabella with the wonderful news of her role as Rosalind. Isabella showed the letter to Denys who looked pleased. He rarely saw Lettice, but he respected her.

"We will arrange to take a box to see your sister," Denys said, sprawling by the open window, waiting for Isabella to finish dressing for a drive in the park.

Rivers, the little maid from Clarges Street now promoted to be Isabella's personal maid, opened a box and took out Isabella's long grey suede gloves.

"No, Rivers. I prefer the dove colour."

She held out her arm and Rivers pushed on the gloves and buttoned them.

"What day does the play open at the Royalty Theatre?" Denys asked, idly regarding his exquisite boots. He had been up for hours, had ridden out in the park with both the children and a groom. He was handsome, slightly fatter, as specklessly elegant as of old.

"Next week or the week after that. I am not sure."

Denys looked surprised, but waited until Rivers had left the room.

"My dearest, surely you know the date of your sister's play?"

"No, I do not. I haven't seen Lettice for weeks and her letter says nothing about dates," said Isabella crossly.

Her relationship with Lettice was something she felt uncomfortable about with Denys. She needed, was given always, her husband's intense love and admiration. The least hint of criticism in his voice made her angry.

"We will find out," he said comfortably.

He always says "we", she thought, when he means I am in the wrong.

Denys idly glanced out of the high windows at a lime tree, its leaves opening, shiny and yellowish. The sky was full of golden-white clouds against pure blue, and the air smelled beautiful. How well Freddy rides now, how pink Betsy's cheeks were when we were in the park, he thought. And my father loves them and is proud of them. He smiled to himself.

Isabella, with one of her sudden impulses, darted across to him and threw her arms round his neck.

16

(1)

EVEN Isabella, young and strong and ready for enjoyment, found the London season tiring. She grew pale after so many late nights and long days full of engagements. Three miles away across London, her sister was weary for a different reason.

Lettice had played no big role since she had acted in the provinces, and she found the rehearsals an intense strain. She must be at the theatre from morning until night, she scarcely saw her children. By nine every morning the carriage was at the door in Kensington, waiting to take her and Buckley to the Royalty.

The journeys were not cheerful, for Buckley was usually morose and silent. Huddled in her seat, Lettice left him to his thoughts and tried to concentrate on her own role. It seemed impossible. Perhaps my talent is lost, she thought. Perhaps Davenant was right when he gave me parts of only four lines. I *could* act once. But that was when I was young, and did not know the dangers. It is like dreaming that one can fly. I used to do that . . . climb to the top of spires and spread my arms and swim through the air. I can never do it now.

During rehearsals she worked with passionate attention, remembering every word that Davenant said. When she watched him playing—he was Jaques—she tried to discover the mystifying secret of his art.

One morning she and Buckley had begun the wooing scene between Orlando and Rosalind when Davenant suddenly stopped them.

"Wait a bit. What are you afraid of, Vernon?"

"I? Nothing," replied Buckley, with a smile Lettice knew was assumed.

"You are afraid of emotion, that is the fact of it. Orlando is lyrically in love. *You* seem to be playing a man who prefers wrestling matches at court to wooing a beautiful woman."

"I do not wish Orlando to be mawkish," Buckley said shortly.

Lettice knew how unbearable he must find being criticised in front of other actors.

"Mawkish?" repeated Davenant sardonically. "Is that what you think Shakespeare is? If you cannot give us lyric rapture, you cannot give us Orlando either. Lettice, your speech, please."

Lettice, drawing a breath, threw back her head and began:

"Break an hour's promise in love! He that will divide a minute into a thousand parts . . ."

But although Buckley played well enough, indeed he improved as the scene progressed, she knew by a sixth sense that he was angry.

When the rehearsal broke she was on her way back to her dressing-room when Buckley called to her. He was at the doorway of his own room and said, "I want you."

She went meekly into the room. He kicked the door shut. Alone with her, he lost the assumed calm he had worn during the rehearsal. He said in a bullying voice, "All that was *your* fault."

"What do you mean?"

"You speak verse badly and you're monotonous, and Davenant sees us together and blames me. You're becoming very practised at upstaging me too, aren't you? I will not have it!"

She went as pale as he. She was outraged at his brutal tone, at his stupid self-deception. Knowing that anything she said would only make him worse, she cried, "Let me alone!" and rushed from the room.

The rehearsal went better in the afternoon and by the end of the long exhausting day, when they returned in the carriage to Kensington, they were both too tired to talk.

On the morning of the first dress rehearsal Gwynyth was waiting for her in the little dark boxroom.

"Mr. Davenant sent you a message. When you are in costume, you're to go and see him."

"Oh, *Gwynyth*."

Gwynyth dressed her in her Rosalind's first act costume, an elaborate court dress of white and gold. She unpinned Lettice's bright hair and threaded it with pearls. The sickly daylight coming through a window small as that in a dungeon shone down on Lettice, turning her painted face into a mask.

Davenant, not in costume, was standing in his salon when Lettice rustled into the room.

"I wanted a word with you."

322

She said nothing.

He frowned.

"You're not to be anxious. You're in the right way of it."

He gestured as if catching things which floated in the air.

"Grace. Ease. Delicacy. True feeling."

They stood looking at the invisible.

"All there to grasp. Off with you. And give it beans."

(2)

The playbills were freshly posted, the necklace of gas lamps hung like yellow bubbles. The night was chilly. Crowds gathered before the performance was due to begin, to stare as the lines of carriages began to draw up. The horses and turn-outs were the finest in the world, they murmured, and as for the crests on the carriage doors—half Burke's Peerage was coming to the Royalty tonight.

Red carpets were laid across the pavement, so that the ladies would not soil the hems of their skirts. Up this red path came gentlemen in black cloaks, ladies in the colours of a fading rainbow, their heads crowned with diamonds or flowers. They moved slowly up the curved stair, carrying fans and flowers, bowing and smiling to each other.

Isabella, on Denys's arm, walked up the staircase among their friends. She looked beautiful in white satin embroidered with loops of pale blue velvet. The gown showed her thin graceful shoulders and the Earl's diamonds which she liked to wear a good deal. She'd noticed how her diamonds still angered Lady Clare.

The Bagots had taken a box on the right, well placed for Lady Fanny to enjoy a good view of the audience. As the family trooped into the box the Earl sidled over to the largest chair in a corner, into which he fell rather than sat. His stooping figure seemed, to his son's saddened eyes, to grow more crooked as time went by.

Isabella, for all the worldly air which in the past she had aped and which was now real to her, was excited at the coming performance. The theatre was filled with exquisitely dressed people. She looked at the red velvet curtains, a wall between Lettice's world and her own. Behind them Lettice must be shaking with fright. Isabella was filled with sympathy and a forgotten sisterly pride.

Down the ill-lit passage in her boxroom

Lettice was being dressed by Gwynyth. The old woman had brought extra candles and the room for once was bright with light. Gwynyth tied the laces of Lettice's costume, low-cut, displaying more bosom than Lettice approved. She gave the dress an unsuccessful tug to hide the division between her breasts.

In the distance they heard the call-boy's voice: "Overture and beginners, IF you please." There was a rap at her door. Lettice felt slightly faint. "Miss Winter. Your call, please!"

She put out both hands, and Gwynyth pressed them. Not looking back, Lettice left the dressing-room with a first step. As she walked down the passage her heart beat so violently that she felt stifled, her breath was short and quick, there was a dazzle in her eyes.

It was the turning-point of her life.

(3)

Lettice woke next morning full of painful uncertainty. The audience had cheered, and after the performance everybody, even Davenant, had congratulated her. But only

325

the morning papers could tell her if she had succeeded.

Buckley was silent during breakfast, and left in a brougham immediately after the meal, saying he had "work to do". She supposed he would go to the Garrick, drink too much and get over his disappointment at the cool applause for his Orlando. Poor Buckley. What stupid creatures we actors are, she thought, egotists, children.

She could not settle, tried to read, changed her dress twice and finally—telling Mary Anne to take the children out into Kensington Gardens—left for the Royalty.

When the brougham drew up at the theatre and she saw her name on the playbills her heart fluttered. It was an emotion she hadn't felt since she was a girl and her name had been posted on the walls. She used to cross the street to avoid passing a playbill with LETTICE WINTER on it. Going through the Stage Door, she averted her eyes.

Davenant's doors stood open, and when she tapped he called, "I wondered how long it would be before you came."

He was sitting comfortably, a silver coffee pot in front of him. Would she take a cup? Various newspapers, the *Morning Post, The*

Times and the *Athenaeum* were on the table.

"Of course, you have read the morning press," he said indifferently.

She shook her head in silence.

"And after your Rosalind last night, you slept like a log."

"Very badly, sir."

"Must be the artistic temperament."

How waggish theatre people are, she thought, inwardly sighing. They'll make jokes on Judgement Day.

"You were worried about me, Lettice, confess it. Do they realise he *continues* to be great, you thought, lying on your sleepless couch."

"You were superb."

"Of course I was, dammit. You may now read the public journals, madam, and judge for yourself if I succeeded. There are also one or two words about you. No more than that, I fear."

She picked up the journals and began to read. All he could see was a little fore-shortened nose and chin, red curls escaping from her straw bonnet. She looked demure. It amused him to think of her last night, face passionate, voice trembling with emotion. She was a mixture of innocence and the keenest apprehension, of soft sensibility and hardness. She intrigued him.

Lettice was reading what the critics had thought of her.

"Radiantly beautiful . . . emotion, grace, spirit . . . the signs of youthful genius," she read. "Exquisitely managed and melodious voice," "high comedy which left nothing to be desired . . ."

"You have gone very pale," remarked Davenant with interest.

There was a knock on the door and Augustus Bryson came into the room. He wore an exaggeratedly waisted dark purple coat and a frilled stock. The scent of eau-de-cologne came in strongly with him

He bowed to Davenant, and then gave Lettice a nicely-judged nod.

"Might I have a word with you, sir?"

"Sit down first," was the barked reply.

Bryson should have known after years with Davenant that the actor would never speak, when seated, to a person standing over him.

"You mentioned the matter of Miss Winter's dressing-room," said Bryson. "I have been endeavouring to ascertain how this may be altered."

"So she's closer to me and the stage."

"Precisely so," said Bryson, frowning; he reminded Lettice of her father. He produced a plan of the dressing-rooms and spread it on top of the notices. Davenant nodded indifferently.

"Ask Miss Winter. You have to start worrying now whether *she* is pleased or not."

Lettice was privately amused. So the little dark boxroom was a thing of the past, was it?

"I thought perhaps here," said Bryson, indicating a room.

"Oh. But that is Mrs. Courtenay's dressing-room," said Lettice.

"Mrs. Courtenay informs me she wishes to be where she can keep an eye on her daughter."

"The redoubtable Kitty," remarked Davenant.

Lettice detested Kitty Courtenay who was eight years old, clever and a perfect brat.

"Exactly so," said Bryson.

Lettice looked at the plan, then up at Bryson and gave him a slow radiant smile.

"It is a lovely room and so close to the stage. Thank you, Mr. Bryson."

"Don't thank him. My idea. You can go, Bryson, when you've told me the state of the Box Office. Good? I'm glad to hear it. Later I mean to talk to you about the size of my name on the playbills."

Davenant watched Bryson go, then leaned back in his chair.

"So you are to be the new one who delights London. They're going to flock. All the men will fall in love with you, that's certain."

She smiled again.

"How shall you like that, mm?"

"I'll be a little sorry for them."

"Hypocrite!"

17

(1)

EARLY in the summer of 1844 Lady Fanny was married. Her husband, the eldest son of a family friend, was suitable in every way. Lord John Ransome was tall, quiet, pleasantly humorous, with one of those skull-like faces which sometimes go with the constitution of an ox. He was probably not in love with Lady Fanny, but he paid her the right gallantries, danced with her at every ball, spent hours of the day riding or walking with her, or sitting at Bagot House with her, and generally played the part a devoted suitor should.

"You certain he's what you want, Fan?" demanded her father after the offer had been made.

"Oh yes, Papa."

"Strong enough to manage him? He's no fool."

"John will manage *me*," was the inevitable reply.

The Earl had to be content with that. He had never understood his eldest child, but she seemed happy and there was nothing wrong with young Ransome or his fortune. Daughters must marry judiciously and maintain the interest and honour of the family.

Lady Fanny was married with pomp and richness at St. Margaret's, Westminster, and left for a Scottish honeymoon.

The family was oddly diminished when she was gone. There was no prim-faced correct little person to pour tea in the drawing-room, wearing her air of head of the household. Even Lady Clare missed her. There were responsibilities in the running of a great house which, despite skilful and devoted upper servants, should be taken on by the mistress. Lady Fanny had enjoyed them. Lady Clare had no intention of doing one of them. She would rule when the household was her own. In short, when she married.

Throughout her twenty-three years, Lady Clare had been ludicrously spoiled. Her beloved old Hopton had begun it; her governess had followed suit; the Bagot servants admired and served her; her family indulged her. From a little child she had been called "the pretty one", as Carteret was "the heir" and her sister "the eldest". Isabella had taken away Lady Clare's claim to be sole Bagot beauty. It wasn't only for her low birth that Lady Clare disliked her sister-in-law.

Society looked on Lady Clare as one of the most interesting prizes in the marriage market. Lady Fanny had a fortune as large, but there was no excitement in seeing her wed, she resembled everybody else. Lady Clare was difficult and men thought it would be challenging to win such a rich beautiful shrew. Young men arrived, one after the other, to pay court to her.

Lady Clare wasted no time in her refusals. She told her family about them, dismissing her suitors with one sentence for each gentleman.

"Papa, the man is a booby."

"Carteret, can you mean I should marry a man who wears scent?"

"Cousin, you have never seen my new suitor on a horse."

It was the Bagots' fault that she behaved so badly, that her opinion of herself was so high and that she became more and more hard to please. Her poise and beauty grew. Despite the large Bagot nose and occasional air of an angry boy, she could look enchantingly pretty. Sometimes her father thought she had a fondness for her cousin, a particular fondness. Certainly Robert was the member of the family who managed her best. On occasions the girl was positively melting when he was about. But only at times. On the whole her character, like that of a vicious horse, seemed to grow worse as she grew older.

The family, with the exception of Isabella, were amused. Clare's dismissal of suitors was a kind of proof of breeding.

"She's taking her time and I'm damned glad of it," said her father to Robert.

The Earl sent for her one morning when she and Robert were about to go riding in the Row. She came into his study, the skirt of her dark habit over her arm. Her fair hair was netted behind her ears.

"Sit down, girl," said the Earl.

"The horses are waiting, Papa."

"I daresay. Let 'em."

There was a pause.

"How's Hopton?" he said abruptly.

Lady Clare looked at him.

"Not better."

"What does the doctor say now?"

"That it's a matter of time."

334

He said nothing. He had an idea she was suffering.

"And don't say," said Lady Clare in a grating voice, "that we all have to die sometime."

He knew the old woman had been ill for weeks; Robert and he had consulted with the doctor but nothing much could be done. Hopton, devotedly nursed, was in the servants' quarters, visited daily by Clare.

"Your cousin tells me Beauchamp's son has offered for you," said the Earl, changing the subject.

"So he says."

"To whom? To you?"

"I would not think much of a man who went to you before speaking to me."

The Earl let her impertinence, and the incorrect manner of the marriage offer, go for the moment.

"Are you interested in Beauchamp's son? What's his name?"

"Lord Paul. He is a clever fellow. No, I shall not marry him."

"You can't spend the next ten years, y'know, refusing every eligible man in London."

"I am two years younger than Fanny," was the sharp reply.

"Not getting any younger, though. All these refusals. It comes to my mind it is getting a silly habit with you."

"I fail to see why this matter is so pressing," she said, quite furious at the unaccustomed criticism. "The last hasty marriage in our family was disastrous enough."

"Carteret's marriage is accepted, miss. We will hear no more of that old story."

She stood up, fastening a button of her tight black glove and turned to her father with the light full on her face.

"Papa, I will marry when I am ready to do so. You need not trouble yourself about my choice. *I*, at any rate, will not bring disgrace on the family."

She swept out of the room.

Robert was waiting, handsome in his bright yellow riding coat and mounted on a magnificent grey. Clare's own horse, fretting and bored, was being led up and down the courtyard by the groom. Robert grinned, and the two set off towards the park, Clare riding stylishly, followed by two grooms who were as much her slaves as every other man in London.

It was one of those mornings of early summer that are almost too perfect. The Row was crowded ... horses and riders, ladies and their tall-hatted escorts trotted and cantered to and fro, throwing up the tan in spurts round the horses' feet; young men leaned on the railings watching the equestrians and judging the horse-flesh. In the centre of the Row people walked, the ladies carefully shaded by silk parasols, moving in a mass of vivid colours.

At the far end of the Row, Robert and Clare dismounted. She tossed the reins to her groom.

"We will walk for a while."

Robert offered her his arm, but she refused. She walked, skirt looped over her wrist, in silence.

"How is Hopton?" Robert said.

"Very ill. I do not wish to talk of it."

Like Denys, Clare's feeling for the family servants was passionate. It was to them she gave her sudden, wonderful smiles. She said abruptly, "I have something I wish to tell you."

Robert gave her a friendly look, but for once her face did not soften.

"It is to do with Carteret's wife."

He stopped walking very suddenly.

"What have you been up to?"

"*I?*"

"You very much dislike Isabella and never bother to conceal it."

For all her farouche ways, he knew that his approval mattered to Clare. But she was unmoved by the sharp tone of his voice.

"What I have to say is none of my doing, Robert. Georgina Sheffield called yesterday. She told me," said Clare, fixing her eyes on him, "that there are rumours."

"Rumours? What rumours?"

"That Frederick may not be Carteret's child."

"*What did you say?*"

She did not reply, for some people passed them and bowed. Robert and she responded automatically. When they were alone again, Clare said, "Do you suppose I like speaking of this? Georgina Sheffield has a spiteful tongue and repeats the merest gossip. I told her the thing was preposterous and that she was a fool, and worse, to repeat it. Perhaps she believed me. She wishes to remain on good terms with me, for some reason. I was very unpleasant."

Robert was aghast. "But what grounds—

surely you asked her where she had obtained—"

"I did not need to," she interrupted, "I know."

"Clare, explain yourself, for God's sake."

They were again passed by some acquaintances; one lady among the group gave them a knowing smile.

Robert said briefly, "We must walk."

They moved under the trees.

"I have known of the matter for weeks, Robert. From Hopton. She had a letter written by Carteret's wife. From years ago. Hopton is so ill, and the letter was on her conscience. She gave it to me. That is where the rumour has come from. Hopton was an old friend of Georgina Sheffield's maid. She must have told her. Swearing secrecy," added Clare, with an arid smile.

"You have been aware of a possible scandal attaching to Isabella for weeks? And done nothing!"

She raised her eyebrows.

"Yes, I did know and I did intend doing nothing. Do you suppose I would render Carteret unhappy? Mention such a matter, even to *you*, unless I was forced to do so? As for his wife, what Hopton told me only proved something I knew by instinct from the first. I merely avoided her. Georgina Sheffield talking of it is another matter. That maid, Banks, is a jealous cat of a creature. I never understood why Hopton liked her. I shall buy her off."

"You will do no such thing."

"But why?" she said, surprised. "Money may persuade her to keep quiet."

He knew her haughtiness hid a distaste of scandal that made her shudder. Yet she had calmly decided to dirty those clean hands.

"Leave this to me, Clare."

She looked at him earnestly.

"You do not think I am afraid—"

"Oh," he said, "I never think that."

(2)

When they returned to Bagot House, she went to her room, and then came to Robert's study. She put a piece of paper into his hand. It was creased and faded but Robert recognised Isabella's handwriting.

"Where did Hopton get this?"

"She did not tell me."

"Clare."

"She took it. Why not?"

340

There was no answer to that.

"I will leave you with it," she said, turning to go.

"You have told Hopton to speak to nobody about all this!"

"She is dying," Clare said fiercely, and ran from the room.

Robert told the footman he was not to be disturbed, and sat down, the letter in his hand. It was dated five years ago, and was no more than a few lines.

"Oh Buck, of course, at twelve or even before. I am going to the Quadrant, then to Jay for silks. *How* I long! Bella."

Buck. Buckley Vernon. The actor her sister had married, whom Robert had seen at the Royalty Theatre occasionally. Robert was filled with horror. Did this scrap of paper prove that the child was not Carteret's? He could scarcely bear to ask himself that. The mere existence of this letter could be tragic. He thought, not of Isabella or the little boy he dearly loved, but of his cousin.

He had known Denys since he had come to live with the Bagots as a child after his parents died. He understood Denys with such

341

intuitive love that he seemed to know, always, what Denys would feel and what he would do. That day when they had rescued a young girl trapped in the mob . . . as Denys had bent over her, Robert had known his cousin would love her.

What now? The dread in Robert's thoughts was not the question of the child's parentage but of his cousin's nature, his deep sense of the old-fashioned quality of honour. If only Denys were a realist, a cynic, like his father. How did one grapple with something as strong and immovable as plain virtue? It might be physically true that Frederick *was* Denys's child. But what terrible wound was this knowledge going to inflict on Denys's trust in his wife?

Poor Isabella. She had grace and spirit, and was in the full tide of social success after taking the near-impossible step into a closed world. If this liaison had happened, and Robert felt sure it had, she was a fool or had remarkable courage. Either way, she was to be pitied.

The old Earl was out at his club or the Lords, both places he enjoyed for company exclusively masculine. At last, when it was time to change for dinner, Robert heard his uncle's voice. The Earl came in with sidling gait.

"Not changed yet? I'm late. Londonderry caught me with some scheme he is putting up for the railways. Waiting for me, were you?"

"Yes, sir. May I have a moment?"

"No more than one. Now, Swayne, off you go. Stop fussing."

He shooed the butler out of the room, and collapsed into a chair.

"Well?"

"Trouble, sir."

"I can see that."

The Earl waited.

"Clare has spoken to me about some kind of servant's scandal."

"*Clare* has?"

"The Sheffield girl called yesterday. And said there are rumours going about. Concerning Isabella."

The Earl said nothing. His face was as hard as stone.

"It seems they came originally from old Hopton. She was maid to Isabella, you remember, when Carteret and she lived here."

"What trash are you talking?"

"Hopton apparently told one of the Sheffield servants that Frederick may not be my cousin's child."

There was a profound silence.

Finally the Earl said, "Evidence? I take it there is something. Or is it just talk?"

"This, sir."

The Earl took the letter and read it. He did not bother to exclaim, but put the letter on to the table as if not wishing to continue holding it. His face was deeply thoughtful. Finally he said, "Carteret will not stand for it. The heir. With such a question, such a possibility, hanging over the child, he will have to be told—he could hear it from others."

"I know, sir."

"Times have changed, that's the devil of it. When I was young . . . I could name you two fellows in society now who are bastards, one of them a Royal bastard at that. But Freddy . . ."

His face twisted for a moment.

"Clare wished to buy the woman off," Robert said. "But I will see to that."

"Do so. Pay her and put the fear of God into her."

The Earl sighed, took out a fob watch and looked at it short-sightedly.

"We must change. I will see Carteret's wife."

Robert noticed the lack of her Christian name.

"Does Carteret ride out in the mornings?"

"Always, sir. Mostly with me."

"Good. Then I will call on her in the morning."

As the two men reached the staircase, the Earl said, "I feel old."

(3)

Isabella was surprised when she was told that the Earl was waiting for her in the drawing-room. She was in the nursery with the children and their nurse, playing with a wooden horse on wheels, pushing it across the floor. Freddy was quite crimson with laughter.

When she heard the Earl had arrived, Isabella thought what a mercy it was that she was wearing her grey and yellow silk, and why was her father-in-law abroad so early. He never called except in the late afternoon for a cup of tea.

The front drawing-room was full of sunlight but when she went into the room, her father-in-law had his back to the window. He wore his customary old-style coat of black, a black satin stock. He was a sombre figure in this room of dove greys and soft blues and little gilded sofas.

"My lord, how kind of you to come," said Isabella, all grace and welcome.

He took her hand for a fraction of a second and no more. They sat down. Like the actress she had been, she sensed that something was different. She was inexplicably frightened as she gave a smile.

"Are you a liar, my girl?" he said suddenly.

"I do not understand you, my lord, are you making a joke—"

"You're in trouble. Grave trouble. Are you going to lie yourself out of it?"

His harshest voice was very harsh, a tone she'd never heard before. He saw with grudging approval that she did not go red as other people did when they were threatened. Her expressive face went pale. She was very still.

"Are you going to ask me what I'm talking about?"

"That is not necessary, my lord, since it must be why you are here."

A cool customer. All the better.

"Carteret knows nothing about this," he

said, "which is why I called while he was out. Word has come to me of a grave scandal attached to your name."

She remained with her eyes fixed on him.

"It is being said that the boy is not my son's child."

Isabella flashed round at him, full of anger.

"Who dares say such a thing?"

He folded his hands over the top of his silver-handled stick, and leaned his chin on it. He had the look of a bird of prey facing some soft creature. A mouse. A mole.

"So you deny it, eh?"

"Deny it! That Freddy is not my husband's son! What a gross, disgusting thing to be said! By whom? To whom?"

Her face was brilliant with indignation. In the role of insulted great lady, she threw back her head.

"There is a letter of yours to an actor," he said, speaking as if the matter was almost too repugnant to be mentioned. "Your maid—"

"Hopton!"

"Indeed. Hopton."

He stood up, giving her a look in which there was no trace of sympathy, even of humanity. "You'd best tell Carteret."

347

"Tell him what? That servants have been spreading lies?"

"Yes. Tell him that."

He gave a brief inclination of the head, and went out.

(4)

Isabella's courage, like that of the actress who must step on stage despite shuddering nerves, deserted her the moment the Earl was gone. She felt deathly sick. She went upstairs to her boudoir, and sat down on the window-seat. She could not keep still, but rocked to and fro. Who knew? What did they know? What letter had she written to Buckley, and how had Hopton obtained it? She sat, thinking of Hopton watching her during those forgotten, lunatic weeks of her love affair. Hugging her shoulders in an unconscious position of fear, she thought of Freddy. "Nobody knows whether he is Buckley's," she thought feverishly. "Not even me. I shall deny it all. Deny it and deny it. Oh God."

Tearless and desolate, she shut her eyes, wondering how she could have done that fatal thing. The fever for Buckley, the desire and its desperately exciting reward were gone.

She could remember nothing. She was frightened and in pain. And worst of all, she had a feeling that she had lost Denys.

18

(1)

SHE had never lacked courage. Denys
came in from riding, wandered lazily
into her room and kissed her. She spoke
at once.

She was indignant, angry but steady.

"You can imagine. I am completely horrified," she finished.

He listened in silence. He had been sitting
by the window in the seat he always used,
long legs stretched in front of him and when
she stopped speaking she waited, almost in
agony, for him to look up. But he did not.
Staring at the ground he asked her questions.
Who had started the story? What had the Earl
said, what had been done to stop it? She could
not tell him.

"Oh Denys—" she instinctively stretched
out her hands as she had done in even the
smallest trouble, for him to grasp them.

He stood up, excused himself courteously,
and left the room.

It seemed to Isabella from that moment as if there was no sunshine any more. She had been happy. It was gone. From the moment the Earl had come to the house, everything was changed. Her life altered, slowly at first and then with terrible swiftness.

In the days that followed she scarcely saw her husband.

Courteously, he explained that it would be necessary for him to stay for a while at Bagot House.

"There are matters to be talked over."

"But Denys—"

"We will meet at the Lennox's for dinner tonight, and I will, of course, bring you home before I return to Bagot House."

For the first time in their lives together, she had no power over him. Nothing she said could touch him, he was a cold stranger. It was all the worse because he was so polite.

At Bagot House, Denys spoke at length to Clare. He did not see Hopton, he knew his presence would alarm her and she was growing very weak. Clare promised to ask the old woman some questions. It seemed, said Clare, returning with red eyes from the interview, that Hopton had followed Isabella on one occasion. Had seen her in the street with

351

a gentleman Hopton did not recognise. Hopton had taken the letter from Isabella's desk. There was no incontrovertible proof but only suspicions, disturbing, uncertain, degrading to listen to.

Robert saw the lady's maid, and gave the woman money. He was very hard on her, hoping he had sufficiently alarmed her to persuade her that silence was wise. But scandals were curious things. Merely by existing in a few people's minds they seemed to come alive like a cloud of mosquitoes, stinging and multiplying. Within a week, other members of society apart from the Sheffield girl were repeating the story.

One wet afternoon when the Earl and Robert were in the study, Carteret came into the room.

"You're drenched," exclaimed his father. "Swayne must fetch you a dry coat."

He rang for the butler. Carteret gave his coat to Swayne and stood in his embroidered waistcoat, mopping the rain from his face. His usually perfect boots were splashed with mud.

"The rain came on while I was riding," he said indifferently. "I hope I do not disturb you both."

His appearance shocked them.

"Gentle heavens, boy, have you been swimming in the Thames? Here's Swayne with a dry coat. Swayne, have the fire lit, the room's cold as charity, and a glass of madeira for his lordship."

"Nothing, I thank you, Swayne."

Swayne looked at Carteret much as his father had done, then bent to put a match to the fire. When he had gone, the Earl and Robert waited for Carteret to speak. They both suffered for him just then. The Earl looked at his son's haggard face. God, he thought, when you marry an actress you take a mad risk. Bagots had done foolish things in the past and a dance it led them. A dance of death on more than one occasion when duelling was the thing. Damn Clare. And damn the boy for looking as if he'd been shot in the breast.

Robert thought his cousin's appearance ghastly. He looked as if he had not slept for days. To see him gave Robert physical pain as if somebody had bruised his own heart.

"I have come from the Temple. I saw Lord Whitfield," Carteret said.

"What in Hades did you do that for?" growled his father.

Denys made a slight movement with his hand. "We cannot leave it as it is. How long is it since Clare told you, Robert? Two weeks? It is beginning to be known in London. Isabella will not go out of the house."

"What did Lord Whitfield say?" Robert asked.

"That it should be kept out of the hands of the lawyers."

"I agree," said the Earl. Neither he nor Robert looked at each other—both had a sense of overwhelming relief.

Carteret said nothing for a while. He held out his hands to the fire.

"She has to be cleared," he said at last.

"From what? A parcel of lies."

"Father. I don't know."

"Some stupid letter which means nothing. And the babblings of an old woman out of her wits."

He used, deliberately, a tone of contemptuous dismissal. Carteret shut his eyes.

"There's no proof Freddy is mine."

"Of course he is yours!" burst out the Earl angrily. "The boy's a Bagot. Any fool can see it. Are you telling me you'll ignore Whitfield and bring in the lawyers like a pack of jackals to destroy us? Submit the family to such a thing? By God, I won't stand for it!"

The veins stood out on either side of his forehead. His usually parchment-coloured face was crimson.

"No, I won't do that, sir."

"Then what shall you do?"

"I don't know."

Denys stared into the fire and his father and his cousin stared at him. He said in the exhausted voice now natural to him, "I have told Isabella I think the children should go to Bagot Park for the present. I am sure my grandmother would go with them. Do you agree?"

"Certainly."

"Thank you."

"I saw your grandmother yesterday," said the Earl. "She doesn't know anything yet, so the sooner they leave the better. Give her something to do, fussing over the children. Better for them too. Get some country air."

"So you agree, sir? With Lord Whitfield?"

"I agree with anything that's best for the family, Carteret. Do you wish me to see Whitfield and have a further talk?"

It was curious to hear the Earl ask such a

question, to hear the Earl ask his son anything.

"If you would, I would be very grateful."

Thanking them, he went quickly out of the
room.

(2)

When the children left London, Isabella was
so crushed in spirit that she didn't know how
to get through the days.

Denys had returned from his stay at Bagot
House but no longer shared her bedroom.
Would she forgive him if he moved out for a
little, he said, he was sleeping badly and
might disturb her?

He also said that perhaps she should not go
about much in society, "for the present".

He only once mentioned the scandal, when
he asked if she would be good enough to see
Lord Whitfield at the Temple sometime.

"Lord Whitfield is a friend of my father's
and a distinguished advocate. He only con-
cerns himself with advice," Denys said. "My
cousin will accompany you." He paused and
added in a colourless voice, "Lord Whitfield
may wish to see that other person, but he will
make the arrangements."

356

That was all.

Isabella had sworn to her husband that she was innocent. Denys never spoke of it again. He was going through a kind of farce, which she supposed was done to protect her. She knew he had been aware from the first that the accusation might be true.

His heart and his senses told him so. He did not necessarily believe Frederick was not his son, but he did know she had had a lover that summer when he had been away for weeks in the North.

What was terrible for Isabella was that Denys no longer loved her. From the moment she'd spoken of the scandal, his love had withered and died. Or perhaps he *did* still love her, which was why he looked so haunted. But he would never take her in his arms again, never make love to her, never be her real husband, never be happy, never laugh, never be Denys again. The thought filled her with terror. Surely to change like that was impossible? Would he not recover, forgive and accept her as a fallible but not despicable woman worth loving and living with?

For the first time since she had unthinkingly married a high-born stranger Isabella was faced with the substance of his nature. He was a patrician, a man of honour, a man to whom betrayal was like treason against one's country, a mortal sin. He might forgive her. He would never take her back.

She was waited upon and maided, dressed in beautiful clothes and Denys took her out in the carriage. They drove to places where there were the least of the season's crowds. Certainly they were bowed to. One or two of Denys's men friends came to dine and were gallant to her. No ladies were invited.

Lonely and frightened, at times filled with hate for Clare and her old, sick enemy Hopton, at other times miserably condemning herself because she had been found out, Isabella dared not see Lettice. How much did Lettice know? Society and the theatre were widely apart, yet now and again the circles intersected. Actresses, particularly successful ones as Lettice had recently become, were invited into society now and then. And men of rank enjoyed the world of the theatre, in the hope that it was as immoral as its reputation.

Isabella wrote to her parents in Richmond, saying she would like to spend the day with them. She ordered the carriage early while

Denys was out riding. It was a relief to leave the house, which was horribly quiet since the children were gone.

The road to Richmond was lined with budding trees, the fields were fresh green, it was sunny. She saw some new season's lambs. In her mood of despondency she thought how little she had seen her parents during the last years. It had been Denys whose generosity had released them from the bondage of the circuits: he had bought them their house. It had been Denys who sometimes arranged for the children to spend the day with them. Denys. Always Denys.

The cottage, with a walled garden, was built at the edge of the park and reached by a secluded path. At the front a flowering currant bush was covered with sweet-smelling pink flowers; there were daffodils in the grass. Isabella told the groom not to come back for her until late. "I will dine with Mrs. Winter," she said.

The groom, whose family had been with the Bagots for years, said politely, "His lordship dines at home tonight, my lady."

"I know, Longstaffe, but his lordship does not expect me."

As the carriage drove away, Ellen opened

the door and Isabella threw her arms round her mother's neck.

Ellen, embarrassed and pleased, laughed as she led Isabella into the house.

"What a change, my child, to see you here. I'm afraid your father will not be home for some time, he has gone to the theatre at Richmond. He cannot keep away from the old life. He tells me the manager may offer him an engagement for the summer. Poor Thomas!"

She laughed in her unsympathetic little voice. She looked older, smaller. Her pale blue dress with gold and blue buttons down the front suited her ageing brown face and still-dark hair tidily coiled. She was so dear and familiar, so far from the rich world in which Isabella had despaired, that she almost began to cry.

The cottage drawing-room was homely and neat, with chintz covers, a piano, a canary in a cage. Isabella, for the first time for years, sank down on the floor. Her mother patted her hair. Not as a caress but to tuck a stray curl in place.

"I am in trouble, Mama."

"So I see."

Ellen looked at her with dark unblinking eyes.

"Don't say anything until you've heard, Ma. I want to tell you exactly what happened."

Isabella sat by her mother's side, and poured out the official, untrue story. Lady Clare hated her and so did the old nurse. Together they had invented lies about herself and Buckley Vernon. What was worse, they said that Freddy . . .

The words tumbled out. She was to see Lord Whitfield. "He is a Law Lord, whatever that means. Everything is frightening, Ma. They have taken the children away. To Sussex."

When Isabella stopped speaking Ellen said, "You have not mentioned your husband."

"He is very upset."

Her own hollow words shocked Isabella. "No, it's worse than that. It is as if he were ill. He is quite changed."

"You mean he believes it."

"He would never say so."

"That makes it worse," Ellen said.

She did not ask whether it was true. Isabella, who had not been able to decide whether to confess or not, realised that her mother had no intention of asking the question. Maybe Isabella had deceived her husband. Maybe the little boy, her grandson, was not a Bagot at all. Ellen's attitude was steady: she accepted on its face value that Isabella needed family love and support. Ellen would give her both, together with penetrating counsel.

They sat without talking while Isabella picked at the braid of her beautiful yellow dress and the canary sang so loudly that its body trembled.

"Do the family stand for or against you?"

"Robert is the only one who speaks to me. He has come to Finstock Lodge to dine."

"Why must you go to this Law Lord?"

"Robert told me it is only for advice."

"Who gains, suppose they decide you guilty?"

"But they can't! I told you—"

"I said *suppose*. Would Freddy be dis-inherited?"

"I don't know. Yes. I suppose so."

"Who is next in succession after Viscount Carteret?"

"Freddy, of course. Oh, after that it is Robert, the cousin, who would inherit."

"Perhaps Cousin Robert began the scandal. He has much to gain."

Isabella gave a shocked choking laugh.

"You don't know him. That is literally impossible."

"Nothing is 'literally' impossible, Isabella," said her mother as cynically as the old Earl.

Ellen, telling her daughter to undo her bonnet or she would get a headache, left the room to speak to the cook. Isabella was alone. Looking drearily round, she noticed that the room was full of objects from her childhood. There was a watercolour of a mountain she herself had painted, a china box with sailors on the lid used by her father for his cigars. A patchwork cushion made by Lettice. Lettice! She had not spoken to her mother about Lettice.

Ellen returned, saying the meal would soon be ready and that Isabella must eat. "You are too thin."

"Am I? I hadn't noticed."

"Your neck is scrawny. You should wear a necklace to cover those salt-cellars," said Ellen, pointing to the hollows at the base of Isabella's throat.

"Ma," burst out Isabella, "do you think Letty knows?"

"I wondered when we would come to your sister."

363

"Oh, I am sorry! Everything is so horrible and I am become so selfish."

The moment she said that her mother's hard expression changed.

"I am sure Lettice and Buckley have heard nothing. They were here with the children yesterday. There was some slight trouble, but it was about another thing." Ellen sighed.

"What thing?"

"Buckley does not enjoy your sister's success. He was quite unkind to her in my presence. Like a silly child. Your father and I think the marriage is not happy at present, and we can only hope it will settle down. But suppose they should hear of this scandal through gossip!" Ellen shook her head with dismay at the thought. "It could do untold harm. I will have to tell them. Or perhaps your father should do it."

"Oh, no! I must do it!"

"Are you sure you're strong enough?" Ellen said. "You'll need tact. You're in no state to use your brains just now."

"I shall tell Buckley at once," Isabella said. "He must know before he hears it from somebody else. I certainly could not—*should* not—tell Lettice. Buck must do that."

By the way she spoke, the determined way

she folded her lips, even the manner of speaking Buckley's name, Ellen knew he'd been her lover. Isabella's no actress, she thought grimly. She never was.

(3)

The next day, while Denys was out, Isabella drove to the theatre an hour before the performance. It was *As You Like It*, and the bills had LETTICE WINTER on them in letters three inches high. Isabella ordered the carriage to wait, and asked at the Stage Door for Mr. Vernon.

She had deliberately chosen dark clothes, a mole-coloured velvet cloak with a hood over her hair, and when Buckley swung down the passage he did not recognise her. He came up, wearing a questioning, merry expression. She had not seen him for years, and his handsome looks struck her with a feeling of forgotten familiarity.

"Isabella! I scarcely knew you. How very pleasant. May I give you a glass of madeira in my dressing-room? Star dressing-room, you know. Bigger than Letty's, as it happens."

He laughed in the old, conceited way, like a boy winning a game played against a stupid rival. He pressed her hand as they walked down the stone corridor.

"If you want to see your sister as well, it will have to be after the performance. She locks herself into her dressing-room before the play—says she has to be alone. You would think she was Sarah Siddons. Poor Letty," he said patronisingly, and she heard an actor's jealousy in his voice.

The corridor echoed with the noise of the cast, talking, laughing, getting ready for the performance; the smell of size and lamp-oil was strong.

Buckley's dressing-room was spacious. Gilded, stiffened costumes lay about, like men collapsed when drunk. There were dishes of coloured powder by the looking-glass. The smell of them, sweetish and dusty, came to her as if she could literally smell the past. She sat down, and the hood fell away from her hair.

"I have come with bad news. People know. About us."

He was so shocked by her words that his mouth fell open.

"What the hell are you talking about?"

She repeated what she had told her mother,

366

but with a difference. He knew the slander was true.

Buckley remained aghast.

"What proof have they? There was nothing!"

"A letter that I wrote you."

"I always burned them, the moment I had read them."

What practice he must have had, she thought indifferently.

"I suppose Hopton stole some letter before I had sent it to you. It is not impossible. And then, perhaps she followed me. They have told me nothing, except that there *is* a letter. It is as if they will not put me on trial. Or are afraid to."

"What does your husband think of this?" he demanded. He was frightened, and she despised him for it. How stupid he looked. She was wrong to think him handsome. Did I sacrifice Denys, she thought, and my happiness and my name and my life for *this*?

"He has not said."

"Has he left you?"

She gave a cold smile.

"People like Denys are different from you and me. He is standing by me."

"He believes you innocent? You've sworn?"

367

"Oh, yes. I have sworn."

He still looked thunderstruck.

"Lettice mustn't find out. My God! What would happen if she knew?"

Isabella stood up. She felt tired and the room, with its scented smell, oppressed her.

"Buckley, I came to say that you must tell her at once. The story has got about, I don't know how, but people are talking. You must tell her before she hears it from someone else."

"Tell her what, for God's sake? Go to her and say I'm sorry, dear, but I slept with your sister and the child she calls the Honourable Frederick Bagot may be my bastard! Lettice would never forgive you."

"You mean she would not forgive *you*," she exclaimed, blushing at his brutal manner. She had forgotten men could behave like that to women.

She held up both hands to stop him speaking again.

"I don't want to hear another word. I came to warn you because we're in dreadful trouble. I shall continue to deny it and you must too. But I tell you, if you don't speak to Lettice in time, she is certain to hear of it. Now, goodbye."

She ran from the room, muffled in her dark cloak like a mourner leaving a funeral.

The streets were crowded with coaches, the journey back to Regent's Park took longer than usual. When she went into the house the butler told her a visitor was waiting for her. For a moment she thought it might be the Earl and a pang of fright went through her. But the butler said it was Mr. Robert.

She went into the drawing-room; Robert, who had been looking out of the window, came over to her quickly and kissed her hands.

"I'm glad to see you, cousin," she said.

"I'm afraid you will not be. I have bad news."

"The children!"

He made a sudden movement of concern and kindness.

"No, no, they are well. Very happy and spending time with their grandmother in the gardens. I saw them two days ago. It is something else. I have just come from Brooks's where I was with Deno. Lord Gough is a friend of my uncle's—they were in the same regiment years ago. Deno applied to serve under him and has just received his papers. His regiment is going abroad. To India."

She stared at him with horror. Half an hour ago she had shocked and frightened Buckley and despised him for the way he had taken her news. As if heaven were revenged on her hard heart she was now the one to receive a blow.

"Oh no, I cannot bear it."

"I asked if I might be the one to tell you," he said, taking her hands again. A feeling of overwhelming grief came over her. Tears rolled slowly down her cheeks. They were the first tears she had shed since that day, weeks ago, when the Earl had stood in this room. So she had been wrong when she said Denys would stand by her. He had given her up in his heart, and had quietly found the best way to cut himself free. She saw his face, his tall lazy figure, heard his voice, felt his arms strongly round her. She began to cry bitterly.

Robert gently stroked her hair.

"Poor girl. Don't cry, Bella, you will break my heart. It is not for ever, you know, only for a while. It really is best just now. The man has been so grieved, so broken up, desperately unhappy. I am sure it is for the best. The army life, work, comrades . . . and he is not leaving you unprotected, he asks me to do everything for you, look after you, care for you. My poor girl. Don't cry. Ah, don't cry."

(4)

When he left her, she went up to her room and asked Rivers to pull the curtains because her head ached.

The Summer evening began to wane.

Isabella lay with her eyes closed. All her spirit, her energetic meeting-life-half-way, her optimism, were gone. She couldn't remember what it felt like to be happy. She imagined, though it was not true, that she'd always known that Denys would go. First the children. Now Denys. She had lost everything, and for what? For lying on Buckley's disordered bed and possessing his muscular white body for a short time—how long, twenty minutes, half an hour? They had never loved for long and "loved" was not the word since Buckley had lusted after her and nothing else. Why, when the pleasure was over he'd sometimes picked up the script of a play! For that she had lost the deep love of a husband she had never understood or treasured sufficiently, the safeness of his home, her children, her name, her honour.

Before she had been discovered she often forgot the past for months at a time. Now it hung over her like a grimacing face, more hideous when she was alone.

I suppose that is being found out, she thought. I'm selfish and I'm a liar. I wanted Buckley and that time when I had him I never even thought of doing wrong or hurting anybody. Now I don't even like him. It is Denys I love.

When she went downstairs, changed into a dark silk evening gown, her hair freshly coiled, she walked into the dining-room as the butler was lighting the candles. It was growing dark. Denys, tall and thin in his black evening coat, was there with his arm along the chimney piece in the indolent way he often stood. The heavy Bagot ring shone on his hand.

He murmured good evening.

During the meal, which neither of them could eat, they managed a kind of conversation for the benefit of the footmen. The farce of this talk told on Isabella's nerves. She was trembling when the butler finally brought in the tray of coffee, extinguished most of the candles, leaving only two burning (something

Isabella in the past had thought romantic). He left them alone.

They sat at each end of a table too long for only two people, separated by an expanse of shining mahogany covered with silver objects so burnished that the silver was almost blue. She poured his coffee and handed it to him. The cup shook in the saucer.

"Robert told me."

She looked beseechingly across the table towards him. He did not respond. He never smiled now, and he had been a man who smiled easily. His round face was like the face of a sick child. With an effort he said, "Robert asked if he might tell you, he seemed to think you would prefer it. I would have told you myself but he insisted."

"It was better I heard it from him. Denys. Oh, Denys. Please, please don't go!"

She hadn't meant to beg or weep and did both. She hid her face in her hands. He did not move, he, the kindest of men, who would have ridden through a storm to save her the slightest headache or disappointment. Without comfort or word she stopped crying. His silence frightened her.

"I am sorry if you are grieved, Isabella. But it is for the best. I do assure you of that. It has often troubled me that I gave up my regiment—"

"You never said so!"

"And Lord Gough is allowing me to be on his personal staff. He is a brave old man, much loved," he went on as if he hadn't heard her. "The children are well cared for with their grandmother and Robert says he will take you to visit them. He is very good. I have arranged with the bankers—"

"Denys, for pity's sake—"

He stood up then and did come towards her, and for a moment, her face piteous in the wavering candlelight, she thought he was going to touch her. She looked up, mournful and lost, but he only gazed at her intently, then gave a kind of bow and went out of the room.

19

(1)

LETTICE had been rehearsing all day, and when she returned to Kensington she was tired. Davenant had decided to revive an old melodrama, *The Orphan of Geneva*, and she was to play the innocent (mawkish, she thought) Thérèse, pursued by a villainous character portrayed by Davenant. The play, Davenant told the actors, was to be "magnificent and spectacular. Storms, castles, ghosts and suchlike to make the audience's eyes pop out."

She came into the house feeling nervous and irritable. The children were in bed, the house quiet. She took off her bonnet and pelisse and went into the downstairs drawing-room in search of Buckley. He was sprawled on a sofa, staring into the garden. He did not get up but turned and looked at her without moving. He was very white in the face and had been drinking.

"Are you well, Buckley?"

He snapped that he was perfectly well. Lettice, never one to continue talking to anybody who snubbed her, sat down and opened her play script.

"Letty. We're in the hell of a mess."

She looked up. Her beauty and poise stung him just then. He said loudly, "It's Isabella. All rubbish and lies but she thinks you ought to know."

Her eyes widened. She said nothing.

"Isabella came to see me at the theatre this afternoon. She says there is some servants' tittle-tattle about herself and me. That we—in short, that we had a love affair years ago. Before you and I were married. A lot of lies. It makes you sick."

He looked at her. He did not know how Lettice would take this or what he expected of her. He was used to scenes with women who wept if they discovered his infidelities, made him promise that *they* were the beloved, rarely even reproached him. Girls in the theatre were easy game. But Lettice said nothing. She sat very still, wearing a ridiculous flounced dress that he thought too young for her. He resented and admired her.

"You're a cool customer, I must say," he

said spitefully. "There is more. They say your sister's boy may be my child."

"Frederick!"

"More lies," Buckley said. "Society people eat and drink scandal. But Isabella said I was to tell you. Warn you."

"Warn me? What has it to do with me?"

He walked over to her, looking at her with a face blurred with drink.

"That's a fine thing. It's your husband they are slandering, isn't it?"

"How do I know it is not true?" Lettice said in a low, icy voice. She stood up and moved away. "Don't come near me, please. Just—just keep away."

"That's a fine thing," he repeated, no longer guilty but beginning to be furious. "That's loyal. I tell you some lying gossip that is going about, and what do you do? You side with the scandalmongers. What kind of woman did I marry, I want to know? You're made of stone."

"Buckley, be quiet!"

She went to the window and stood with her back to him. She felt sick, a mixture of shock and nerves, very like stage fright. She waited for the feeling to go. What was curious was that after that first moment of horror and disbelief, she was not surprised. She remembered things about Buckley and Isabella from the past, things she had been too self-absorbed to notice closely. Her sister's manner with Buckley, long ago in the North, had been strangely uneasy . . . Isabella's excited white face once, when was it?—at the theatre before she and Buckley were married. Buckley's own manner sometimes when she talked of Isabella . . . it was forced. She thought of the little boy she had only rarely seen, a spoiled, handsome little person, perhaps her own children's half-brother, her own husband's bastard.

She felt a hand on her shoulder. He turned her round to face him. He was resentful, angry—but at a loss, and she had never seen him like that before. He liked to arrange life so that he shone. She had a pang of regret because she was stronger than he.

"I shall write to Isabella and say I cannot see her," she said coldly. "Please do not talk of this to me again. Ever."

She left the room.

(2)

Denys's regiment, the Fourth Cavalry, had

378

been mustering in Gravesend for the last couple of days. As soldiers did at the end of leave, the men and their families arrived in the town haphazardly. Lodging-houses were crammed, the streets full of soldiers in scarlet and wives in tartan shawls. Many of the young women carried babies in their arms or led little children by the hand. The soldiers had brought their parents too, grey-haired men who had known other campaigns and thin-faced women.

The *Durham* would be sailing before dawn, when the high tide was just on the ebb. She was a handsome new steamship, but twin-masted and with plenty of sail as well. The old slow East Indiamen of the past would have taken months to reach the Indian Ocean but the *Durham* was fast. The red-coated soldiers would be in India in a matter of weeks. So far away. The atmosphere in the little riverside town was hectic, tense and sad.

On the evening the *Durham* was due to sail, Denys and Robert arrived at Gravesend in the Bagot coach. The Earl had wanted to accompany them, but somehow Robert had dissuaded him and father and son had said goodbye at Bagot House. Robert knew Denys was

379

too wretched to bear a long-drawn-out parting from his father.

When the cousins arrived at the *Nelson Arms* on the quayside, the old-fashioned inn was as crowded as the town. Boxes were heaped in corners, candles shone, laughter was loud and waiters rushed by carrying loaded trays. Robert and Denys were taken up a crooked staircase to a room reserved for them. Like the inn it was beamed, panelled, askew, the floor at an angle, the windows so low that the young men had to stoop to look out of them. It was a bedroom, but Denys would leave it before dawn.

Robert ordered supper and then joined Denys at the window.

"There she is."

The *Durham*, twin masts topped with single lamps, was high in the water, the ship as bright with light as the inn. The stretch of water between ship and shore was bobbing with boats. They plied to and fro, packed with people, and Robert could see the crowd swarming up the ship's side on to the deck.

Denys stood leaning on the windowsill. His scarlet tunic altered him, he was no longer the indolent companion who rode every day in the Row or went to Tattersall's, joked or talked of horses. Robert could feel what Denys was feeling. Everything happening just now, in the inn, in the boats, on the quayside, in the ship, the tears and goodbyes, the feeling of love heightened by coming separation, the families clasping each other close, made Denys's own state worse. He stood, serious and sad and longing to be gone.

(3)

Robert always breakfasted with the Earl in the mornings. It had been something insisted on when he and Denys were boys, punctiliously continued by Denys when they were older although the Earl was morose at breakfast time, almost daring either young man to utter a word.

On the morning following Denys's departure, Robert went to the breakfast-room where the Earl was silently reading his letters. There was the usual sideboard of hot dishes but Robert ate little.

"Have some salmon," said his uncle suddenly.

"I don't think so, thank you, sir."

"Stewed kidneys. You like those. Swayne. Give Mr. Robert a dish of kidneys."

After Robert had again refused the Earl returned to his letters.

The old man was offering him a kind of challenge as if to demand proof that nothing was upsetting him. It's hard for him, Robert thought. He loves Deno and never showed it and is suffering in consequence. There is nothing to be done.

In the afternoon Robert rode to Finstock Lodge. It was sunny, misty, hot. His thoughts were with Denys. The sea would be calm for the beginning of that long journey.

Finstock Lodge lay in the sunshine, looking rich and well cared for. It was a pleasant house with its velvety lawns, a pretty aspen tree in a corner and a bronze statue of a nereid that Denys had brought from Sussex. The statue, Denys said, reminded him of Isabella; Robert, glancing at it now, thought that in the nymph's short nose and high cheekbones there was a look of her . . .

He was shown into the drawing-room which overlooked the park. He found Isabella, in a rose pink dress, sitting on the window-seat with her hands in her lap. It was an effort for her to smile.

"When did he sail?"

"On the ebb. From Gravesend."

"And you saw him off?"

"Yes. The *Durham* was packed to the gunwales with troops. You never saw such crowds. It was pandemonium when the ship was about to move off—"

He realised what he had unwittingly told her.

"Many women came to say goodbye to their men?" Isabella said. "I wish I had been there. I do wish I had."

He was about to answer, but she said, "Don't say it is for the best. Denys kept saying that and we all know, Robert, that it is *for the worst*. Don't let's talk about it."

"I'm afraid we must for a little," he said matter-of-factly. "We have an appointment this afternoon with Lord Whitfield. Don't start like that, Bella. He won't eat you. He's one of those bluff down-to-earth people, everybody likes him. Best get the visit over, don't you think? Unless you have other plans for this afternoon?"

"I am doing nothing."

"Then that's settled," said Robert. "Now. About you. Lady Quenington told me she had invited you to dine with her but you refused. The old Countess of Bovill was also enquiring."

"They are very kind."

He gave a slight grin.

"I doubt that, Bella. Well, old Bovill is rather a duck; Lady Q. is another matter. You know about scandal, you've heard enough of it in past seasons. It can turn into a hurricane and pull its victim up by the roots. Or it can just die away. We may be able to weather the storm."

"We?"

"You and I. My uncle. Deno—at a distance. Even Clare, who incidentally has left London and gone to Bagot Park. Poor old Hopton died last week."

"I am sorry."

The conventional reply was a shock spoken in that empty voice. He would have preferred her to say something almost wicked—that she was glad Hopton was dead, for instance. It was like being with a sleep-walker.

"Shall we go, then?" he said. "Put on your prettiest bonnet to charm Lord Whitfield. He has an eye for a handsome woman, my uncle tells me."

During the journey to the Temple Robert talked and Isabella listened, sometimes faintly smiling when he made one of his disjointed Robertish jokes. The carriage took them through the crowded streets, passing four-horse omnibuses full of people, phaetons, riders, carriages lined up at the bonnet shops and lace warehouses in Regent Street. Riding down Regent's Circus, helmets flashing, plumes waving, was a cavalcade of scarlet-coated Household Cavalry. The scene was cheerful, and Isabella had a curious thought she half-believed: that every single human being in the busy streets was happy. Save herself.

The carriage drew up in the hush of the Temple gardens. Telling the coachman to wait, Robert escorted her into an ancient house in King's Bench Walk. A clerk bowed them into a large dark room, and a man at a table stood up.

"Lady Carteret, Mr. Bagot. My service to you."

He greeted them pleasantly and Isabella was given a chair facing the lawyer.

Lord Whitfield was a ruddy-faced man in his sixties, with curling white whiskers and curling white hair. There was something sporting rather than legal about him. He wore a white cravat fastened with a gold horse-shoe pin, a red rose in his buttonhole.

His manner was as brisk as Robert's but without Robert's grace.

"Best come to the point right away, Lady Carteret, don't you think?" he said, having dismissed the clerk. "Robert here, and Carteret himself, have laid this thing on my desk. I've been spending some time on it. I have seen the party in question—"

Isabella wondered who that was. Buckley? Clare?

Lord Whitfield picked up a sheaf of closely written papers.

"The old nurse's evidence. Well, you cannot call this evidence, it is mostly tittle-tattle that she repeated to Clare, poor old thing. I gathered she died last week, Robert?"

"Yes, sir. Clare was very upset."

"Of course, of course," was the uninterested response.

"Clare was deeply anxious that the whole thing should be silenced, and that there should be no reflection on the family," Robert said.

Isabella looked up. She did not believe him.

Lord Whitfield was examining the papers again. He said, as if speaking to himself, "There is no strong case here."

"My cousin never intended there should be a case at all, sir," put in Robert.

"I know that, my boy. Like his sister, he wanted it silenced. Cleared up. If there was anything actually to clear, if you take my meaning."

He put on some small round spectacles and looked over the top of them at Isabella.

Now and again he'd had cases, curious and interesting they were, that involved dealing with women of quality; he was accustomed to inevitable feminine denials. Tears too. The woman sitting opposite him did not behave in the expected way. If it were not for the letter on the desk Lord Whitfield could have believed her innocent. He admired her pluck.

"Of course," he said, "I haven't consulted my colleague yet, he's the great expert in these things. If he advised it I'm in duty bound to inform the Viscount that the child should not—*could* not by law—be the Bagot inheritor."

"Yes, Lord Whitfield, my cousin and my uncle are perfectly aware of that," said Robert, in a voice as practical as if discussing the transfer of an estate, not Freddy's future life. "But I take it from your remark just now that there *is* no real case?"

"I couldn't say that," said Lord Whitfield with a lawyer's perversity. "Now, this letter, Lady Carteret."

He picked it up. She could see, upside down, her own writing of five years ago. "Foolish," he said, reading it. "Very foolish."

"Buckley Vernon was a friend of Lady Carteret's before she married. They were in the theatre together," said Robert. It was curious to hear him mention such a thing. Isabella thought from his voice that he had also read the letter.

"*Oh Buck, of course, at twelve, or even before,*" Lord Whitfield read aloud. He passed the letter to her.

"I daresay you don't remember a word of it, do you?"

The letter had the look of paper, even paper as thick as this was, which has been much handled. The ink had faded. It could have been a hundred years old.

"According to a colleague, and I agree, that letter can be read in six different ways," Lord Whitfield remarked. "It has taken a deal of our time. I said that the matter is not exactly closed, but I do not wish to sound despondent. We'll see what can be done to mend things. That is all I have to say at present. I wished to make your acquaintances, Lady Carteret. It is always necessary in matters like this. Feel assured of my best services."

He stood up, and grasped her hand firmly, almost fiercely.

She had surprised Lord Whitfield by her self-command, and on the journey homeward to Regent's Park, she surprised Robert by her silence. She sat very straight, very composed. She didn't turn to him and exclaim, as would have been human, that thank God it looked as if there was a little hope, that perhaps everything might even return to normal. Robert saw that Isabella accepted that things, now, could never be the same. However weak the evidence against her, who believed her innocent? Poor Deno never had. The old Earl, he himself, Lord Whitfield, all suspected she'd been that actor's mistress. Between the Bagots and this beautiful woman lay only her rather admirable lie.

The carriage turned in at the park gates and trotted under the shady trees. When it halted at Finstock Lodge he saw Isabella give a slight shudder.

20

(1)

BY the time Lettice's second important season at the Royalty had begun, she was what they called in Green Rooms a star. The town adored her. She now had scores of ardent friends while in her days of obscurity she had scarcely had three. She played Viola in *Twelfth Night*, Beatrice in *Much Ado About Nothing*. Boldly ignoring the difference in their ages, Davenant played Benedick. They were the most fascinating pair of actors in London. Lettice had become so famous that crowds collected at the Stage Door every night to see her arrive and leave. When she stepped onstage the audience roared, as if welcoming a lover; when the play ended it was like a Roman triumph, with flowers thrown in bright heaps at her feet. Letters arrived begging her to meet foreign marquises and English baronets.

Davenant was pleased by the adoration, since he had discovered and trained her.

Lettice was the toast of London, but it was him they were actually toasting. The roars for him, in any case, never lessened. Why should they?

Lettice was not hardened by the stream of light and money pouring down on her. She became rather softer now that she was the acknowledged queen of the London theatre. But her life altered. She and Buckley moved to a larger house in Kensington. There was a walled garden and an orchard, a fountain in the courtyard outside the drawing-room, a covered entrance from the road to the front door. The Vernons had their own carriage now, which took them daily on the country drive to the theatre, and was waiting for them at night after the performance. Matilda and Billy had a nurserymaid to help Mary Anne, who had been promoted and wore a dark frock and neat white collar which suited her fair looks very well. Lettice's clothes were created by a fashionable dressmaker.

Lettice's looks flowered. Her russet hair was worn, in imitation of the young Queen, parted in the centre and plaited over her ears. Her pale skin had a glow, her luminous eyes were bright. She entertained a good deal. More than fame and accompanying wealth, what made her happy was playing opposite Davenant. Her life was filled with work, with Davenant and work, one inseparable from the other. He taught her to "plaster her voice" as he called it "on to the back wall of the gallery". He taught her that if a costume was to cling, it must first be wet, then knotted and left to dry so that it became clinging and wrinkled. He taught her—while acting—how to laugh. He never needed to teach her how to cry, for her eyes brimmed when her speeches were sad and her voice made audiences weep with her.

Two things darkened the brightness round Lettice. She had refused for more than a year to see her sister. And Buckley had begun to drink too much.

Ellen had told Lettice that Lord Carteret had left England. Neither her mother nor she wished to talk of the matter, but Ellen had said that pretty little Frederick could lose his title. He might be Buckley's child—her own children's half-brother. What a tragic mess Isabella had made. All for a stupid, stupid love affair probably lasting a few weeks.

Playing the great passions upon the stage, to Lettice "real" life was much less real than make-believe, and such insane folly as her sister's was beyond her understanding. Lettice was wonderfully practised at imagining herself into the skin of others—but not when she thought of her sister and her husband together. She knew well enough that Buckley had had affairs with actresses in the company. Once, early in their marriage, she had taxed him with something about another woman and Buckley had lied so outrageously that she had been shocked. When he became involved with an actress for the second time, Lettice had ignored it. But her affection for him began to wane. It was as if a chill, a layer of cold frost, had fallen on the tenderness she used to feel. As for his past relationship with her sister, she pushed that firmly out of her thoughts and fixed them on her work.

She was dressing for the theatre one afternoon, with her maid waiting on her, when Buckley came into the room. Looking quickly at him, Lettice said, "Thank you, Janet. I can do the rest for myself."

The maid left the room, and Lettice calmly tied the wide green silk ribbons of her bonnet in a bow under her chin.

Buckley leaned against the wall. His face had the blurred look she had begun to hate. Never tidy or cared-for in his person, his expensive green coat was marked with dust as if he'd been lying on the ground.

"Buckley, don't you think you should rest?"

He gave a jeering smile.

"Go on," he said, "hurry off to the theatre and give the mob a treat. They'll be hanging round the Stage Door by now, won't they? Do you know something? Your acting makes me sick. You're Davenant's puppet, that's all you are."

"You are drunk."

Her collected manner infuriated him. She was small, neatly and fashionably dressed, calm, everything about her invulnerable. Did she think she acted better than he did? Did she conspire with Davenant to rob him of importance?

"Yes, I'm drunk and I'll get more drunk," he said, coming towards her. "And don't look at me like that, you stupid vain little—"

Using a filthy word he struck her hard across the face. Lettice tottered and almost fell, then with a kind of gasp ran out of the room and down the stairs.

She had no veil to her bonnet and huddled in the corner of the carriage, her hand against her face. The bruise throbbed, and when she dabbed her cheek there was a little blood. She was too angry to feel any pain and when she had hurried with bowed head through the Stage Door to her dressing-room, the first thing she did was to look in the pier glass at her face. A great bruise was forming on her cheek round the thin gash of dried blood. She began to cry, not from pain but from helpless anxiety. How could she play now? She was examining the bruise when there was a loud knock at the door.

"Don't come in!"

"Why not?"

It was Davenant. He saw her standing by the glass and at once came over to her. He took her chin in his hands.

"That's some black eye you are going to get there. Don't waste time explaining. I came in to ask you to have supper with me after the performance. No, no, don't speak—"

He continued to study the reddening bruise.

"Sit down," he said. "We'll see what we can do in the way of repairs."

On a clean linen cloth on Lettice's dressing-table were the small pans and dishes of moistened water-colour which she used for her make-up. Gwynyth prepared them freshly

395

for every performance. A large dish held the flesh tint which Lettice put on with a sponge, and when that was dry she painted with a brush the lines to stress bone structure, the white for highlights.

"Now," he said, skilfully beginning to make up her face, "I had a black eye myself once when I was playing Hamlet. Had a few words with a nincompoop playing the Ghost. The man hit me. It would have been a fine thing to appear in customary suits of solemn black with an eye to match. I did it like this . . ."

He went on working at her upturned face. "There."

When she looked in the glass, there was not a mark on her face.

"We can show them a trick or two," he said. "I don't know what they'd make of Benedick if they thought he'd been knocking the lady about before the play started. Don't forget. A little supper in my dressing-room after the performance. Just a few friends . . ."

When the play ended, Gwynyth helped her to dress in an evening gown. Lettice's dressing-room on the first floor was scarcely less grand than Davenant's, and she and Gwynyth often laughed over the end-of-the-passage boxroom. In a cupboard running the full length of the room, Lettice kept a number of gowns into which she changed when she was going to suppers after the play.

Gwynyth knew nothing about the blow and Lettice was not going to tell her. She couldn't bear to discuss it. She merely said she had decided to keep on her stage make-up. Gwynyth accepted this without comment. Anything Lettice did was right.

"Did you see the lilies?" she said. "Aren't they magnificent? Can't make out the writing, it looks foreign to me. There's red roses again. And all the little violets, and that big basket of camellias in the corner."

"Lovely, dear," said Lettice, accustomed to living in a room full of flowers sent by people to show that they adored her. "Do you know who is to be at Mr. Davenant's party tonight?"

"Haven't heard," said Gwynyth. "Funny, I usually do."

The two women kissed affectionately, and Lettice went down the corridor, arranging her silk gauze scarf. She had taken a long time to dress and the theatre was settling into its midnight silences. She was tired. Now the performance was over, she felt shaken and shocked again.

In Davenant's suite two waiters were laying a table and Davenant was supervising, examining plates and cutlery. "This fork has a crooked prong. No, the flowers and candles go there, if you please."

He had changed into evening dress. The dandyish style of his clothes showed off his stocky powerful figure. His hair, parted at the side and curled, was greyer than when Lettice had first met him. His face was more lined. But his eyes were as blue, his voice as alluring as ever.

"Here you are, madam. Not before time. You are the most unpunctual of my actresses. That will do," to the waiters, "I will ring when I need you. No, I prefer to pour the champagne myself. Off with you, but remember to ice the Chablis correctly. And no bits floating in the turtle soup. The lady dislikes them."

He shooed out the waiters.

"I considered my favourite supper, kippers and champagne," he said, "but somehow I thought it might not suit."

"Where are the other guests?" asked Lettice.

"Did I say there would be any?"

"A few friends, you said."

"A good description. Sit down. This champagne is passable. It was brought to me from France by the Comte de Chambrunier. Try it."

She accepted a glass in silence.

"Are you feeling better?"

"Thanks to you, yes."

"You'll need to paint thick for ten days, I fear."

"As long as that?"

"Bruises hang about, Lettice. Going to tell me about it?"

"I would prefer not to. A private matter."

"Very proper," he agreed, filling his glass.

The meal was enjoyable because nobody in the world could resist Davenant if he set out to capture their approval. He had an extraordinary way of combining energy, exuberance, a teasing wit, a satiric turn of phrase. Her thoughts about Buckley faded. But there was something in Davenant's manner which put her on her guard. She had not acted with this man, playing lover, wife, daughter, mistress, without having strong intuitions about him.

When the meal was over he pushed back his chair and sipped a glass of brandy.

Putting down the glass with deliberation he said, "Did I ever tell you I was married, Lettice?"

She said coolly enough, "Everybody says that you are."

"Why do you suppose they've never met this invisible wife of mine?"

"There are various rumours."

"I can tell you every one of them. That she left me for a foreigner. That she's mad and locked up. That I divorced her. One kind friend suggested that like the Earl of Leicester with poor Amy Robsart, I'd made away with her. That was after we had been playing *The Pit of Hell* to full houses."

"Why are you telling me about your wife?"

"Why not? We are friends. There's something sympathetic about you."

She was still on her guard. The bruise, too, worried her. It ached now she was no longer keyed up by the evening's performance. I'm sure my face is swollen, she thought, I must look a fright.

"Yes, Lettice, I did marry years ago," Davenant said. "A pretty little creature who fell sick within a year and nearly died giving birth to a stillborn son. She has been in Wales on a mountain top ever since, living with an old aunt of hers. I go—I went—to see her as often as I could. Sometimes I had to travel all night to visit her and then return for a performance. Poor child, it was pitiful to see her fading. She lingered on for years, but there was never much hope from the doctors. Last month she died.''

"I'm so sorry,'' Lettice said in a low voice. He shook his head.

"No need. It was the best thing. Terrible to be so ill, bedridden, in a kind of swoon most of the time. I gave her the best I could. But I've wished, God knows, that I'd never met her. It was bearing my child that ruined her health. It is my fault she is dead.''

He stared into the brandy glass. He was deep in thought.

Lettice was moved. Yet there was nothing she could say about this hidden part of his life. She waited for a little. He did not stir. At length she stood up. He roused himself, came round the table and with a kind of push made her sit down again.

"Don't you make a missish speech and then say good night, Lettice, because I decided to tell you Eliza is dead. I'm not a block of wood. Of course I am grieved. But the poor thing was never a wife and scarcely knew me during that years-long illness. What is reality is my work, the theatre, the friends who understand me. I suppose you're remembering those improper suggestions I made years ago."

"I have forgotten them."

"What a Miss Prim," he said satirically. "You remember the occasion perfectly. I can see it in your eyes. Have some more strawberries?"

She shook her head.

"I see I have taken your appetite away. Now we come to the matter on hand. I am, as I've told you, Lettice, now a widower. Why not marry me?"

Her usually pale face blushed scarlet. Even her nose and ears went red.

"What on earth can you mean?"

"What I say, of course"

"But I am married!"

"Not much of a husband, is he?" he said, touching his own cheek at the spot where Buckley had hit her.

"He's unhappy, he didn't mean it, sometimes he drinks—oh, how could you say such a thing?" she cried hysterically, sprang to her feet, and a glass of wine tipped up, spilling in

402

a crimson stain across the skirt of her white satin dress. She burst into tears.

He put out his arms and clasped her, his hand on her hair, pressing her head against his chest.

"Cry away. Cry away."

"I don't want to cry," she sobbed angrily. "Let me go. Leave me alone."

"No, I will not. You don't love that self-indulgent man you married. I know you have two pretty children and why shouldn't you keep them? But Vernon doesn't suit you. Didn't I hear talk about him and that titled sister of yours? Vernon's a woman chaser. He drinks, too. In my experience it is drink in men that makes them brutal to women. What is more," he said, releasing her, "he's not the actor he was."

"He would improve if you gave him a chance."

"If he improves, I will."

She sniffed and mopped at her skirt with a small lace handkerchief. She had utterly lost her poise.

"Poor Buckley. He needs me."

"Lettice, Lettice," he said, "Buckley is an egotist. He'll find another woman tomorrow. If I am a judge of men, there goes one who never thinks of any single human creature but himself. Are you simple-minded enough to think he needs you? He bitterly resents you. Now, now, turn off the tap for heaven's sake. You're not crying because you are shocked at my suggestion. Or because I've hurt those delicate feelings you're so proud of. You are crying because you want *me*. As I want you. Stupid, talented, tiresome, beautiful, steady-hearted woman. I want and need you. Between us, what can't we do? Come. You've kissed me onstage often enough. That's it. That's better. And if Vernon lays a finger on you again, tell him I'll shoot him with Edmund Kean's duelling pistol on the wall yonder."

(2)

Buckley was astounded when his prudish wife calmly informed him she was considering a divorce.

"What do you mean? You have no evidence."

It seemed she had found out about a recent affair Buckley had had with a dancer in the Royalty ballet. The girl, Lettice said, had "confessed".

"A woman can't divorce a man for that," exclaimed Buckley angrily. "You'd need to cite cruelty!"

He was so flabbergasted that he had forgotten the bruise on her face.

"That too," said Lettice. She left the room.

For the first few days after this conversation he simply could not believe that his wife would go to the lengths of divorcing him. It was out of the question. He behaved, on the whole, rather well. He apologised for striking her and said he would stop drinking to excess. She merely listened. He did not mention Floss Buxton, who had vanished from the ballet without trace—he supposed Lettice had put the fear of God into the poor child.

After a few days of guarded peace he was astounded when Lettice said at breakfast, "I am afraid, Buckley, you cannot live here any longer. You will have to leave as soon as it is convenient for you to do so."

"You actually mean you want a divorce!"

"I think so. I am considering it. But you will have to leave in any case. You can see the children, of course, whenever you like."

"That's kind," he said, so bitterly that she sighed.

"I'm sorry. You did bring this on yourself, though. If you want any extra money . . ."

That really stung. He'd never loved her, although once he had liked and respected her. He'd married her because he had been afraid of the very scandal which had now broken over Isabella, damned near drowning her. Lettice had been dutiful rather than passionate. She was a brilliant actress and could be a good friend. But she played the part of wife and mother rather than feeling either very deeply. As for taking her money—how dare she!

"Listen to me," he said viciously. "I wouldn't touch a sovereign of yours if I was starving in a ditch. I've put up with a lot from you. Only a lunatic marries an ambitious woman. You don't like that, do you? Your duty was to *me*. You should have thought of me, your husband. All you did was push yourself into the front of the stage. What's more, I act better than that old played-out Davenant and I'm twenty years younger. Keep your money for him when his hair and teeth fall out. I don't want to hear another word."

406

He slammed out of the room.

He left that afternoon, when most of the servants were out and the children in Kensington Gardens. The carriage was heaped with boxes of clothes, guns, fishing tackle. A set of rapiers with chased steel handles. Some portraits. Neither Lettice nor Buckley had ever stopped him having any possible thing he wanted.

He opened the drawing-room door but did not come into the room and said loudly, "Goodbye."

She started up and ran towards him, suddenly troubled.

But he did not give her time to speak. He was gone.

Something like remorse came over Lettice for the rest of the day, every time she remembered him. When she arrived at the theatre she talked to Gwynyth earnestly about what had happened, but Gwynyth was full of prejudiced encouragement. Lettice was dressed in her costume as Beatrice, made up her face and went down to the wings. The overture began.

She stood in her vaporous green dress, her hair loosed from its plaits and falling round her shoulders, listening and musing. Two hands laced her waist and a voice muttered in her ear, "Don't think *they* have come to see *you*."

She was pressed so close that she was breathless.

21

(1)

ISABELLA did not close Finstock Lodge in the autumn when the rest of society left town. She stayed. London emptied and in a way she welcomed it. She lived a lonely life. During the winter her children were sometimes brought from Sussex to stay with her but she knew herself a dull companion, and was well aware they preferred the merry country life of a great house.

Robert visited her as often as he could and what he saw of her disturbed him.

Finally, when the Bagots returned to London at the beginning of the season in the following spring he rode to Regent's Park determined to help her in some way. But how?

The park looked fresh, children shouted and ran about, Finstock Lodge itself was crisply white as he rode up to the door. In the drawing-room he found Isabella sitting on the window-seat. She wore a green dress which did not suit her.

"How is it with you, cousin?" he said, taking her hand.

She said she was well enough.

He sat with her in the window and talked of family matters. To make things natural he spoke of Denys. Isabella must have received a letter, as he had, telling of the terrible storms and of how the regiment had been cut off by floods.

"A serpent in his riding boot!" Robert said, laughing. "His news is so dramatic. Ours must be very tame to him."

There was the kind of silence which was better broken.

"Well, Isabella, what are your plans?" he asked in his energetic way. "Do you intend to stay here at Finstock?"

She looked round the room and he thought he saw her give a slight shudder. She'd done that once before. Marriage is the devil, he thought. This room is full of Deno. There was a pencil portrait of him on the wall, a silver box for his cigars on the table beside them. There was the Bagot crest on every damned piece of silver one looked at. There was even Denys's much-thumbed book of form in its old place where he could pick it up

410

and flip through it, commenting on horses and owners.

"Why not pack up and leave here?" he said suddenly.

"Where could I go?"

He thought the question, from this beautiful woman in her unbecoming dress, very pathetic.

"What about Brighton? It's cheerful there, I'm told. There are all kinds of entertaining things to do. Sea-bathing if you are brave enough! You might persuade your mama to go with you. Let me arrange things. Yes?"

Ellen agreed to go with her daughter to stay at Brighton—Robert suggested the fashionable Bedford Hotel. Ellen had hesitated at leaving Thomas but he insisted. The post he had obtained at the Richmond theatre interested him (now that Viscount Carteret had settled some money on the Winters, Thomas was less fussed about his work). He would be well looked after by Ellen's two servants at the cottage. Of course she must be with their daughter.

"The girl's made an unholy mess of everything and the more she sees of you, my dear, the better for her."

Ellen was inclined to agree.

411

Ellen liked Brighton at once. The climate was kind, the sea breezes refreshing. She enjoyed the fashionable crowds, the carriages and riders going by on the road by the sea, the ships, the feeling of being somewhere lively, modish. The hotel was comfortable and well furnished; members of the nobility sometimes stayed there.

"What more can we want?" Ellen said with her upward trill of a laugh.

But in the months that followed, although Ellen was a practical and not weakeningly sympathetic companion, although her father came to visit them and everything was done for her well-being, Isabella remained listless.

A misty autumn look began to come to the sunny mornings. Soon, Ellen thought, she must return home. Sitting by the window, looking at the calm sea, she wondered if the Michaelmas daisies were out in her Richmond garden yet.

It was too early for the morning parade of carriages or horsemen and when Ellen heard the clatter of a carriage arriving, she looked down curiously.

Isabella had come through the archway leading from her bedroom.

"Are you expecting a visitor, Isabella? I

think the Bagot carriage has just drawn up."

Isabella sat down very suddenly.

Moments later Robert was announced. He entered in his quick way, greeted Isabella with affection and Ellen with respect. She had met him once before and was charmed. She would have liked to stay and talk, but knew she must not. Regretfully, she curtsied and left the room.

Robert looked sharply at Isabella. The strong light from the sky shone full on her. He had not seen her for weeks and she had grown even thinner. There were rings under her eyes and her skin was no longer olive but yellowish. Her grey embroidered dress hung round her, emphasising her wasted figure.

"I was not expecting you, Robert. It was good of you to come. How are the children? Are they still at Bagot Park?"

"Yes, and thriving. But they would so much like to see you. May I take you there? It is only two hours from Brighton and in this fine weather—"

"I don't feel quite strong enough at present."

He leaned forward.

"Cousin, are you ill? May I send you a doctor? Tell me what I may do for you."

"I am perfectly well, Robert. A little thin, I suppose." She grimaced and bunched the loose waist of her dress. "Mama scolds me and Rivers wants to alter the dress but I don't wish it."

There was a trace of the old, wilful girl in her insistence on wearing a dress which emphasised how she was changed.

He still looked at her concernedly and she said, "Have you heard again from Lord Whitfield? I do wonder if the Earl has decided poor little Freddy must be sent packing."

"Bella!"

"Why not? If they decide he is not the *heir* any more, why should they give him house-room?"

"You're very bitter," he said, at a loss—something rare for him. "I don't like to hear you talk like this. Do you hate us now, Bella?"

She twisted a heavy emerald ring Denys had given her years ago. It, too, was overlarge and the stone slipped from the front to the back of her finger.

"I don't hate anyone. Not even Clare. I've thought about what happened with Clare. Hopton adored her so. I suppose she knew

Clare was in love with you and thought her secret might straighten the path of true love."

"Bella, you know that is nonsense."

She gave a smile of such irony that he was shocked.

"You and I both know Clare was attached to you. I suppose she still is. She must have been glad when Hopton told her those things. With poor Freddy out of the way—Denys too—you would inherit. And maybe Clare with you."

He did not reply for a moment or two. Poor Isabella. So her old enemy Clare must take the burden for what had happened. Yet Clare had known of the affair and kept silent for weeks until it was repeated to her from outside the family. But was there any use in reminding Isabella of that? She was looking at him as if he exhausted her. Her words could not hurt him, since what she had said was ludicrous. It was true that Clare was fond of him, but not too fond, he had decided.

He stood up, walked about, opened the window wider, bent to sniff some roses in a bowl on the table. He came back and stood beside her.

"Forget this nonsense, Bella. You must not sit about getting so thin and sad-looking and spend your time on sick fancies. You do not look well, cousin. My clever idea about the healthy Brighton air is a great failure, I see. Why not go home?"

"To Finstock Lodge? Please don't ask me to."

"Do you still dislike it so much? Then let me sell it for you."

She shook her head, saying merely, "Oh, Robert."

"Where would you like to live?" he said, ignoring that. "I went to dine at Twickenham last season. It's an enchanting place. Pope used to live there, they tell me. And Lady Mary Wortley Montagu and all kinds of last-century grandees. Why don't we go to Twickenham and look together?"

Isabella was about to refuse. She was too worn out with misery to make any kind of decision. But Robert raised her to her feet. Clasping her hands, he seemed to force some of his own energy through his fingers into her own.

"That's settled, then."

(2)

It was early winter when Isabella moved into

the new Twickenham house, a twenty-minute ride from her parents' cottage in Richmond. Lockton House had been built in the early 1700s. It was a rambling old place full of irregularly-shaped, oddly attractive rooms. Sloping lawns ran down to the river's edge. It had been built for one of George II's ladies-in-waiting.

Robert spent all his time with Isabella, helped her to choose the house (just as the old Earl had done, Isabella thought wryly), and waited on her with unselfish kindness. No detail was too small to interest him.

She had dreaded returning to Finstock Lodge in the autumn, even for a short time, but somehow the combination of Robert and her mother, neither of them sympathetic, made the ordeal less terrible. Robert's common sense, his lively company, most of all an unspoken championship, helped her to recover her health and spirits a little.

At first she was only glad to see him because he reminded her of Denys and the days when she'd been happy. Then she began to look forward to his visits and to enjoy the long chilly drives to Twickenham, the shopping, the unaccustomed activity.

When Isabella was settled in her house,

Robert broke the news that he must return to Sussex.

"My uncle is getting crochety. He keeps saying in his letters that he's not getting any younger. What he means is that I'm behind in my work on the estate."

Isabella sighed. They were in the dining-room of her new home, having luncheon together. Looking at her, he had a feeling of satisfaction. She wore a creamy velvet day dress with a scalloped skirt and a beautiful rose-patterned shawl. She was almost the girl who had been Deno's wife. If Deno had seen the poor thing looking so ill, Robert thought, he must have relented.

"Fanny and her husband are at Bagot at present," he said. "The Lord knows who Fan has invited, the place is bursting with visitors. I shall miss you and this nice house and the fun we've had."

"I shall miss you too."

Robert disappeared from Isabella's life as suddenly as he had appeared. For weeks he had been her companion, coaxing her back to life. Then he was gone. He arranged for the children to return to her. They were taller, noisier, more beautiful than Isabella remembered. They seemed delighted with

418

their new home, soon forgot to mention Bagot Park. They brought their nurse with them, a fat country girl all smiles. But although Isabella hugged them and went for riverside walks with them, she did not feel close to them. It was to their nurse they ran, crying, when they fell over.

She began to receive a few cautious invitations from people in society, and once or twice nerved herself to accept. But at a small dinner at Lady Quenington's the talk was of the Queen and Prince Albert and a ball at the Palace. One deaf old lady from the country said loudly, "Why weren't you there, my dear?"

Isabella went scarlet. She was more conscious of her curious situation now that she had half-entered society again.

The children had been with her for a few weeks when she received a letter from Robert suggesting they should come back to Bagot Park for Christmas "if she could spare them". When she told Freddy he fixed his dark eyes on her and said, "Mama, I think we *need* to go. Our ponies miss us."

"And I'll be with Freddy," chimed Betsy.

In the way of children, when the moment of parting came they gave her desperate hugs and kisses and danced off into the Bagot carriage as if on their way to a party.

It was late November and had begun to be very cold. On the day the children left Isabella went for a walk by the river, returning before it was dark. A fire was lit in the drawing-room and she sat staring into the flames and thinking of Denys. She had received another letter, creased, travel-stained. It had been written on a journey to the North of India. It was brief and dutiful and meaningless, ending "Affectionately yours, D." All his letters ended like that.

She read it again. Tears stood in her eyes. He'd been away now for much more than a year. She had thought when he closed his heart against her that she passionately loved him, but perhaps that had not been so. Perhaps what she had ached for had been *his* love, which had so surrounded her that when he took it away she felt vulnerable and un-protected. That feeling, that she had pos-sessed something infinitely precious and had lost it for ever, came back whenever she received a letter. Even his slanting hand-writing made her cry.

It snowed in the night, and when Isabella woke the world outside was changed. There was a strange glare, a kind of light from below. Garden, trees, lawn, were a blazing white. The house was bitterly cold, and she ordered fires to be lit in every room, including those which she did not use. Isabella's fits of extravagance were much approved of by her servants, many of whom had worked for rich people who counted every penny. Footmen and maids bustled to and fro with logs. There was a smell of woodsmoke, a crackling sound, and the air grew faintly warmer.

Isabella came downstairs wearing a dark red braided dress with many petticoats, and a great white fringed shawl which Denys had given her. She went to the window-seat and sat down, looking out. The morning was hushed. Then she heard the muffled sound of hooves on snow, and a moment later a familiar carriage turned into her gates. Yellow and black, with two footmen on the box. Robert.

He came into the room with his quick walk, and kissed her hand. She smiled but he did not return the smile, and as they sat down a slight shiver ran down her spine. Did she imagine that he had an air of haste and sadness?

"How pleasant to see you, cousin."

It was as if he had not heard her.

"Isabella. Deno is on his way home."

Her eyes widened. She swallowed.

"But I didn't know the regiment had been ordered home—"

"It is not that. He is invalided out. He is ill."

She started, and touched his hand.

"Oh. I am so very sorry."

"A kind of fever. He has had it for weeks. The doctors do not understand it, but he is very ill."

She pressed his hand, but said nothing.

Robert looked at her steadily. "I have come from the Earl. He begs you to return."

"But that's impossible!"

"Isabella, listen—"

"The *Earl* asks me!" she interrupted. "He cannot stand to see me, nor can any of the family. Imagine Clare, should I enter the house! I am deeply sorry poor Denys is ill, but he is young, he will be nursed back to health. All the family know that the last person he would want near him is me. You know how it is with us, Robert. The Earl knows it. How could you ask me such a thing?"

"You are wrong."

"It is not to be discussed."

"Yes, it is. Because Deno loves you."

She recoiled involuntarily as if he had burned her.

"Don't say such things to me. Don't upset me."

"Why not? Why should I not upset you, as you call it?" he said harshly. "Deno needs you. He always has done, and how much more, now that he is gravely ill, might even die. Were you blind enough to think he stopped loving you when all that happened? Isabella, I beg you. Be at the house when they bring him home."

She shook her head. She was mute.

"Are you afraid of the family? That they would not be kind to you? If I promise—"

"I am not afraid of them."

There was a pause.

"I can see you are not," he said. "Very well. Isabella, once again, please come."

"Don't ask me. Don't ask me again."

He looked at her coldly. She had never seen such an expression on his face.

"Robert. Try to understand, Denys *cannot* want me, and I cannot bear to come. Please, please understand."

"I understand this, Isabella. You have been hurt and your marriage is broken. Whether it was your own fault or not, whether the world believes you innocent or not, it is time you thought of somebody else for a change."

"You think me selfish."

"Very."

"But . . . if I went . . . I would have to suffer all over again."

"*You* suffer?" he repeated, with such disdain that she went crimson. "Are we talking of *you*? Deno loves you. It was because he loved you that you cut him to the heart. Try. For once in your life try to think of somebody other than yourself."

Her eyes brimmed. "You can't ask me to bear it for a second time."

There was a pause. The clock ticked. A door closed somewhere in the house.

"Can't I?"

22

(1)

THE windows of the old house glowed, but the park and gardens, fields and woods lay in a waste of whiteness. Isabella had made the long journey alone, leaving Robert to wait for the arrival of the ship at Gravesend.

Tired and grey-faced, she was shown into the long drawing-room which seemed to her dazzled eyes too brightly lit with dozens of candles.

The old Earl and Lady Clare were by the fire. The Earl sidled over to take her hand.

"You're half frozen."

"The carriage was stuck in the snow for a while."

"By the marsh? Did they manage the horses? Come to the fire, girl, you look perished. Clare, are you going to greet your sister?"

Lady Clare pressed a thin cheek against Isabella's. It was the first time she'd done such a thing. She murmured something and then returned to her chair.

Sitting in the elaborate room filled with the treasures and trophies of the past, the most composed person was Isabella. She was poised and calm. She had made a decision and after that everything had become curiously simple. She had no resentment or dislike left for the Earl or Lady Clare. Lady Clare had wronged her in the past. She had wronged Denys. They were suffering more than she. Denys had lived in their thoughts all the time he had been away, because he still loved them.

The Earl sat down in the old way, as if falling. Lady Clare began to sew.

"Robert says the ship is expected in Gravesend in a week or so," Isabella said, holding her hands to the fire.

"Might be sooner," said the Earl. "If they have a following wind."

"I always forget the wind."

"Sailors don't," said the Earl.

A second later he fell suddenly asleep. He began to snore.

Lady Clare put the embroidery frame down on her knee.

"He often does that. He is getting old."

426

"He looks quite well," said Isabella involuntarily, with the old trick of needing a happy end.

"I do not think so. If Carteret dies it will kill him."

"Don't say that, Clare!"

It was the first time Isabella and Clare had talked normally.

"He's been so sad since my brother went to India," Clare said, beginning to sew again. "He blames himself, you know, because he was not good to Carteret. He never appreciated him. He treated him like a fool. Now he's unhappy. The thing that upsets him most is that it was he who persuaded Lord Gough to get Carteret back into the regiment . . ."

Clare talked of Denys and his father. The old Earl lay deeply asleep. How different Clare is, Isabella thought. Everything is changed because I am changed. Only this huge old house is the same as when I was seventeen and acted in that play with Lettice and I thought everything here so beautiful. Like paradise.

A log in the fireplace fell in a shower of sparks. The Earl stirred.

"He won't wake for another half-hour," Clare said.

Isabella looked at her.

"Your father must not blame himself, Clare. Denys went because of me. He couldn't bear to be with me. He chose to go as far away as possible. To the other side of the world."

Clare looked into the fire. Her face, with its odd look of a daring boy, was sombre.

"If somebody I loved hurt me, *I* wouldn't run," she said. "Nor would Robert. Carteret was never very brave."

Clare didn't seem to find anything curious about the conversation. If I am changed, Isabella thought, so is she. I suppose, because she won, she forgave me. Yet I lost, and I don't hate her. Isabella wondered if it was Denys whose wounded spirit altered everything. But he wasn't here yet: she couldn't tell.

Clare picked up her sewing. As she pulled the silk through the taut fabric it made a snapping sound.

"It was good of you to come here. I am sure Carteret will need you. I remember when Freddy was born he said you were brave. I hope it's true. Because you're going to need to be again."

428

In the days that followed, Isabella resumed the pattern of living she'd known during her marriage and which the Bagots had set generations ago. She remembered it as an actress might recall a role played years before. The family had formal meals together. In the mornings or the afternoons they rode out, or walked in the park despite the bitter weather. They visited the nursery. The children were brought in by their nurse for tea. In the evenings the family often played backgammon. They always played cards in the Music Room, where Lettice had acted in *The Welsh Girl* so long ago and where the marble Venus stood in its unchanging place. Clare and the Earl behaved to her with a marked courtesy. They felt in her debt. Freddy and Betsy took her presence with the marvellous lack of surprise of people under six years old, merely asking would she please read to them, she was so much better than Nurse.

The snow didn't melt. It fell again, freshly white on the top of the old frozen snow, thickening along the windowsills, its surface starred with the tiny feet of birds. One day colder than the rest there was the sound that everybody in the house from the Earl to the youngest servant was waiting for. Wheels in the drive, a carriage with four tired horses at the doors.

A weary man, grey-bearded and in uniform, alighted from the carriage with Robert, and together they supervised carrying the stretcher into the house.

Clare and Isabella had been in the drawing-room, and when they heard the carriage wheels they stared at each other with an identical expression of dread. Clare didn't move. But Isabella ran to the door and opened it in time to see two footmen, Robert and the unfamiliar figure of the doctor going by with a kind of pallet, which was slowly carried up the main staircase. All Isabella could see was a motionless figure covered in blankets.

She watched the procession disappear up the staircase.

Coming back into the room she said in a low voice, "Clare. What must we do? Wait?"

"We will do a great deal of that," Clare said. Her voice shook.

Isabella went to the window and watched the horses steaming in the cold air and the grooms running to blanket them, leading each horse away with a sweet coaxing whistle. Everything about Denys was mysterious, his sickness, his nearness to death, the long journey on the sea, the far-off places he had come from, the battles he had witnessed. He no longer seemed either the indolent nobleman who had married and loved her or the stony stranger who had made her suffer, but someone else into whose presence soon— today—she must go as if to face the Day of Judgement.

The door opened and Robert came in. He still wore his long coat trimmed with fur, and mud-splashed boots.

"When he has rested, you may see him."

Clare remarked severely, "You look exhausted."

"The ship didn't dock until two. I was up and about quite early."

"All night, you mean."

He smiled slightly and then spoke to Isabella in the window-seat, "I see Denys is in his own room."

"I have moved next door. If it troubles him that I am close I shall move to the nursery wing."

"I did not mean that."

431

"Robert, you cannot seriously imagine he would wish me to share his room."

Denys's presence, Denys's sick presence, came into the house like the snow from outside. Neither his wife nor his sister was allowed to see him for the rest of the day. The nurse engaged by the doctor, a tall elderly woman, sat beside him, cared for him expertly. Servants came and went. The house was quiet. The Earl sat for a while by his son's bed while Denys slept, then sidled out in silence.

When Clare and Isabella had dressed for dinner and were in the drawing-room, Robert came to them. He had slept during the afternoon and looked more like himself. He was also in evening dress; its black and white suited him, Isabella thought. He is like Denys. It is something about his eyes, I think.

"Clare. If you'll forgive me, I will take Bella up first."

Robert walked beside her up the marble staircase and along the corridor to the room Denys and Isabella used to share, where both Freddy and Betsy had been born. Robert opened the door.

Only two candles burned. The room was as

quiet as a church at night. Denys lay in the big double bed with heaped pillows arranged to support him. His eyes were shut and he was very pale but the moment she saw him she lost the feeling that this was a stranger. It was dear, familiar, sleeping, stricken Denys. His night-shirt was open at the throat and she could see the dark hairs on his chest. His hands on the counterpane were whiter than the sheets. They were beautiful.

The nurse stood up and said in a low voice, "I think his lordship is awake."

"Thank you, nurse. You may leave us for a while."

Isabella sat down, took the pale hand in her own and pressed it against her cheek. She did as she used to do, rubbing his hand backwards and forwards against her face. He opened his eyes.

Faintly, through the luminous haze of the candles, he saw a girlish oval face, a small straight nose like a child's. He sighed.

"Ah. My dearest," he said.

(3)

Isabella moved, not to the nursery wing to be away from him, but into the sickroom. She slept in a bed at the foot of his own. Until now always afraid of sickness, she stayed with him all day, slept in the room at night, would scarcely stir from his side. She learned from the old nurse, and was alone with the patient for hours, holding his hand until her own became so numb Robert had to chafe it back to feeling.

Sometimes Clare or Robert came in and forced her to go out for a walk in the snow or ride round the park or spend an hour with the children or have tea with the Earl. But Isabella was always fretting, impatient, and ran back up the staircase to Denys's room like a dog to its master.

Denys was often in pain and glad to take the chloral which made him sleep and relieved his suffering. He drifted like a soul aswoon, but followed her with his eyes when he was awake. When she put her cheek against his hand he somehow managed to move his other hand and touch her.

Young, sanguine, healthy, hopeful, how could she help believing she could make him better?

"Robert, he *must* live, I shall *make* him!" she said.

434

She was in the hall, having come in from impatiently walking up and down the snow-covered terrace. Her fur-edged cloak was sprinkled with snow. She looked up the stair-case, about to hurry back to the sickroom that she could not bear to leave.

Robert said slowly, "Dear Bella. Don't hope."

He took her hand.

"But I must! I shall!"

She wrenched away her hand and ran up the stairs two at a time. She slipped through the door into the room where Denys lay. The room was full of love and suffering. It smelled of flowers and chloral, it was airless and still. She could hear a dying fall of music there but she blocked her ears against it.

Denys died a week later. He had seen the children, but Isabella knew he had scarcely known them although he tried to smile. Once or twice he had seen his father, he had pressed his sister's hand, spoken to Robert. But it was Isabella, jealous, tender, passionate and calm, whose figure he looked for with his dying eyes. She was alone with him when, so quietly, his breathing grew slower and slower and then stopped.

Isabella had been the solitary centre of Denys's dying; she carried the whole weight of his illness and death, never letting go of an ounce of the burden. When he was dead the centre shifted to Clare. Isabella did not become ill. She was always about the house, pale and collected in her black dress. But she knew nothing about such things as a Bagot funeral. The Earl was ailing, and Robert and Clare took over the house and organised the coming funeral as if it were for a royal prince. People would come not only from all over the county but from London, every room in every neighbouring mansion would be crowded with distinguished visitors, Bagot Park would be full, not a bedroom of the seventy or more unoccupied.

Fanny's child was due soon and her doctors would not allow her to travel from Cumberland, to her deep grief. But every other relation and friend in the great world would be there. Everything was arranged with formality. Isabella listened in silence as they chose the music and the flowers. There was a letter from Her Majesty and one from the Duke of Wellington. There was mourning for the children. Isabella thought Freddy and Betsy's little figures pathetic, clothed from head to foot in black serge.

On the day of the funeral there was no sign of a thaw. The air was clear and bitter, with winter sunshine cold as the snow.

Isabella, with the Earl, Clare and Robert, travelled to the church in the old Georgian carriage brought out for Bagot state occasions. Isabella had last sat in it for Betsy's christening and she remembered how she and Denys had laughed because the carriage was so huge, the baby so tiny in her yards of cambric and lace.

The Earl said nothing during the drive. Clare looked at him and said, "Papa. Would you like some air? Shall I open the window?"

"Don't be a fool, girl. Do you want to freeze us to death?"

The small old church was crammed with black-clad sad-faced people, only half of whom Isabella recognised. She and Clare were shown with reverence into the high-backed Bagot pew, and the Earl collapsed beside them, bent and pale. The choir of children, some scarcely older than Freddy, sang with a piercing sweetness as the coffin, covered with white flowers, was carried in.

Isabella's heart ached. What was all this, so mournful and austere, so comforting because of prayers, so comfortless because of the silence of death, to do with Denys?

It is my fault he is dead, she thought. It is my fault that lazy, sweet man had his life ruined. For Buckley. For Buckley and something I wanted and can't remember. The voices of the children rose higher and she remembered Denys exactly as he had been when they were happy. He moved again in her imagination. She heard the lazy voice, saw him stretch out his long legs and stare idly at his polished boots. She saw him laugh, smelled his eau-de-cologne, felt his gentle passionate kisses.

Then, with a swish of black silk skirts and the sound of feet on cold stone, everybody rose and went out of the church into the icy graveyard.

(5)

Some of the guests stayed on for a while. Most were elderly relations whose presence Isabella found comforting. Denys's grandmother, old Lady Bagot, now in her eighties, was kind to her for the first time since they had met. She took her grandson's death with more steadiness than the Earl, who spent his time shut up in his study with Robert or riding on the frozen roads round the estates.

When Isabella returned to the house on the afternoon of the funeral her husband's sick-room was transformed. The bed in which he had died was gone, a small eighteenth-century four-poster was in its place. Curtains and covers were changed. There were fresh-covered cushions on a chaise-longue. The altered room banished the days she had spent beside him. She said nothing.

A week later she went into the library one dark afternoon and found Clare sitting wearily at a desk lit with two branched candlesticks.

Clare looked up.

"I am trying to answer some of the letters. Papa has taken the most important but there are five hundred still to do. I try to do thirty a day."

"I will do thirty as well."

"Would you? Are you sure?"

"I will be glad to."

Clare gave a brief smile which altered her face, making her beautiful for a moment or two.

"I know they must write and we must

answer. But every time I read a letter it still makes me cry."

Isabella suddenly leaned forward and kissed her.

They were both startled by the embrace. Clare said in an uneven voice, "I never apologised to you. For the way I treated you."

"Perhaps I deserved it."

"Carteret didn't. I can't forgive myself for that."

"You mustn't be like your father. Denys would hate you to be unhappy, wouldn't he? Clare. I want Denys's bed back in my room."

"But I thought—"

"Oh, I know. You were right. I couldn't have slept in it the very next night or even after a week. Now I want to."

It was Clare whose eyes filled with tears.

The desk was wide, and Isabella pulled up a chair beside her. With the candles lighting both of them, she picked up one of the letters and began to read.

(6)

It seemed to everybody at Bagot Park that the rest of their lives would be spent surrounded by snow.

440

The thaw came suddenly. One morning when Rivers pulled the bedroom curtains, Isabella knew that something had changed. Then she saw there was no longer a six-inch white bar along the window-ledge. The air was full of the sound of dripping water. She heard children laughing on the terrace and the sound of a puppy barking.

It was like the transformation scene in a pantomime, she thought, as she came down to breakfast. The park was already turning green. The sun was shining. When she went into the breakfast-room her father-in-law nodded at her. Robert smiled. Swayne looked disappointed when she refused any of the five hot dishes on the sideboard.

Robert glanced at her during the meal. How silent she was these days. In the past she was never quiet, it had been one of the things about her Denys had liked when they first met, her friendly, frivolous chat. Now she sat, upright and graceful in her deep black, like a figure in a mourning ring. She seemed to take on the colour of life around her, to became a part of it. Was it the actress in her? Robert asked himself what her future would be.

The Earl shuffled some documents which

had arrived that morning. He cleared his throat.

"Isabella. I have something to say to you."

She looked up. It drifted into her mind that perhaps he no longer wished her to be here.

"Whitfield has written to me. In short— about that damned thing."

She saw he was upset and wishing to save him pain said, "Would you rather we did not speak of it?"

At this strange sentence, proof of her own strength and indifference, he stared.

"Of course I wish to speak of it. To get rid of it. Whitfield says, *I* say, that it's to be forgotten. Never a word of truth in it."

He blew his nose fiercely.

"So Freddy is still—"

"For God's sake!"

He stood up, muttered, "Kiss me," gave her a peck on the cheek and sidled out of the room.

"He's more glad than he shows," said Robert, who had watched in silence.

"Then I'm glad too."

"Bella, do you suppose you could wake up? It is very unsatisfactory talking to you nowadays. Like being with somebody who has been mesmerised."

"I am quite awake, Robert."

"Then you must be relieved that the miserable thing is finally over."

"Yes. For Freddy's sake. But Denys is gone. And then, you know, one gets used to having no reputation."

"All that will be mended now," he said vigorously. He spoke, she thought, as if planning to repair a farmer's damaged roof.

"There's more news. It's a day for news. First the thaw. Then Lord Whitfield. And now Clare. She told my uncle last night that when the mourning time is over she wishes to be married. He knew about the offer, of course, but not whether she would accept. He's very pleased."

"Oh, I'm so glad!"

It was the first time she had shown any vitality. It was ironic, he thought, that her reaction to the sister-in-law who had hated her was warmer than that about her own good fortune.

"The Duke of Blackwell's heir," he said and laughed. "Clare will be a duchess one day. Fan is already jealous."

"Clare will make a fine duchess."

"She'd agree to that."

There was a pause. In his usual way Robert

was walking about, now standing at the long window, now coming back to collect the papers the Earl had left scattered on the table.

"May one ask what your plans are, Bella?"

"To go back to my house quite soon."

"This is your house."

She shook her head.

"No, it is not. It is the Earl's. Clare's. Yours. Freddy's one day. It is nothing to do with me."

"You proved the contrary when Deno was brought home."

"Yes. I was glad to be here. Glad you brought me—forced me to come. I think it *was* mine for a little. But not any more. Everything is changing. I can feel it and so can you."

"Perhaps."

"So I must go back to Twickenham and make the house live and see my family, and the children shall be with me when it's spring. I must make something of my little life."

"I hope I shall be part of it."

"I daresay a cousin is a small part," she said with her tired smile.

444

23

SEEING him almost every night of her life, Lettice rarely visited Davenant's house. He invited her to luncheon one Sunday in early spring to show her some costume designs. He looked sly when he mentioned the designs, which she guessed meant that his—for a new production of *Love's Labour Lost*—were going to outshine her own.

Davenant lived in a rambling old house in Chelsea. Along the riverside were beached boats, willow trees, old men with tattooed arms mending upturned skiffs. Steamers puffed by on their way to Cadogan Pier.

Lettice waited in the upstairs drawing-room. A visitor would have wanted to spend an hour staring round the room which was full of the treasures collected by a great actor. Portraits of Davenant as Hamlet, Shylock, as Sir Edward in *The Iron Chest*; framed programmes printed on satin, silver boxes engraved with admiring verses. In a glass-topped table was an embroidered shoe of Garrick's, a Spanish comb which had belonged to Sarah Siddons.

The room's romance left Lettice untouched. Artists also painted her, distinguished visitors brought her offerings. She spread out her velvet skirts and stared into the fire. She was thinking about Buckley.

After all these months she had still not begun proceedings for the divorce. Gwynyth and Laurie Spindle loyally assured her they would give evidence proving Buckley's infidelities. Davenant was a witness that Buckley had struck her. But divorce! Society had set its face against it and the mass of the people, her beloved audience, agreed. They demanded probity, chastity.

Buckley had left Kensington months ago. Occasionally he visited the children for whom he had a noisy overstated affection. In good fortune or bad, Buckley always overstated things. She knew all his failings. But he hadn't left her conscience.

Davenant stepped briskly into the room.

"A glass of madeira, Lettice?"

She gave him the radiant smile which was perhaps the most potent of her spells.

"I won't drink anything, but thank you."

"I shall," he said. "You inform me rather too often that you consider even small quantities of wine dull the artistic perception. But why do you need perception today?"

"I always do when you are about."

He took her to a table and spread out the costume designs. He talked of work. He made her laugh, mimicking the designer. He picked up a copy of the play and read a passage aloud.

"So you like the designs? Excellent," he said at last, putting them away without hearing her opinion.

"Some of my costumes may have to be changed a little."

They both laughed.

When they went back to the fire and sat down he asked, "Did you see *The Times* yesterday?"

"No."

He looked at her ironically.

"But I see that you know the news. Your sister has lost her husband."

"Gwynyth told me. I shall write to her."

He was not impressed.

"You're a hard little creature on occasions. You remind me of a peach. Your sister, from what I gather, is an egg. Well-shaped. Smooth. Firm shell. But if you close your hand upon it, what happens? A peach is very different. Juicy and luscious. But if you bite too deeply, by God, you crack your teeth on the stone."

"You think I'm hard-hearted?" she said, actress-like, taking up only the description of herself.

"Not for your audience. You're all melting womanhood and virtue to *them*. And I like my peach, juice, flesh, even its danger to my teeth."

It was weeks since he had spoken of the divorce. Would he do so now? And would he take her in his arms? He did neither.

"It's time you saw that sister again. Write and tell her so."

"I have refused to see her for two years. She knows why."

"Lettice, Lettice," he said, raising his eyebrows. She knew he perfectly understood her. Her weaknesses and prejudices, her sometime lack of heart.

"Do as I tell you. Write to your sister. It's your cue now. As you are very well aware."

(2)

Isabella decided not to take her children back

448

to Twickenham when she left Bagot Park. She wanted to get the house ready. Besides, now the thaw had come, Freddy and Betsy were riding out with their friends every day, looking comic and red-faced on their shaggy ponies.

Robert and Clare were both relieved the children were to stay.

"Freddy's such a comfort to his grandfather," said Clare.

"Betsy's rather a comfort to Clare," added Robert.

The family came out on the terrace to bid Isabella goodbye. They embraced her fondly. Swayne fussed over her. Mrs. Judge had packed a travelling basket of food. The groom wrapped her in a sable-covered rug. Every member of the family, every servant, treated her like that. It moved and at the same time oppressed her.

It was late and dark when the carriage trotted into her own drive. The brougham, following with the servants, pulled up, and there were voices, stamping hooves and figures scurrying with boxes. Isabella, who had been asleep, woke up and shivered. She walked into the ice-cold house with the servants round her like a queen among courtiers.

Rivers brushed her hair and wrapped her shoulders in a filmy shawl and Isabella went to bed and blew out the candle. The new-lit fire scarcely warmed the icy room. She lay back on the pillows which were damply cold. She had a feeling of yearning sadness.

But next morning the sun was an orange disc above the trees and she woke to Rivers's cheerful face and a tray with a pot of hot chocolate.

"A letter, my lady. Delivered early."

Rivers looped back the curtains and lit the fire.

Isabella picked up the letter. It would be another among the hundreds that she and Clare had painfully answered already. But when she looked at the envelope she flushed—it was Lettice's writing. It was a long time since she had seen that rounded girlish hand . . .

"My dear Isabella,
"I was grieved to hear of the Viscount's death. He was a wonderful man, and so very kind to our parents. It is sad for your children to be fatherless.

"Our lives have been much severed, and perhaps it is time to try and mend this, before we grow older and it is too late. I am quite willing, at least, to attempt to do so. If you would like to see me, come to the theatre on any afternoon, about four o'clock, if that time is convenient to you. I do not work at that hour."

Exactly as Denys used to do, in the same abbreviated and meaningless way, the letter ended "Affectionately, L."

While she had been in Sussex, Robert had given her a spaniel puppy—a little black creature called Chloe. "She will look after you," he had said, putting the puppy into her arms. Isabella took the dog for a walk that morning by the towpath. Lettice's letter had made her nervous. She was not sure she wanted to see her, she shied away from the meeting. But she knew she must accept the hand coolly offered. And it would please Ellen if it did nothing else.

"I suppose Robert will be quite pleased, too," she thought. Robert, it seemed, had become part of her conscience.

When Isabella arrived at the Royalty Theatre, she asked her coachman to wait, and sent up her card at the Stage Door. Almost immediately a little woman with dyed hair came down to meet her.

"Lady Carteret? Lettice said would I fetch you. I am her dresser."

Gwynyth took her into an enormous room so filled with flowers that it was like walking into the hothouse at Bagot Park. The air was scented and heavy, the room more gilded and fussy than those Isabella was used to.

Lettice, in costume, was at her dressing-table. She wore a bluish-green silk robe with huge sleeves and a four-inch gold sash round her waist. Her feet were bare, her coppery hair strangely dressed and threaded with pearls. She wore full stage make-up, her freckled skin white as alabaster, her lips reddened. Her sister's black-robed figure startled her. She had forgotten the mourning.

She stood up and walked over, saying kindly, "Do sit down. Would you like tea? Gwynyth always makes me some at this time."

"Thank you. That would be nice."

They could have been strangers.

When the old woman came in with a tray and Lettice absently thanked her, she was given a look of adoration. Isabella had never seen such a look on the face of any servant of the Bagots, even those who had worked for the family all their lives.

There was an embarrassed pause as Lettice poured the tea.

She's changed, each sister thought. To Isabella her sister had become curiously larger. Physically she was still small, but there seemed an invisible aureole about her. Perhaps it was fame. She moved and smiled as the Queen might do. I know nothing about her any more, Isabella thought. And her face is masked with paint.

But although Isabella found her sister's look and manner unfamiliar, Lettice was far more affected by the change in Isabella. With the artist's sharp eye, she noticed infinitely more. She could scarcely recognise this woman, with her delicate pale face and mournful eyes, her repose, a kind of aristocratic detachment. Could this really be her sister, who had embraced Buckley, perhaps mothered his child, been through a disgraceful scandal, and was now a widow?

They talked banalities for a while, but Lettice did manage to make her smile, and the sallow face altered. That horrible black, thought Lettice. I suppose, as she is a Viscountess, she will wear it for months—even years.

"What are your plans, Bella?" she said.

Isabella sighed.

"You sound just like my cousin Robert. Must one have plans?"

"It would not do for you to be lonely."

"Oh, I shall manage, I daresay."

Lettice looked at her thoughtfully.

"You have talked of your cousin Robert, as you call him, quite a lot. Shall you see him, perhaps? I only met him rarely, but I remember he was very handsome."

"I suppose he is. And clever and kind. But one cannot impose . . . I really could not . . ."

Privately, Lettice did not agree.

There was a sharp rap on the door.

"Ten minutes, Miss Winter! Ten minutes!"

"Bother," said Lettice, standing up. She arranged the peacock robe, which dragged behind her as she walked barefoot across to her sister and touched her hand.

"I am glad to see you. But I won't kiss you, or you will be covered with paint."

Isabella left the dressing-room. Doors stood open, and actors called to each other. Somebody began to sing in a voice of perfect pitch which its owner knew was beautiful. As she

walked along the passage she had a wave of
memory, full of lost friends and clapping
hands, of tawdry finery and dusty theatres
half asleep.

(3)

The next morning a watery sun was shining,
and Isabella again took her puppy to walk
along the towpath by the river and the leafless
willow trees. She thought of Lettice. She was
walking homeward along the muddy path
when she heard a rider, and stood to one side.

A voice said mockingly: "Greetings!"

She had a moment of intense shock. It was
Buckley, reining in his horse and smiling
down at her. He dismounted and took her
gloved hand.

"Imagine finding you," he said, "when I
was on my way to leave a card at that mansion
of yours. I only heard yesterday that you lived
here. Your father told me."

He laughed boyishly.

She gave a constrained smile. Her heart had
ceased to thud from shock, she was her collected self again. Although his presence had
been totally unexpected, and certainly she
had never wished to see him again, she looked

on him now as a friend from a past almost forgotten.

Buckley led his horse, walking beside her and chatting animatedly. He had an engagement at the Richmond theatre, and the first person he had set eyes on had been her father. Was that not astonishing?

She listened, as they walked slowly along the path together. Glancing at him, she saw that he was not as handsome as he used to be. His face, his thick girlish mouth, were coarser. There was a dissolute, worn look about him. But he still had panache. It was not easy for him to explain why he had left the brilliant Royalty Theatre, and after a time in the provinces taken an engagement at a little theatre on Richmond Green. But he made it sound rather a clever thing to have done, showing good judgement. His bravado was touching.

"I am to play the lead in a new burletta. Did you know that I can sing?" he said, smiling and showing his white teeth.

They had come to the riverside gates of her drive. Buckley nodded towards the distant house on its rise of ground.

"Very magnificent. I hope I am invited to drink a glass of madeira?"

It would have been easy enough to give some polite reason why she could not invite him to the house at present. But when she looked at him again, she felt a stab of pity. She said pleasantly that she would be glad for him to come.

He had not yet mentioned her widowhood and she disliked the omission. Perhaps he was embarrassed? Buckley, she remembered, never dealt well with tragedy.

She did not know how changed he found her. The deep mourning she wore made a barrier. Her black silks, her pale reposed face, were unfamiliar. Mourning, to Buckley, was something onstage in melodrama, or worn by strangers passing in the street. Actresses tried to avoid it or struggled out of its dark confines because they needed engagements, and it might spoil their chances.

When they arrived at the house, Isabella left him to take off her bonnet and cloak. As she returned across the hall, her butler, Dixon, spoke to her. He was an elderly man chosen by Robert, very quiet and thoughtful.

"Will the gentleman take luncheon, my lady?"

"Oh, I don't think so, Dixon—"

But something in Dixon's face, a fatherly

look which plainly said that the visit of a friend might be good for her in her solitary life, made her hesitate. And she remembered again the uncomfortable feeling of pity. Life had not dealt well with Buckley and it showed.

"Perhaps I should suggest it," she said, sighing. "Mr. Vernon is an old friend, Dixon. He is my brother-in-law."

"Yes, my lady," was the unsurprised reply.

Buckley talked a great deal during luncheon. He set out to amuse her, and at first he succeeded, but he drank too much and as the meal progressed she was embarrassed. When they returned to the drawing-room he was in excellent spirits, warmed by wine, good food and rich surroundings, and just drunk enough to lose any caution that might be needed to get what he had decided he wanted very much.

He said expansively, "Bella, I was sorry to hear your news. I haven't spoken of it until now because—well—I wanted to give us both time to be friends again. I hope you are not grieving too much. You always had a soft heart."

She recognised, from long ago, the look on his face. Just for a few moments he meant what he said, he actually did feel a sympathy.

He waited for her to respond, confident that he was on the right ground. But she had been with people whose feelings were deep, and recognised the difference.

"Thank you, Buckley," she said. But no more.

He was at a loss, giving an uncertain smile. Isabella felt a little sorry for him. Buckley needed so badly to shine and be sought-after, and at present was doing neither. Feeling she should be kinder, she told him that Lettice had written to her. He had scarcely mentioned his wife, keeping the talk to his hopes and plans in the theatre, and when she spoke of Lettice's letter he laughed.

"I'll wager you and she will patch it up. By the by, you know your sister and I are living apart now?"

"Mama did say something, but she hoped—"

"Oh, no," he said heartily. "It is quite over. We didn't suit, you know. Not one bit." He added with heavy roguishness, "There is only one woman for me. Can you guess who *she* might be?"

Isabella was so taken aback that she stared. At her expression he laughed aloud, and the sound literally hurt her. Too late she realised she should never have invited him here. Nothing about him, his hungry demand for admiration, his lack of formality, his coarseness and egotism, was bearable. And now this.

"Don't look so thunderstruck. I know you have not been long a widow, but you are still a beauty, do you know that? Particularly when you no longer have to wear that Hamlet rig."

She started up as he came across the room. But he was already close to her and grasped her hand.

"You don't have to be coy with *me*," he began in a caressing voice, "I will wait as long as you think proper, but you are mine. Aren't you? Aren't you?"

She tried to withdraw her hand but he clutched it more tightly in a strong, damp grasp.

"Please."

"Is it Letty that's troubling you?" he said, lifting the imprisoned hand and brushing his mouth against it. "You can forget her, Bella, just as I have."

"It is nothing to do with Lettice."

Her voice was low and shook slightly, and he misinterpreted it. He looked at her, his

460

lips apart, tracing her face with a caressing, drunken glance. He liked her pretended resistance, it excited him.

At last wrenching away her hand, Isabella backed away, shuddering violently.

"Please go."

"What did you say?"

"I mean it. Please leave my house."

He stared at her, thunderstruck.

"What are you talking about?"

"I do not wish you here. Go now. Or do you want me to ring for a servant?"

She spoke with such contempt that he froze. He stared stupidly at her, scarcely recognising in the dark-clad woman the beautiful creature of the past whom he had still believed existed and desired him. The glow of the wine died and he began to be angry.

Standing farther away from him she looked at him fixedly.

"Did you actually imagine I would accept such a suggestion, now, after all these years? Did you really think such a thing possible? That I would again sacrifice my life, my children, my name, everything Denys stood for—for *you*."

He looked so savage, taking a lunge forward, that for one incredible moment she thought he was going to strike her. But he gave a kind of gasp and rushed out of the room. There was the slam of the front door.

(4)

Lettice wrote some weeks later to invite Isabella to spend a day with her in Kensington the following Sunday. Driving along the country roads from Twickenham, Isabella thought how green the trees and fields were now. Winter was gone, and Denys had been dead for nearly five whole months. When she thought of him, as she did many times a day, it was with a deep and honest sorrow. Her heart ached, yet it did so tenderly. He had held her hand. He had called her "my dearest".

Separation between Lettice and herself had done curious things to the past. There must always be gaps now, things which had happened to each of them the other could never know.

Lettice's house, which she had never visited, had a handsome entrance gate, and in the front garden a bronze statue of Neptune. The laburnums were in flower.

462

"Bella!"

Lettice kissed her, and took her to the upstairs drawing-room. It was long and spacious, with windows overlooking the bronze Neptune at the front of the house, and more windows framing a vista of lawns, rosebeds and a line of yew hedges.

To make her sister feel at home, Lettice rang for the nurse to bring in the children. When Matilda and Billy came shyly into the room, Isabella clasped her hands.

"Oh Letty, how they've changed!"

Matilda, pretty and self-conscious, was startlingly like Buckley, with the same mouth, the same melting eyes. Billy had Lettice's red hair and freckles; he was plump and timid. When Lettice encouraged him to kiss his aunt, he looked as if he might cry. As with her own children when they had been away for many weeks, they seemed strangely tall: they reminded her of flowers with long stems.

When they had gone she said, "They're lovely. Matilda is going to be a beauty, and Billy is a darling. Poor boy, he was frightened of my black. You wouldn't recognise my Freddy and Betsy, they look pathetic all done up in black serge. But Robert and Clare say they will be allowed to come out of it in a month or two."

"And how long shall you be in mourning, Bella?" asked Lettice. The laws of the nobility were unknown to her.

"Maybe a year. Then I shall be in half mourning, which is lilac and white. I shall wear Denys's amethysts. He always liked me to wear them. Of course I must not go about, you know, although Robert says he will. He told me women always mourn longer than men," Isabella said drily.

"Do you mind? Black for so long, I mean?"

"Oh no. I prefer it."

Conversation during luncheon was pleasant but constrained. After the meal Lettice showed her the nurseries, the garden room, a panelled library where two full-length portraits of Lettice hung, one as Beatrice, the other as Rosalind. They went into a conservatory full of exotic flowering plants.

When they were back in the upstairs drawing-room Isabella said, "You must be happy here."

"I think Mama enjoys it more than I do," Lettice said. "She goes round on every visit suggesting improvements. She does enjoy spending money."

"And Pa?"

"He likes to be with the children. He is teaching Matilda to speak verse. Do you know, she is quite gifted. The other day when I went into the nursery, can you guess what I heard her reciting to him?"

"*Not* the Ten Dramatic Passions!"

"You are right."

They both smiled.

There was a pause. Isabella thought how young her sister seemed. There was a kind of veil of innocence round her. How did she keep it?

"I have something to tell you, Letty. Buckley came to see me."

Lettice gave her the oddest look. Warning? Sympathy?

"Did he . . . ask you to return to him?"

It was delicately put.

Isabella clasped her hands.

"I thought you would guess. Yes, he did. Oh, Letty, how could we possibly have loved him? How did you? How did I? Of course I sent him away, as you did, and of course he was angry! I should think he went straight off to Richmond to the arms of some ballet girl or other. He is *ridiculous*, isn't he?"

She began to laugh. It was a sound that

465

Lettice had once known very well and heard every day when they were children, a low giggle, impossibly infectious.

"Poor Buckley," said Isabella, mopping her eyes. "He just has to have everybody worshipping him and nobody must say a word of criticism or he snarls like a dog. He is so *funny*, Lettice."

She was still laughing and Lettice couldn't help joining her.

"Do you think he will ever forgive us?" said Isabella, dabbing her eyes again.

"I am sure he won't."

Everything could be talked about after that. Lettice spoke of Davenant and confessed ruefully that she was in love with him. She was sure Isabella would be very surprised, and added that when the divorce, which she dreaded, was over she had agreed to marry him.

"He knows I am afraid of what people think. Do you know what he said to me? 'We are the makers of manners, Kate.'"

"You're very brave to take on such a fierce fellow."

"That is what he tells me," Lettice said.

There was a little pause.

"Now tell me about your cousin Robert,"

Lettice said. "You like him. I am sure of it."

"Letty, I see you are still a little sentimental. That is a comfort," Isabella said. Leaning her chin on her hand, she talked of Robert. She described how he differed from yet how he resembled Denys. He had done so much for her, stood by her when things were at their worst, persuaded her to move away from Finstock Lodge where she had been so unhappy . . .

"And then—most of all—he made me go back when Denys was ill."

"Made you?"

"He is stronger than I am. Now, Letty, why are you making me speak of him? I told you I must not lean on Robert any more. *He* has everything before him . . ."

Lettice nodded, saying that it was getting dark and she really must ring for the lamps to be lit. It had begun to rain; they could hear the sound of raindrops falling on the spring trees in the garden.

But they stayed in the half dark, talking of the past. Of their childhood, and the coaches jolting them through so many nights. Of the North Street theatre, and the winter evening when they had played *The Welsh Girl* at Bagot Park. Of the fire and the snow. Of

Newcastle, the corn riots. Of Davenant. Of Denys. They had not talked together like this since they had shared an attic bedroom.

Suddenly Isabella lifted her head.

"I think you have visitors, Letty."

They heard the familiar noise of horses, the slam of a carriage door.

"I wonder who it could be. Shall we look?" Lettice said.

As if on cue, they stood up and went together to one of the front windows and looked down.

The rain was heavy now, and it fell steadily on a yellow and black carriage at the door. Everything about the carriage shone, from its brass fittings to the wet, glossy coats of the chestnut horses.

A man had descended from the carriage, and was walking to the front door.

"Robert!" exclaimed Isabella, her cheeks suddenly pink. "Letty, *what* have you been up to?"

"Nothing in the world," said Lettice, in a voice of childlike innocence. "May one not invite a kinsman of yours to dine?"

The Trial of Charles I   *C. V. Wedgwood*
Royal Flush   *Margaret Irwin*
The Sceptre and the Rose   *Doris Leslie*
Mary II: Queen of England *Hester Chapman*
That Enchantress   *Doris Leslie*
The Princess of Celle   *Jean Plaidy*
Caroline the Queen   *Jean Plaidy*
The Third George   *Jean Plaidy*
The Great Corinthian   *Doris Leslie*
Victoria in the Wings   *Jean Plaidy*
The Captive of Kensington Palace
                              Jean Plaidy
The Queen and Lord 'M'   *Jean Plaidy*
The Queen's Husband   *Jean Plaidy*
The Widow of Windsor   *Jean Plaidy*
Bertie and Alix   *Graham and Heather Fisher*
The Duke of Windsor   *Ursula Bloom*